P9-DDA-180

PRAISE FOR NANCY BOYARSKY'S NICOLE GRAVES MYSTERIES

"full of page-by-page surprises"
–Kirkus Reviews

"...nail-biting adventure whose thralls are difficult to escape"
–Foreword Reviews

"a hold-onto-the-bar roller coaster of a mystery"
—RT Book Reviews

"a charming and straight-shooting heroine"
–Foreword Reviews

"Well written, non-stop, can't-put-it-down suspense."
–Charles Rosenberg, bestselling author of *"Death on a High Floor"*

"Taut, suspenseful, and fast-paced..."
–Laura Levine, author of the *Jaine Austen* mystery series

"Well developed characters in a rich English setting brings ample twists throughout and all the way to the final pages."

–Eric Hoffer Award Gold Winner 2018 for *The Swap*

LIAR LIAR

a Nicole Graves mystery

NANCY BOYARSKY

 Light Messages

Copyright © 2018, by Nancy Boyarksy
Liar Liar
Nancy Boyarsky
www.nancyboyarsky.com
nboyarsky@lightmessages.com
Published 2018, by Light Messages
www.lightmessages.com
Durham, NC 27713 USA
SAN: 920-9298
Paperback ISBN: 978-1-61153-254-8
Ebook ISBN: 978-1-61153-253-1

ALL RIGHTS RESERVED
No part of this publication may be reproduced, stored in a
retrieval system, or transmitted in any form or by any means,
electronic, mechanical, photocopying, recording, scanning, or
otherwise, except as permitted under Section 107 or 108 of the
1976 International Copyright Act, without the prior written
permission except in brief quotations embodied in critical
articles and reviews.

*This is a work of fiction. All characters, organizations, and
events portrayed in this novel are either products of the author's
imagination or are used fictitiously.*

For Bill, always and forever,
and for Jeff and Cathy, whose advice and counsel
made this book possible.

ONE

LATER, NICOLE WOULD PONDER THE TRUTH and its illusive nature. She'd realize how many lies people would tell to protect themselves from it. And, worst of all, how many she herself would tell to get at it. She'd always considered herself a truthful person. Yet she'd find herself lying to others, to her fiancé, and even to herself.

She'd wonder if there was such a thing as the actual truth. Or was truth relative, the product of incomplete or faulty memories, or the limitations of the observer? How often was the truth tainted by what an individual wanted, or needed, to believe?

On this bright day in mid-March, Nicole stepped into the United Terminal at LAX and encountered a situation she could hardly believe. It was as if she'd slipped back in time to the previous year when the media was stalking her. This morning, they were massed in a corner of baggage claim. After the initial shock of seeing them, she noticed they weren't looking in her direction, hadn't noticed her at all. They were waiting for someone else, someone they expected to come down the escalator from the arrival gates.

The great hall was a hub of activity, unusually crowded even for a weekend afternoon. The noise was overwhelming. It wasn't just the buzz of the luggage carousels and thud of suitcases dropping from the chute. The source of the commotion was the corner packed with people carrying microphone-equipped cameras.

Nicole had an urge to walk out the door, find her car in the lot, and leave. But she had a job to do. She was here to pick up a passenger, and that passenger was no doubt the reason for the welcoming committee.

Her charge, Mary Ellen Barnes, was suing a fellow student for rape as well as Oceanside University for failing to protect her after the authorities refused to take action. It was a classic he-said, she-said, rape scenario, and a national anti-rape organization was footing the bill for the trial in civil court. The case had captured national media attention, and the tabloids were featuring it along with movie stars' affairs, marriages, and divorces. Little wonder that Mary Ellen's arrival would stir up a mob.

Nicole's job was to look after the girl for a day or two and keep her away from the media. She could see it was a lost cause. The tabloids had already found Mary Ellen. They had an uncanny ability to track down those unlucky enough to attract readers, or clicks, as online news sites referred to them. Somehow, they'd discovered when Mary Ellen would be arriving and at which terminal. The tabloid *XtraHotNews* probably had an airline employee on its payroll. Or one of the paparazzi had hacked into Mary Ellen's phone or her lawyer's. She thought back to the year before when her own cellphone had been hacked by the tabloids. She'd suddenly become an heiress, murder suspect, and target of the media's spotlight. What a nasty experience that had been.

Nicole took a step back. The automatic door opened. Another step and she was outside again. A warm breeze ruffled her hair. The weather was a balmy eighty degrees, not unusual for L.A. at this time of year. She reached into her bag and scrabbled about, pushing aside the can of pepper spray she always carried. She found her sunglasses and sun hat. She put them on and tucked her hair into the hat. She hoped this would grant her a degree of anonymity. Even though the reporters and paparazzi weren't looking for her, the fact that Nicole Graves was picking up Mary Ellen Barnes wouldn't go unnoticed.

She took a deep breath and reentered the terminal. She should have refused when Jerry, her boss, had called her at home that morning and asked—no, begged—her to take this assignment. "It's just for a day or two," Jerry had told her. "Joanne was going to do it, but she woke up feeling sick. She thinks she'll be able to take over tomorrow, Monday at the latest." Reluctantly, Nicole had agreed. When she hung up, Josh had said, "What was that about?"

"Jerry needs me to pick up a witness at the airport and look after her for a day or two."

Josh had immediately picked up on the word "witness." "Witness for what?"

"Mary Ellen Barnes in the—"

"The Oceanside U. rape case?" Josh had said. "For God's sake, Nicole. Have you lost your mind? Call him back and tell him you can't do it. The paparazzi will be all over you again."

"There won't be any paparazzi," she'd said. "Besides, they've forgotten all about me. My job is to keep the girl away from the press. It's not going to be a problem."

"If some stray mutt with a camera spots you," Josh had said, "there will be a problem." He'd paused a moment, looking at her. "Please don't do this."

"I have to. Joanne's sick, and there's nobody else. I'll be fine; you'll see."

But she wasn't fine—not caught in this mob of reporters and photographers. She shivered, then pulled herself together and began to push her way toward the front. She was petite and slender with sharp elbows, distinct advantages in a crowd like this. Even so, her progress was impeded by those going in the opposite direction—ordinary travelers, tired and cross, fighting their way through to claim their bags. A woman dressed in gray sweats rammed Nicole's knee with her suitcase. Moments later, a young man on his cell phone ran his bag over her foot. A few steps forward, and a heavy metal case collided with her thigh.

Nicole shoved steadily forward until she reached the front. Here she found herself next to drivers holding up signs with the names of the VIPs they'd come to pick up. Instead of bringing a sign, she'd told Mary Ellen what she'd be wearing: jeans, a red top, red sneakers. Behind her, the throng of reporters, photographers, and cameramen seemed to be growing. She could feel them pressing against her. The place grew hotter, and sweat began to trickle from under her hat.

She kept an eye on the electronic arrivals board overhead. At last, the board blinked, and the status of Mary Ellen's flight changed from "on time" to "arrived." Nicole pulled out her phone and alerted her driver to stop circling the airport and pull up to the terminal. She was glad Joanne had thought of hiring the limo. It would spare her and Mary Ellen from being chased to the parking structure by paparazzi.

She jumped when she felt a hand on her shoulder. It was Greg Albee, a reporter from the *L.A. Times*. He'd helped her when she was in the media's crosshairs, and they'd become friends.

"Hey, Nicole," he said, pulling her into a hug. "Small world! What are you doing here?" Greg Albee was short, with freckles, thinning brown hair, and an enigmatic smile. His easy, laid-back manner hid a relentless drive to beat the competition to the next big story.

Nicole gave him a smile. "I'm meeting a friend. Guess she chose a bad time to arrive."

He regarded her with a knowing look, as if he'd just administered a lie detector test and she'd failed. She liked Greg well enough, but the last thing she wanted right now was to be talking to a reporter.

"Hear you've gone to work for a private investigation company," he said.

"Right. Colbert and Smith Investigations—mostly corporate stuff. I'm putting in hours so I can qualify for a private investigator's license. Oh, I have news: Josh and I are engaged."

Greg was congratulating her when her phone rang. It was Mary Ellen. "I'm off the plane and on my way down to you." Mary Ellen spoke with a soft Southern accent. She had a little-girl voice and ended the sentence on a high note, as if it were a question.

"Great," Nicole said. "See you in a minute."

She knew what Mary Ellen looked like. The girl's picture had been in the paper and online tabloids. Mary Ellen had gone home to Georgia for a few days at the start of spring break. She was returning early to prepare for her court appearance.

Mary Ellen and Doshan Williams, the quarterback, had been freshmen together the year before. Both were scholarship students, but they had little else in common. She was a deeply religious Baptist from a small town in Georgia. Her scholarship had been sponsored by her minister, and she was majoring in religion.

Doshan was African American and a jock. Mary Ellen's parents would be considered working poor, but Doshan's family was much more prosperous. They lived in middle-class Leimert Park, a predominantly African American and Latino area of L.A. Doshan's father owned a successful auto repair business, and his mother was a public school teacher.

Doshan himself was known for his leadership qualities. In high school, he'd organized his fellow classmates into a group that helped the homeless in South Central L.A. Articles about him in the sports pages focused on his charisma, good looks, and sunny nature. These qualities, along with his performance on his high school's football field, had raised him to the status of local hero. His athletic talent had gotten him a free ride to Oceanside. There, he'd continued to stand out as a student leader and gifted athlete.

More importantly, he was a big draw at Oceanside alumni events that raised money for the school.

At the start of their second quarter, Mary Ellen filed a complaint with the university, stating that Doshan had raped her. The school appeared to investigate the case but nothing came of it. At first, they'd refused to explain. Outrage from feminist groups on and off campus, as well as news coverage and editorials, had forced the school to issue a statement. They said there simply wasn't enough evidence to act on Mary Ellen's complaint. Then someone leaked the investigation report online, and it went viral. The report said that Mary Ellen Barnes hadn't reported the assault until two months after it happened, which made it all but impossible to gather evidence.

An even stickier point was this: There was no dispute the two had sex—both admitted that. The issue rested on whether the girl had given her consent. In the end, the report concluded, it boiled down to "she said, he said," without substantive proof on either side.

While this was going on, Doshan had become a football superstar, earning a national reputation. He was golden, expected to be drafted in the first round by a National Football League team. Now, his future was in doubt, depending on the outcome of this trial. NFL teams were unlikely to accept a man found guilty of rape.

The trial had taken almost a year to make its way into court. It was big news and not just from the sports angle. Oceanside was a Christian-affiliated university in Malibu; its reputation as a safe and wholesome environment for young people was also on the line.

The proceeding was to begin in Los Angeles County Superior Court in Santa Monica on Monday, the day after tomorrow.

The moment Mary Ellen stepped off the escalator, cameras began flashing, and people were shouting her name, trying to get her to turn in their direction. Nicole waved, then started pushing her way toward the roped-off area where the girl would emerge. Albee followed along with his hand on Nicole's shoulder. "I'll help you get her out of here," he said. Nicole started to refuse, then reconsidered. She'd never manage to get Mary Ellen through this horde. The girl herself appeared on the verge of collapse.

As Mary Ellen walked along the rope divider, reporters shouted at her and poked camera-mounted microphones in her face. The unwanted attention made her turn a deep shade of pink, and she looked as if she were about to cry. As soon as she spotted Nicole, she headed in her direction.

Nicole and Albee positioned themselves on either side of Mary Ellen, each with an arm around the girl's shoulder. They started shoving their way toward the exit. When they reached the door, it occurred to Nicole that she should have directed reporters' questions to Mary Ellen's lawyer. But it was too late. All they could do now was make a quick exit.

The doors slid open, and they dashed for the black limo waiting at the curb. Albee opened the back door, so the women could pile inside. He put his hand up, fingers pointing to his mouth and an ear, signaling that he and Nicole should talk by phone. She nodded, and he closed the door. The women were still fastening their seatbelts when the car started up with a lurch. A squad of paparazzi on motorcycles—apparently circling the airport in hope of catching the girl on her way out—were not far behind. Reporters and paparazzi were running for their vehicles. They were parked in a marked-off area two terminals down and didn't stand much chance of catching up.

The limo sped to where the airport's inner ring forked. Two left-hand lanes led back around to the terminals, while the one on the right led onto city streets. At the last minute, the limo darted across the left lanes—soliciting a chorus of honking—to exit the airport. The maneuver lost the paparazzi, who were stuck recircling the inner road. Mary Ellen's face was shiny with sweat, and she looked terrified. Clearly, when she'd signed up for this, she had no idea what she was in for.

Nicole's heart went out to her. "You OK?" she asked.

"I guess." Mary Ellen leaned her head against the backrest and closed her eyes. Her bangs, damp with sweat, stuck to her forehead.

As they reached the junction of the San Diego and Santa Monica freeways, Nicole's phone rang.

It was Greg Albee. "Where you headed?" he said.

"Sorry, Greg. I can't you tell that." She paused, then added, "I don't know what you're planning to write, but I'd consider it a huge favor if you wouldn't mention my name."

"I thought of it," he said. "But sure. It's not germane to the story."

"Great," she said. "I promise I'll share anything I can with you. By the way, how did you know what flight she was on?"

"I heard it from a shooter we sometimes buy photos from. He occasionally gives me tips. I don't know where he got it. But you know how it works. The tabloids pay for information, and the paparazzi somehow get wind of it."

By the time she hung up, they were in Santa Monica, exiting the freeway. The limo driver turned into an alley and parked behind the Windward, one of the city's boutique hotels. He pulled Mary Ellen's roller bag and Nicole's overnight case out of the back seat while Nicole called the desk. A few minutes later, a uniformed attendant opened a door to admit them. Nicole, who'd checked out the hotel's logistics a few hours before, led Mary Ellen to the service elevator and, once inside, punched the button for the tenth floor.

As they were riding up, she had her first chance to study Mary Ellen. The girl was about five-seven—at least half a foot taller than Nicole—with long, straight, fair hair. She had a lovely figure, slender and willowy. At the airport, surrounded by shouting reporters, she'd been flushed, her face pinched in distress. Now that things were calmer, Nicole could see what the girl really looked like. She wore no makeup, but her skin was a glowing ivory set off by the natural pink of her cheeks and full lips. Mary Ellen might have been beautiful but for the way she held herself with her shoulders slumped and her head thrust forward. She exuded a sense of haplessness, vulnerability, and defeat.

Part of it was what she was wearing: a pink, flowered dress with puffed sleeves that appeared to be an old Laura Ashley. It was so out of fashion, it might have been regarded as trendily vintage. But it showed signs of wear, and Nicole had a hunch it was a hand-me-down. The girl wore it awkwardly, occasionally pulling at the skirt and smoothing it out as if she wasn't used to wearing dresses. Across her chest, bandolier-style, she wore a white plastic purse. A small gold cross hung on a chain around her neck.

No doubt Mary Ellen's virginal, fundamentalist appearance was what Women Against Rape needed for a case like this. She looked like someone a jury would want to protect against a big, hulking athlete. Nicole wondered how much race would weigh in this trial since Doshan was African American and Mary Ellen was white. Even in this post-millennium age—in the bluest of blue states—race prejudice was very much alive. And the Santa Monica jury pool was overwhelmingly white.

They exited the elevator; Nicole led the way to a door at the end of the hall and unlocked it with the key card she'd picked up earlier. Impressed by the size of the suite, Nicole had inquired at the desk and discovered it was costing Women Against Rape a staggering $1250 a night. But that probably was a pittance compared to the cost of bringing this case to court.

Once inside, Mary Ellen collapsed into a chair and blew an upward breath that lifted her bangs off her forehead. For the first time, she seemed to notice Nicole.

"Oh, my goodness!" she said, in her high, little-girl voice. "That was awful! It isn't going to be like that at the courthouse, is it?"

Nicole took this in, the "my goodness" instead of the "Oh, my god" or "wtf" most girls Mary Ellen's age would use.

"I'm afraid there will be a lot of media," Nicole said, "but you'll be using a side door, and security will keep them away. While you're here for the trial, the media will be looking for you. They'll want to ask questions and take your picture. So it's probably best if you stay in the hotel when you're not in court. If you go out, the paparazzi will find you. As you saw, it's pretty unpleasant to be cornered by them."

Mary Ellen straightened up and looked at her incredulously. "What about my friends? We have plans. I mean, I'm free to go out if I want, aren't I?"

"Of course," Nicole said. "You're not our prisoner. Your lawyer will be here in a few minutes. You can ask her advice about going out, that kind of thing." She got up, heading for the minibar. "I'm going to have a Coke. Do you want something?"

"No, thanks," Mary Ellen was quiet for a moment, then said, "Um, what—? I mean, are you staying here with me, ma'am? I don't mean to be disrespectful, but are you, like, my babysitter or something?"

Nicole shook her head. "My job is to get you settled. Joanne, the woman who was supposed to pick you up today, is sick. She's the one who arranged for the limousine. She reserved this hotel suite so you'd have a place to stay where the media can't find you. She'll be out for a day or two, so I'm filling in. If you want anything, I'll help you get it. I'm here to make sure you're safe and comfortable. But I'm certainly not your babysitter."

This wasn't true. Nicole's job was to stay close, keep an eye on the girl, and look after her needs. More importantly, she was to make sure Mary Ellen, who was young and inexperienced, didn't get into the clutches of the media or into any kind of trouble. In fact, Nicole was Mary Ellen's babysitter, and "babysitting" was the informal term the firm used for this assignment.

At that moment, the doorbell rang. Nicole got up and looked through the peephole. It was Mary Ellen's lawyer, Sue Price. She was a tall redhead, who'd helped Nicole when she'd been at the center of another case.

Introductions were made, and the three of them settled in the sitting room. The decor was both luxurious and informal. The restful blues, greens, and golds echoed the colors outside, visible through French doors that led to a small balcony.

After some small talk, Sue repeated what Nicole had told Mary Ellen about sticking close to the hotel.

"What about my friends?" Mary Ellen repeated. Her face had gone pink again, and her lower lip trembled. "We were planning to go to Hollywood and, like, see the clubs. Are you saying I can't go?"

"I'm simply advising you." Sue spoke softly, but her voice was firm. "I strongly recommend you stay out of the public eye, Mary Ellen. The paparazzi are on the lookout for you. They hang around those Hollywood clubs, looking for celebrities. It won't be much fun with people poking microphones in your face, asking questions about what happened to you.

"I know!" Sue's tone brightened, "Why don't you invite your friends up here? Nicole can stay in her room, and you'll have the place to yourselves. Order anything you want from room service and rent some movies." She gestured toward an enormous TV mounted on the wall.

Mary Ellen pulled a tissue out of her purse, dabbed her eyes, and blew her nose. "That's a good idea, ma'am," she said. "Maybe we'll do that. I'm pretty tired anyway."

"I want to explain two very important matters," Sue said. "First and most important, do not talk to anyone, especially the media. If someone approaches you, even to ask how you are, tell them you've been advised by your attorney not to answer any questions. Have them call me, all right?"

The girl, staring out the window, gave no response.

"Mary Ellen," Sue persisted, "are you with me?"

The girl turned toward Sue and flushed. "Yes, ma'am. I'm

listening. I'm just so tired. It's been such an awful day."

"I know," Sue said, "and I'm sorry about that. I just want to be sure you remember not to discuss this case with anyone. Not your friends and especially not the media or anyone associated with the accused."

Sue sat forward in her seat, intent on keeping the girl's attention. "On Monday, you'll be delivered to court. I'll be there. This first day is voir dire. That's when the lawyers select jurors to hear the case. Voir dire could take most of the day. Your only job is to sit quietly and look like a sweet, innocent girl who's been terribly wronged. Image is important to jurors. You want them to like you." Sue paused to study the girl. "Do you have any questions?"

"No, ma'am. I understand. I have to look like a nice girl who's been victimized. I'll do my part. I promise."

"Good," said Sue. "And that gold cross you have around your neck? Perfect. Be sure to wear it to court. That's all for now. Nicole, why don't you walk me to the elevator. I have a couple of things I want to go over with you."

Nicole picked up her key card and followed Sue into the hall.

"What do you think?" Sue said as they walked toward the elevator.

"Well, she certainly looks the part," Nicole said. "She makes the perfect poster child for the Women Against Rape organization. But I feel bad for her. She was completely freaked by the media at the airport. Did anyone let her know what she was in for?"

"Of course," Sue said. "They described the whole process, even the fact that the defense team would try to dredge up dirt to make her look like a tramp. She insisted she was up for it." Sue drew in a deep breath. "I just hope she stays put and keeps her mouth shut."

"She was pretty shaken up by the scene at the airport," Nicole said. "I doubt she'll step foot outside."

They were both silent, watching the elevator's progress on the display. The car was making a long stop on the third floor.

"I've been wondering," Nicole said. "Where are her parents in all this? You'd think they'd be here to support her."

"Her parents are divorced," Sue said. "Neither has much money. Her mother is a waitress; she was afraid she'd lose her job if she took time off. Her father's some kind of handyman; he's refused to have much to do with Mary Ellen since the civil case was filed. Hard to tell what that's about. Mary Ellen is on her own."

Sue stabbed the button for the elevator again. "By the way, WAR is sending a lawyer of their own to chair. I'm local counsel."

"War?" Nicole said.

"WAR is the acronym for Women Against Rape. At demonstrations, they wear T-shirts and hats identifying themselves as WARiors. It has a certain ring to it." Sue paused and gave a smile. "And how's Josh? How are the wedding plans going?"

"Josh is great, but the wedding plans are still up in the air. All the best venues are booked for June and July. We're still trying to come up with a date," Nicole said. "I wonder when Joanne will be able to take over with Mary Ellen. Have you heard anything?"

"Not a word," Sue said. "Why don't you call and ask?"

"Good thought," Nicole said. "I'm dying to get home."

"I don't blame you," said Sue. "If I had someone as gorgeous as Josh waiting for me…"

Not for the first time, it struck Nicole how little she knew about the attorney's personal life. Sue was tall and beautiful. But she didn't wear a wedding ring, and although she had family photos in her office, they included no one who looked like a significant other. She was a mystery to Nicole, who was always curious about people. She'd looked Sue up on one of her office's databases but had found little other than Sue's law credentials, professional affiliations, home address, and date of birth, which was about fifteen years earlier than Nicole would have guessed.

With anyone else, Nicole would have simply asked. Yet, despite her warmth, Sue had an air of formality that discouraged questions about her personal life.

The elevator arrived, and Sue reached out to give Nicole a hug before stepping inside. As the door started to close, she said, "Take care, Nicole. Keep an eye on that girl."

"Will do. See you Monday. Good luck with the case. Or is it unlucky to say that?"

"What makes you think luck has anything to do with it?" Sue laughed. The elevator door closed, and Nicole headed back to the room.

Two

BACK IN THE SUITE, the sitting room was empty. The door to one of the bedrooms was closed, and Mary Ellen seemed to be on the phone. Nicole could hear the low murmur of her voice but couldn't make out what the girl was saying.

Outside, the sky was growing dim as sunset approached. Nicole checked her watch. It wasn't yet 6:00 p.m., but in mid-March, the days were short. She opened the door to the balcony and stepped outside. She could see the busy traffic on Ocean Boulevard directly below. On the other side of the road, the beach was relatively deserted. The palms lining the beach and city streets were gangly and almost comical from ground level. From her tenth-floor balcony, Nicole looked down on two of these trees. Their green, arching fronds ruffled gracefully in the wind. They leaned toward each other, like lovers waiting to watch the sun set behind the mountains.

She took in a breath of salt-scented air and waited. The water turned slate gray as the light waned. To her right was the Santa Monica Pier, where twinkling lights delineated the merry-go-round and Ferris wheel. As the sun sank, it turned red, casting a deep pink glow in the water and the sky around it. It seemed to pause a few seconds, then slid behind the mountains; dusk arrived. The transformation had taken less than a minute.

Without the sun, the temperature dropped, and Nicole went back inside. She helped herself to a bag of nuts and a small bottle of white wine from the minibar. All at once she remembered that she had to call Joanne to find out how she was feeling.

After a couple of rings, Joanne picked up and croaked, "Hello."

"My god, Joanne," Nicole said. "You sound awful."

"Not as awful as I feel. I think it's the flu and it's hit all systems. Sorry you got stuck filling in for me."

"That's okay," Nicole said. "I'm guessing you won't be back tomorrow."

"I don't think so. My temperature is 102. God, I sure hope this doesn't drag on—" Joanne's voice cut out. Then: "Oh-oh. I've got to go." The phone went dead.

Whoa, Nicole thought. *This is not good.* With the trial only two days away, she realized, she might very well get stuck with Mary Ellen when it began. She'd have to call Josh and let him know. She wasn't afraid of his reaction. Not exactly. He was sweet natured, rarely cross or angry. But this one issue—the idea she might put herself in danger or within the sights of the tabloids—upset him.

His attitude bothered her. The past was gone; there was nothing she could do about what had happened last year or the year before that. She'd learned from those experiences and had promised she'd keep out of harm's way. Josh didn't seem to believe her.

Nicole hadn't seen this side of him until she decided to take a job with Colbert and Smith Investigations. Josh had done his best to dissuade her. It took awhile to convince him that the firm bore no resemblance to the private detective agencies portrayed by Raymond Chandler. She'd be doing research on a computer and an occasional interview with a witness or expert of some kind.

Her new firm's assignments came from corporations and law firms. That meant she wouldn't be dealing with criminals, putting her life in danger, or doing anything to attract the media. In deference to Josh's concerns, she'd made it clear to Jerry, her new boss, that she wouldn't babysit witnesses in high-profile trials.

Yet here she was.

At that moment, Nicole noticed that Mary Ellen's room had gone silent. She went over and knocked on the door. "I'm going to order dinner from room service," she said. "Why don't you take a look at the menu?"

"I'm not hungry, ma'am, but thanks for asking," Mary Ellen said.

"OK," said Nicole. "Are your friends coming by?"

"I'm too tired. I'm going to take a nap. I'll probably sleep through 'til morning. Y'all have a good night, ma'am."

"You, too," said Nicole. "Sweet dreams." Only after she said it, did she realize how unlikely this was.

She ordered a salmon entree with a salad, then sat a long moment staring at the phone. At last she dialed Josh. He didn't answer their home phone. That meant he was probably at the office. He was an architect and sometimes met clients in the evening. She called his cell, and he picked up.

"Hey, you," he said.

"Where are you?"

"At the office. I figured work was better than being home alone."

"Working, eh?" she said, in mock disbelief. "So you say." They both laughed. "Do you have time to talk?"

"My clients should be here any minute, but I'm yours until then."

When she told him about the media at the airport, he said, "Christ! Did anybody recognize you?"

"Of course not," she said. "They don't care about me anymore. Oh, I did run into Albee. He sends his congratulations on our engagement. Listen, Joanne is still sick. Looks like I'm stuck here for at least another night, maybe two."

"Damn it, Nicole!" His tone was uncharacteristically irritable. "This kind of stuff makes me crazy. Call Jerry and tell him to get someone else." There was a silence before he added, "Please!"

"There is no one else. Joanne and I are the only women in the office this week. Besides, I'm already here. Stop worrying. We're safe. The press has no idea where we are."

"Okay. Fine." But there was an edge to his voice. "What about the trial? It's day after tomorrow. What happens if Joanne's still sick? You'll end up in the courtroom, won't you?"

"No way! It's up to her lawyers to look after her in court. I won't have anything to do with that. I promise."

"I know what." His tone softened. "I'll sneak up for a visit. Climb in a window so nobody knows I'm there."

"Good idea," she said. "Keep in mind we're on the tenth floor."

"Thanks for the warning," he said. "I'll bring my Spider-Man gear. So, what's this girl like?"

Nicole lowered her voice, "Seems like the quintessential pious good girl. Actually calls me "ma'am," if you'll believe it. Straight from central casting. I don't think she's going to present any problems."

"I can't wait until this is over." He sighed. "I miss you. If you're not home by tomorrow night, maybe I'll have dinner with my folks."

"I'm sure Mum will enjoy having sonny boy to herself," Nicole said. It rankled that Josh's mother still didn't like her. Oh, she made a pretense, calling Nicole "dear" and including her in the conversation. But Nicole could tell—when Carol's cool gaze met hers—that she wished Josh had fallen for someone else, someone who wasn't divorced, someone without a "past."

"Don't be silly," Josh had said, whenever Nicole brought it up. "Of course she likes you. It just takes her awhile to warm up." Josh's younger sister, Alison, had been more forthcoming.

She'd explained that their mother had never liked any of Josh's girlfriends, and Nicole shouldn't take it personally. Even so, it was hard not to.

"Hey, my clients are here," he said. "Call me at bedtime, okay? I love you."

While Nicole waited for room service to deliver her meal, she went to the XHN website on her iPad. There at the top of the page, under a banner headline, was a story about the trial with a photo of Mary Ellen at the airport. Nicole could see her own arm around the girl's shoulder. To her relief, the rest of her had been cropped out. Next to Mary Ellen's photo was one of Doshan in his football uniform.

She picked up the book she'd been reading, a thriller involving an emotionally damaged cop, his glamorous but inexperienced female partner, and a serial killer. After the events of the day, it was hard to focus, and she found herself thinking of Josh. For the first time—after a failed marriage and a doomed long-distance romance—she'd found the right guy.

He was perfect, except for those moments when he became overly protective. But she was sure this would pass—once things were calm for a while and he finally understood that her past mishaps had been pure blind chance.

She picked up her book and gave it another try, half listening for any sound from Mary Ellen's room. The suite remained quiet. Around 10:30, Nicole began to doze off. She put down her book, called Josh to say goodnight, and went to bed.

She was half asleep when she thought she heard the sound of a door closing. She went into the sitting room and turned on the light. Mary Ellen's door was shut, and everything was just as Nicole had left it. Then she noticed that the chain lock wasn't fastened. She secured it, went back to her room and fell asleep.

She was startled awake by someone banging on the front door. The clock said 3:00 a.m. She got up.

She peered through the peephole. To her shock, it was Mary

Ellen. Nicole looked at the chain lock. It was still fastened. That meant the girl had left the suite earlier, perhaps when Nicole was in the bathroom getting ready for bed. She unlocked it and opened the door.

Mary Ellen was wearing jeans and a light-weight jacket. Her face was flushed, and she looked as if she'd been crying.

"What's up, Mary Ellen?" Nicole was careful to keep her voice neutral. No accusation, just a reasonable tone. "I thought you weren't going out tonight."

Mary Ellen refused to meet Nicole's eyes, and she wore the expression of a little kid caught doing something forbidden. "No. I mean, I just met a couple of friends—um—down in the lobby. I'm on my way to bed now." She looked down at the jacket she was wearing. Her eyes met Nicole's, only to dart away again.

"I didn't leave the hotel, ma'am," the girl went on. "I promise. I told my friends I'd go out, but then I remembered what you all told me—about the media? So we just sat in the lobby and talked."

"I hope you didn't run into any problems," Nicole said.

"No, ma'am. The place was empty. Nobody bothered us. I'm really tired. Goodnight." She went into her room and softly closed the door.

Back in her own room, Nicole dialed the front desk, described Mary Ellen to the night clerk and asked if he'd seen her and her friends in the lobby.

"I did see a girl like that. She came down around—" he was silent, apparently thinking about it "—I'd say around midnight and left by the front door. I think she came back a few minutes ago, but I was on the phone, so I'm not sure. When I saw her earlier, she was alone. And we haven't had anyone sitting in the lobby. I would have noticed."

Nicole set her alarm for 7:00 a.m. As soon as she woke up, she checked on Mary Ellen. The girl was fast asleep. Since it was Sunday, Nicole planned to let her sleep until 10:00 before waking her. Then they'd go shopping. Today was their one chance to buy clothes for the girl to wear to court.

Her next order of business was to call Sue and tell her about Mary Ellen's outing and the fact that she'd lied about not leaving the hotel.

"Damn," said Sue. "I had a hunch all that humility and 'ma'am-ing' were too good to be true."

"Look at it this way," said Nicole, "now that we know we can't trust her, we'll take precautions. I'll sleep in the living room tonight. The couch pulls out into a bed, and I'm a light sleeper. If she attempts to go out, I'll try to talk her out of it. If she goes anyway, I'll follow her."

"Good idea," Sue said.

Nicole ordered breakfast from room service and was just finishing when the phone rang. "This is Geneva Ford," a woman said. "I'm an attorney with WAR. I'd like to speak to Mary Ellen Barnes."

"She's asleep," Nicole said. "Can I take a message?"

"I'm downstairs in the lobby. I'd like to meet with her."

Nicole introduced herself and said, "I'll come down and talk to you, but I have to get dressed first. Give me ten minutes."

"Oh, all right," the woman said, clearly annoyed. *Too bad*, Nicole thought. She wasn't going to let a stranger talk to Mary Ellen without checking her out. Why hadn't the woman called ahead?

Nicole phoned Sue. "That is the name of the attorney," Sue said. "But go down and make sure she's the real thing before you bring her up to the suite."

Nicole cleaned her teeth and ran a brush through her hair. She checked her reflection in the mirror. Her hair was still wavy from yesterday's hot-roller session. She made a mental note to have her highlights touched up. She wasn't beautiful, but she could do a fairly convincing job with makeup. No time for that now. Instead, she dabbed on some lip gloss and pulled a fake smile at her reflection. Her dimples appeared. *Damn*, she thought, they made it hard for people to take her seriously. As soon as they saw those dimples, they jumped to certain conclusions: that she was sweet, a pushover. Well, let them think so.

She pulled on one of the outfits she'd packed: a pair of white jeans, a blue knit top, and woven-leather sandals. Then she was on her way down to the lobby.

Even at first glance, it was clear Geneva Ford was the real thing. She was a well-preserved woman of indeterminate age who gave off a vibe of negative energy, impatiently tapping one of her strappy high heels and glancing around the room. Her close-cropped white hair was spikey on top, and she was wearing a smart, asymmetrically cut black dress with big buttons down the front. The outfit made her stand out among the casually dressed guests in the lobby. This was Santa Monica a.k.a. Silicon Beach. No one dressed up here, especially on a weekend morning.

"Let's have some coffee," Nicole said after she and Geneva exchanged introductions. A waiter was tending a nearby table; Nicole gave him a wave and he hurried over to take their orders. Nicole ordered a latte; Geneva just shook her head and motioned the waiter away. After he was gone, Geneva asked about Mary Ellen, and Nicole told her of the girl's late-night excursion.

"That's completely unacceptable." The woman's words were clipped with disapproval. "Mary Ellen promised us this case would get her undivided attention and that she wouldn't contact other students until the trial was over."

She stopped talking when the waiter arrived with Nicole's order. The two women remained silent while he placed a small white china tray on the low table with the latte and a plate of assorted biscotti.

Geneva was tapping her foot again, clearly impatient to get back to business.

"You don't have to worry," Nicole said. "I've got things under control. I'll sleep on the fold-out couch in the front room. She won't be able to sneak out without waking me."

Geneva went on as if she hadn't heard. "I'm going to have a talk with that girl. We decided to back Mary Ellen's case because we felt she'd make a convincing witness. She seemed so determined to see justice served. Frankly, I'm shocked."

As Nicole listened, she selected a chocolate-dipped biscotti from the plate.

"We have five of these cases in progress." Geneva spoke in a voice that reminded Nicole of Mrs. Fox, the dean of girls at her old middle school, unable to converse in a tone that wasn't hectoring and argumentative. "Our goal is to make colleges and universities more sensitive to rape cases. They've improved, but they still fall down when college athletes or prominent academics are involved. I'm sure you know how much money top college football teams attract in TV rights, sponsorships, and alumni donations."

They lapsed into silence. Geneva was gazing out the window at people strolling along the beach. Nicole wondered if the attorney was regretting her wardrobe choice. Probably not. She didn't seem like the kind of person who'd kick off her shoes for a walk in the sand.

When Nicole finished her latte, she said, "If you're ready, I'll take you to the suite and wake up Mary Ellen."

It took a while for Nicole to get Mary Ellen out of bed. "I'm so tired," the girl said. "Just give me another fifteen minutes." She burrowed head under the pillow while Nicole pulled back the covers.

At last Mary Ellen emerged from her room wearing the pink, flowered dress from the day before, now more than a little wrinkled. She wasn't wearing shoes.

"Well, young lady." Geneva didn't bother to hide her irritation. "I don't like what I've been hearing about you—leaving the hotel in the middle of the night. And then lying about it."

Mary Ellen flushed and looked down at her feet. As if suddenly noticing they were bare, she covered one foot with the other and curled her toes under. "Yes, ma'am," she said. "I'm sorry. It was such a hard day. I couldn't sleep, and I thought the fresh air—" her voice trailed off. "I won't do it again." She sat down on the couch, tucking her feet under her.

"I should hope not," Geneva said. "But I think I have the right to know where you went and who you saw."

Mary Ellen worked her mouth a few times, but no sound came out. Finally, she managed, "A couple of girls from school. We were planning to go to Hollywood, but Ms. Graves here and that other lady said I shouldn't do that. So we just sat in the lobby and talked. But I didn't say anything about the case, and no one saw us."

"I'm sorry, Mary Ellen, but you're not telling the truth," Nicole said. "I checked with the night desk clerk, and he said he saw you leave the hotel, and there weren't any people in the lobby while he was on duty."

The girl flushed again. "I didn't want you to worry about my going out. But we didn't run into anyone. We just sat on the beach and talked."

"Well, I'm astonished," Geneva said. "After everything we've done for you, you're sneaking out and lying to us. Not only that, but you agreed not to meet with anyone from the university, and you did just that. You might inadvertently say something that would damage our case. It would also be bad if the paparazzi caught you running around in the middle of the night. A lot depends on your image, the idea that you're a nice, clean-cut girl."

Geneva nodded before continuing, "Now we asked you this before, but I want you to think very carefully before you answer. Is there anything in your past—anything at all—that could undermine this case?"

Mary Ellen met her eyes. "No, ma'am."

Apparently satisfied, Geneva stood and picked up her purse. "All right then. I'll see you in court tomorrow morning at 9:00. Don't even think of being late." She paused to take in Mary Ellen's wrinkled dress. "You have something more appropriate to wear in court, I trust."

Nicole saw Geneva out. As soon as the door closed, she turned to Mary Ellen and they both spoke at the same time. But Mary Ellen said, "What a witch!" to Nicole's "What a bitch!" They laughed.

A little while later, Nicole and Mary Ellen were in the limo, heading toward Century City to outfit the girl for her coming ordeal.

THREE

THE DAY'S SHOPPING WENT WELL. Mary Ellen let Nicole choose the outfits she was to wear. When they were back in the limo heading for the hotel, Mary Ellen said, "Thank you for the beautiful clothes."

"Don't thank me, Mary Ellen," Nicole said. "The WAR organization is paying."

"I know," the girl said. "But you have such good taste, ma'am, and you found some really nice things. You're so pretty and well dressed. Do you think you could help with my hair and makeup tomorrow morning?"

Nicole wished the girl would stop calling her "ma'am" and trying to ingratiate herself. But she simply said, "I'll be happy to."

Back in the suite, Mary Ellen's mood sank. Barely responding to Nicole's attempts at conversation, the girl kept her eyes glued to the TV. After a while, she got up. "I'm tired. I'm going to take a nap."

Nicole read for a bit, then went into her room to call Josh. They discussed how each had spent the day. Josh was just heading out to his parents' for dinner.

After they hung up, she returned to the living room. Everything appeared in order, but she suddenly realized that she shouldn't have left the front door unwatched. What if Mary Ellen had snuck out again? She knocked on the girl's door. When there was no response, she knocked again and opened the door. Mary Ellen, lying on the bed, lifted her head and gave Nicole a startled look. "What?" she said. "Is something wrong?"

"I just wanted to be sure you're okay."

"I'm fine. I was asleep."

"Sorry," Nicole said, gently closing the door. She killed some time reading the paper and doing a crossword puzzle. She called her sister. When the call went to voicemail, she left a message. Stephanie, she imagined, was probably out with a new boyfriend, of which there seemed to be an endless supply. To Nicole, they were all alike: incorrigible slackers. To a man, they displayed negative attitudes toward just about everything except Stephanie. Until she broke up with them. Then things could get unpleasant. Steph currently had two restraining orders against rejected suitors who refused to take "no" for an answer.

As soon as Steph acquired a new boyfriend, Nicole would do a background check on the office database. So far, none of them had criminal records, but they often had bad credit ratings and piles of unpaid traffic tickets. Many were divorced, some several times. A few had outstanding warrants for failure to pay child support.

At first Nicole had shared this information with Stephanie, who didn't appreciate what she called Nicole's *snooping*. "I'm not going to marry him," Steph would say. "Do you think I'm that stupid?" More recently Nicole kept these background checks to herself, vowing not to say anything unless one of these men seemed truly dangerous.

Nicole was feeling restless. She wished she could somehow arrange for Josh to visit or, at the very least, get out of the hotel for a walk. But it was her job to stay close to Mary Ellen, and the girl couldn't risk going out. Even if the press didn't find her, anyone with a smart phone might recognize her from the news, take her picture, and tweet her location to the world. Nicole picked up her book again.

Late in the afternoon, Mary Ellen emerged from her room. Her eyes were red, her face swollen from crying. She immediately went into the bathroom. After a while she came out, looking slightly better. Nicole patted the couch next her. "Let's have a chat and get your mind off things."

Mary Ellen sat down, sniffling, and blew her nose on a tissue wadded up in her hand.

"Tell me about home," Nicole said. "I've never lived in a small town. What's it like?"

Mary Ellen considered this, then shook her head. "I hate it. When I started Oceanside, I hoped I'd never have to go back. Can we talk about you instead?"

"Sure, what do you want to know?"

"Do you have a boyfriend?"

"I do," Nicole said. "In fact, we're getting married later this year."

"You are?" For the first time Mary Ellen smiled. The smile lit up her face, erasing the downcast expression she'd been wearing since she arrived. "Are you having a big, white wedding? What's your dress like?"

"No white dress, I'm afraid. You see, I was married before, so I'm wearing lavender silk with a wreath of flowers in my hair instead of a veil. Actually, I can show you." She flipped through the photos on her iPad to locate the one her sister had snapped of her in her wedding outfit the day they'd gone shopping.

Stephanie had been so excited about news of Josh's proposal, that she'd insisted they visit some bridal shops right away. She'd tried to talk Nicole into a purple velvet sheath that bared one shoulder.

"Why don't you get it?" Nicole had said. "It's more your style."

Steph had looked at the price tag and said, "Whoa! $900. No thanks."

"Don't worry," Nicole had said. "I'm buying. You're my maid of honor."

When Nicole located the photo, she handed the iPad to Mary Ellen. "It's beautiful," the girl said. "Do you have a picture of your fiancé?"

Nichole nodded, searching through her photos until she found her favorite shot of Josh. Mary Ellen drew in a deep breath. "Oh, he's so good looking, and he looks really nice."

"He is. He's wonderful." Nicole smiled and flipped through some of the other photos of him and the two of them together. She never tired of looking at him. He was tall with wavy, light brown hair. He had expressive blue eyes fringed with pale lashes. His most striking features were his prominent cheekbones and an easy smile that started at one side of his mouth before spreading to the rest of his face. He was always smiling, except when—she dismissed the thought.

"You're so lucky," Mary Ellen was saying. "How did you meet?"

"By chance, on the street," Nicole said. "A car was speeding around the corner, and Josh pulled me out of its path. After he saved my life, he asked me out."

"What about that guy who helped us through the mob at the airport?" Mary Ellen said. "At first I thought he was one of the paparazzi, but it was like you two were friends."

"We are friends," Nicole said. "He's a reporter. I met him about a year ago, when the paparazzi were after me."

"They were? How come?"

Nicole sighed. "It's a long story."

"We've got all day."

"That's true," Nicole said. She described what had happened after a workmate was murdered and inexplicably left her a fortune. It got into the news, and the story went viral. She'd had to hide from the media and the killer, who thought she knew more than she did.

"Everything eventually worked out," Nicole said. "I gave a final, exclusive interview to Greg Albee, the man you saw me talking to. He works for the *L.A. Times.*"

"What about the money you inherited?" the girl said. "Does that mean you're rich?"

"Hardly. The estate is all tied up. The man who left it to me earned his money by blackmailing people, and he never paid taxes. The IRS has a hold on his property so they can collect what he owed them. Law enforcement is trying to confiscate the rest because he was involved in criminal activity. My lawyer is appealing, so I may get something after the house is sold, if it ever does. It's been on the market for almost a year, but there aren't many buyers for a house someone was murdered in."

Mary Ellen's eyes grew wide. "You mean he was murdered there?"

"Exactly," Nicole said. "That's one reason, among many, I'd never live there. The whole thing was pretty traumatic. I wasn't as lucky as you. I didn't have anyone to keep the media away or protect me from his killer; I had to go into hiding. I ended up staying with Josh. That was the real beginning for us."

"Wow! That is so romantic," Mary Ellen smiled again, leaning over to hug Nicole. "I'm so happy for you."

"Why don't we watch TV and order something to eat?"

Room service and romantic comedies took up what remained of the afternoon and evening. They started getting ready for bed around 10:00. As Nicole made up the fold-out bed in the living room, Mary Ellen said, "Aren't you going to sleep in your room?"

"No," Nicole said. "I have to make sure you don't go out again."

"But I won't," Mary Ellen said. "I promised."

"I believe you. But your lawyers insisted I sleep between you and the front door."

"Okay," Mary Ellen said. "But you can trust me. I'm not going anywhere."

The night passed peacefully, and Mary Ellen was true to her

word. There was no repeat of the previous night's outing.

When morning came, Nicole called Josh before she got out of bed. As they were about to hang up, he said, "Look, why don't we meet for lunch?"

"I'd love that," she said. "But I have to stay within an easy drive of the courthouse. They want me to look after Mary Ellen when today's session ends, and there's no telling what time that will be."

"If I'm not too swamped, I'll come to you," Josh said. "Will you be at the hotel?"

"No. I think I'll go into the office. I'm sick of this place, and I won't have anything to do after I drop her off at court."

"Wait a minute." His voice had that edge to it. "You told me you wouldn't have to go to court with her."

"Quit worrying," she said. "I'm just delivering her. I'll stay in the limo; it has dark windows. No one will see me."

"Promise?"

"Promise."

"Okay, then," Josh said. "I'm heading for work. I'll see you around noon."

Nicole dressed and ordered breakfast. Around 7:30, she knocked on Mary Ellen's door. There was no response. She went into the girl's room and found her hunched under the blankets.

"Time to get up," Nicole said.

Mary Ellen moaned and pulled the covers over her head.

Nicole sat down on the bed, put her hand on the girl's shoulder, and gently shook her. "Today's the day, Mary Ellen. You have to get up."

"Just a few more minutes," the girl said. "Please."

"OK, but next time you really are getting up."

Nicole set her phone to alert her in five minutes. When she went back, the girl still wouldn't budge. Finally, Nicole pulled Mary Ellen's arm until the girl sat up and swung her legs over the side of the bed. She stumbled into the bathroom.

Twenty minutes later, Nicole knocked on the door. There was

a long pause before it opened.

"Mary Ellen!" Nicole said, thrusting the girl's clothes at her. "You have to get dressed! The limousine will be here in half an hour."

At 8:30, she knocked on the bathroom door again and went in. Mary Ellen was in a fog. She was dressed, but her hair wasn't brushed, and she was still barefoot.

"Have you cleaned your teeth?" Nicole said. When the girl nodded, she said, "Wash your face. I'll help with the rest." She went into the bedroom to find a comb and brush. She quickly fixed the girl's hair and had her sit on the toilet lid to put on her shoes.

"Wait!" Mary Ellen stood up. "I'm going to be sick." Indeed, her face had gone white, and beads of sweat dotted her forehead.

"Sit down, put your head between your knees, and take long, deep breaths," Nicole said. Then she added, "I know what you're going through. Appearing in court is scary. But you aren't on the stand today. You won't have to do anything. Jury selection starts in thirty minutes. We can't be late."

At 8:50, they were in the hotel's back alley, getting into a black sedan with dark-tinted windows.

"How long does it take to get to the Santa Monica Courthouse?" Nicole asked the driver. "We have to be there by nine."

"It's not far," he said "You'll make it."

Nicole glanced over at Mary Ellen. Her face was ashen. Nicole told her to put her head between her knees again. The girl complied.

A few minutes later they pulled up in front of the Santa Monica Courthouse, a three-story block of utilitarian architecture from the 1950s. The front lawn was packed with reporters, photographers, and camera crews. Several news vans were double parked, tying up traffic. Their driver wove his way past the confusion, turned the corner, and pulled up to the curb.

Nearby was the side entrance where they were to drop off

Mary Ellen. Barriers manned by six police officers created a wide path to keep reporters and trial junkies at a distance.

Waiting on the sidewalk was Sue's paralegal, Alise. Nicole recognized her from the office. Mary Ellen was about to get out of the car when she got a good look at Alise. Tall and rangy, the young woman had a long face and dark, intense eyes. Her hair was pulled tight into a bun. Nicole was sure Alise was good at her job, but her severe appearance was off-putting. Indeed, the sight of her seemed to throw Mary Ellen into a panic. She sat back down and turned to Nicole, eyes brimming. "Please come with me. I can't do this alone."

"You won't be alone. Alise will take good care of you. I promise. I'll be back to pick you up as soon as it's over." Nicole pulled Mary Ellen into a hug. She was actually shaking. "You'll be fine," Nicole said, as she patted Mary Ellen's back.

Mary Ellen looked out the window. Her eyes were enormous, darting around at the noisy crowd and then to Alise, who by now had opened the door and taken a firm grip of Mary Ellen's arm. After a moment's resistance, Mary Ellen allowed herself to be pulled from the car. Reporters were waving microphones in their direction and shouting questions. The police and the barricade kept them away so the two women could dash into the courthouse. Nicole waited until they disappeared inside before she told the driver to take her to her office.

Colbert and Smith Investigations was located in a tall white building across from the Los Angeles County Museum of Art. Nicole didn't really have to come in, since she'd worked all weekend. But she was at loose ends, and this would give her a chance to keep up with her assignments.

Josh called at 11:30 a.m. to say he wasn't going to make it; he had too much work. "I'm sorry," he said. "I really miss you."

"I know," she said. "I miss you, too."

"TMZ had a video this morning of Mary Ellen arriving at the courthouse with all those paparazzi outside," he said. "Just knowing you were in that car—."

"Well, they didn't see me, and there's no way they're going to," she said. "Call me tonight, okay?"

Sue called Nicole at 3:00 to say that the jury had been chosen, and the judge had adjourned for the day. Nicole summoned the limo. They picked up Mary Ellen at the courthouse, then took a circuitous route to the hotel in order to lose the paparazzi tailing them. Back in the suite, the girl was subdued, spending the rest of the day in her room. She came out for dinner, played with her food, and went back to her room. Nicole could hear her murmuring on the phone. Although she kept her voice low, it sounded like she was arguing with whoever was at the other end.

Around 10:00, Mary Ellen came out again, carrying her pj's and a cosmetics bag. She disappeared into the bathroom to get ready for bed. Nicole, who was waiting to do her own bedtime regimen, wondered why such an expensive suite would have just a single bathroom. Once Mary Ellen was done, Nicole showered, figuring it would save time in the morning. Then she made up the couch into a bed.

Before turning in, she went to check on Mary Ellen. She knocked gently on the door, and, getting no response, opened it. The room was partially illuminated by the lights on the pier a ways up the beach. Nicole could see Mary Ellen lying in bed, fast asleep. She closed the door

Climbing into bed, Nicole glanced at the clock. It was 11:30. Her mind was racing, and despite how tired she was, she couldn't sleep. She kept thinking about the girl and how frightened she must be. She wished she could go in to court to offer her support. But, no. That wasn't possible—not without exposing herself to a lot of nasty publicity. Still, given the girl's emotional state, Nicole wondered how she'd be able to testify. Oceanside's sports-minded alums had hired a top defense attorney for Doshan. If Mary Ellen was falling apart at the prospect of sitting through jury selection, how would she hold up under cross examination?

Nicole tried not to think about it. She was too tired. Then a new worry popped into her head: Joanne was pretty sick. What if she didn't get better in time to take over this week? The care of this frightened and unpredictable girl would fall to Nicole. Worse yet, she might very well catch the attention of the tabloids and paparazzi. She lay awake a long time, wondering if she'd made a terrible mistake agreeing to this assignment.

FOUR

TODAY WAS THE DAY the lawyers would present their opening statements. But the main event would be Mary Ellen's testimony. Her performance was crucial to the trial's outcome.

Nicole rose early, dressed and sat down to the breakfast she'd ordered the night before, perusing the *L.A. Times* while she ate. An article about the trial was featured on the front page of the California section, accompanied by a photo of Doshan on the football field. Mary Ellen's picture was relegated to the continuation page. It had been taken while the media was mobbing her at the airport. She looked miserable, and the photographer had caught her at her worst.

She turned to her iPad to see what the tabloids had to say. They each carried briefs about the upcoming trial. One was accompanied by yet another bad photo of Mary Ellen. It also featured a video clip of one of Doshan's feats on the football field. Even Nicole, who knew little about the game, could see what a gifted athlete he was.

Mary Ellen was awake when Nicole went in to get her up.

"What a night," she complained as she got out of bed.

"Didn't you sleep?" Nicole said.

"Hardly. I kept having nightmares. You know, about being cornered by those guys with cameras. I don't think I've ever been so scared in my life." Mary Ellen paused, and added, almost as an afterthought: "Except when Doshan..." She left the sentence unfinished.

Room service had delivered Mary Ellen's breakfast along with Nicole's, but the girl refused to eat or even have coffee. "I'm sorry, ma'am, but I don't think I can keep anything down," she said. "Would you mind helping me choose what to wear?"

Nicole picked out a simple black A-line skirt and a blue crew-necked sweater with black boots. She pulled the necklace with the little gold cross out from under the sweater.

Once Mary Ellen was dressed, Nicole took time to fix the girl's hair. Instead of letting it hang straight, she pulled the front sections back, fastening them with a clip at the crown of her head. The style made her look childlike and innocent, one hair bow away from Alice in Wonderland.

They were already in the alley behind the hotel when their driver arrived. At the courthouse, the crowd had grown from the day before; there were now six TV vans, even more people armed with cameras, and a throng of spectators.

Once again, Alise was waiting at the curb. As soon as they pulled up, she opened the door, leaned in, and held out her hand. Mary Ellen shrank back, sliding across the seat toward Nicole.

"This is all a terrible mistake," Mary Ellen said. "I thought I could do this, but I can't."

"You have to," Alise said. "WAR spent months preparing this case. Now it all depends on you."

Nicole could see this was the wrong approach. Applying pressure was just going to upset the girl more. "It's okay, Alise," she said. "Why don't you give us a minute."

After a slight hesitation, Alise stepped back and, at Nicole's gesture, closed the limo door. "What's going on, Mary Ellen?" Nicole said. "Tell me."

The girl started to cry, and her words came out in a rush. "I can't go in there and talk about it in front of all those people. And him there…" she paused and seemed to gain a little more control of herself. "I thought—I guess I thought it would be different. A small room—just the judge and a few lawyers."

"Listen to me," Nicole said. "You've been very brave. You've spoken up, and you're in the right. Something bad happened to you, and you want to prevent it from happening to anyone else."

"I don't care. They can drag me in there, but I won't testify. They can't make me."

Now what? Nicole thought. She reached across the weeping girl and opened the door. "Alise," she said. "Go find Sue. Tell her we need her."

As Alise headed into the courthouse, Nicole closed the car door and put her arm around Mary Ellen. "You're going to be fine," she said soothingly, as if talking to a child. "Go ahead and have a good cry. It will make you feel better. Everything's going to be okay."

It wasn't long before Sue arrived at the car, along with another woman. It took a moment for Nicole to realize it was Geneva Ford, completely transformed. In place of the white, close-cropped hair, she now was sporting a brunette bob, which had to be a wig, although it looked real enough. The do was flattering, making her look younger and more hip.

Sue opened the car door. "What's going on?"

"Just a bad case of stage fright," Nicole said. She looked back at Mary Ellen. The girl had stopped crying and was snuffling into a tissue.

"I'll do it if she comes with me," Mary Ellen's voice was hoarse from crying. She turned to Nicole. "You're the only one who cares. I'll be okay if you're there."

Sue and Geneva were looking at Nicole expectantly. "But I

can't—" she began. Then, realizing this could blow the case, she reluctantly agreed. She did a quick inventory of her appearance. She was already wearing her sunglasses. She reached into her bag for her hat, but it wasn't there; she'd left it at the hotel. She took a deep breath and got out of the car, pulling the girl with her. As they hurried up the path to the courthouse, a murmur went through the crowd, and someone shouted her name. Other reporters joined in. "What are you doing here, Nicole?" someone yelled. And "How do you know Mary Ellen?" "What's your connection with this case?"

She never thought she'd have to endure this kind of attention again, but here it was. Was it coincidence, bad luck, or karma for something she'd done in an earlier life? And why hadn't she seen it coming? She thought of Josh and her stomach churned.

The hubbub faded as the courthouse door closed behind them. Once they were inside, no one seemed to recognize them. They headed up the crowded stairway and went through an unmarked door. It led to a hallway that brought them to the front of the courtroom.

Alise started to propel Nicole to the front row of the visitors' gallery, but Mary Ellen grabbed Nicole's arm. "She has to sit next to me," she said.

"The front table is reserved for counsel and plaintiff, Mary Ellen," Alise said. "Nicole doesn't belong there."

"Then I'm leaving!" The girl got up as if to head for the door.

Sue stepped forward and put her hand on Mary Ellen's shoulder. "It's okay. We'll tell the judge you need her for emotional support. He'll understand."

Just then, Doshan and his attorneys entered on the opposite side of the room and sat at the defense table. Mary Ellen glanced at Doshan, then looked quickly away.

From the Internet, Nicole knew what he looked like. But seeing him in person was completely different. He was enormous—six-foot-five—dwarfing the lawyers who were with him. Doshan was dressed in a slim-fit navy suit, white shirt, and gray-and-navy tie. He had close-cropped hair and his skin was a dark, burnished copper. He was very handsome. If he had a flaw, it was his ears, which fit closely to his head at the bottom and flared out at the top, like sugar-bowl handles. Most of the photos Nicole had seen showed his broad smile and deep dimples, but he wasn't smiling now. Staring straight ahead, he looked grim and unhappy.

She hadn't really thought about his fate in relation to this trial. Until now she'd assumed he was guilty and deserved to pay for it. But if the case went against him, the stigma and, most likely a financial penalty, could wreck his life. With his beauty—for he was indeed beautiful—his athletic talent, and his leadership qualities, it seemed a terrible waste. What a stupid way for someone to throw away his life.

It wasn't long before spectators began to file in. Two young men, almost as big as Doshan, were among the first. They sat in the third row, immediately behind the seats reserved for the media. When Mary Ellen saw them, she stiffened, drew a deep breath, and flushed.

"What's wrong?" Nicole whispered, but the girl didn't answer. In response, Sue jotted something on her yellow legal pad and turned it for Nicole to read. "Doshan's teammates," it said. "The one on the left is his best friend."

Nicole glanced at them again. They were big guys. One was a Latino who was wide as well as tall. The one on the left—Doshan's buddy—had buzz-cut blond hair, flat on top like a marine's and a tattoo that ran up the right side of his neck from under the collar of his shirt. It was a snake's head, which made her wonder if the creature's body was tattooed on his chest. As if he sensed her stare, he looked at Nicole and their eyes met. He gave her a sardonic smile and winked. She was the first to look away.

By now Mary Ellen had swiveled her chair around and was openly staring at the men. Her lips were parted slightly, her expression unreadable. Sue leaned over, whispered in Mary

Ellen's ear, and turned her chair so she faced front again.

After court was called to order, Geneva stood and asked to confer with the judge. She approached the bench, and one of Doshan's lawyers joined her. They kept their voices low. When they were done, Geneva nodded at Nicole, who moved up to take the seat next to Mary Ellen.

Geneva then turned and faced the jury to begin her opening statement. After introducing herself, she delivered an impassioned speech about how Mary Ellen was raped and, almost as bad, Oceanside University refused to believe her story and give her the support she needed. The university had also failed to protect her by neglecting to have campus police patrol the grounds on the night in question and then failed to address the crime by refusing to punish the perpetrator. Nicole was surprised by how different this Geneva was from the person she'd met two days before. The hard edge and argumentative tone were gone. Her voice was soft, reasonable, and persuasive. She focused on the jurors, making eye contact with each. Whenever she turned her head, her shining, dark hair swung forward on one side or the other. The effect was almost hypnotic.

Doshan's attorney, George Goodman, was a tall, grey-haired man with a smooth voice and an air of authority. He explained that he would prove there had been no rape. "This encounter was nothing more than consensual sex between two adults. For her own reasons—embarrassment, shame, or something we don't know—Mary Ellen Barnes invented this fiction of forcible rape."

Each attorney spoke for about a half hour. The rest of the morning was taken up by a forensics expert, who introduced the evidence furnished by Mary Ellen's attorneys. One item was the underwear she'd been wearing the night of her encounter with Doshan. She'd brought it, unwashed, to the university health center when she reported the rape, two months after the event. The expert said there was semen on the underwear, but no blood. He read from a DNA report, which identified the semen as Doshan's.

Next, the forensic witness used a projector to show photos of bruises on Mary Ellen's arms. These were selfies she'd taken after the rape. The photos had been downloaded to a computer and printed out. Each was stamped with the date it was taken. The witness explained that the bruising was consistent with Mary Ellen's being grabbed and held by someone stronger than herself, someone with large hands.

Under cross-examination by Goodman the forensics expert agreed that, aside from these photos, there was no other evidence that Mary Ellen suffered any physical injury.

"Can you tell us with complete certainty when these photos were taken?" Goodman said.

"Well," the witness said, "the date stamp says January 22, which would be the day after the alleged incident."

"Isn't it true that date stamps like these can be changed on a cellphone or computer?"

"On some. Yes."

"So, this date is open to question, isn't it?" Goodman said.

The witness seemed unwilling to concede the point. "I suppose you could say that."

"'Yes' or 'no' is the proper answer," Goodman said.

"Yes."

Goodman turned away. "No more questions for the witness at this time."

The judge banged his gavel and said they would break for lunch and reconvene at 1:00. Nicole and Mary Ellen were shown to a private waiting room. After a few minutes, Alise bought them some plastic-wrapped sandwiches and soft drinks from the cafeteria. All Mary Ellen would take was a Coke. Alise was brusque to the point of rudeness. She seemed angry, no doubt because of her demotion from Mary Ellen's caretaker to waitress. After asking if they needed anything else, she left.

Lunch was all but inedible. Nicole's chopped-egg sandwich turned out to be soggy and tasteless. She took a few bites, rewrapped the remains, and threw it in the trash.

There was no conversation. Mary Ellen was busy texting on her phone, and Nicole wondered who the girl was communicating with. She wasn't supposed to discuss the trial with anyone, and there was always the danger that the paparazzi had hacked her phone and were reading her texts as she wrote them.

Nicole was about to ask her to stop when her own phone dinged with a new message. It was from Josh. "I've got some time," it said. "Want to meet for lunch? I could be there by 1:00."

She bit her lip, trying to think of a way to tell him she'd ended up in court with Mary Ellen without provoking him. But there was no way around it. "ME had a meltdown in the limo," she typed in. "Refused to go to court unless I came with her. I'm stuck for the day."

Almost instantly, a reply popped up. "Shit! I knew it!"

"I know. I hate myself for agreeing to do this," she wrote. "You were right. I should have listened."

"The media knows you're there?"

"Yes."

"Damn it!" he wrote back. Then, "I've got to go."

"Wait!" she texted. "Call me." He didn't reply, nor did he call.

After a few minutes, she decided to call him. But she couldn't do it in front of Mary Ellen. She'd know Nicole and Josh were fighting because of her, and that would add to the girl's burden. Nicole got up. "I'll be right back," she said. Mary Ellen was too busy texting to look up.

Nicole went into the hallway that led back to the courtroom and closed the door. She tapped in Josh's cell number. It rang several times and went to voicemail. She tried his office number with no better result. Had he seen her caller ID and refused to pick up? She called him again and left a message: "On top of everything that's gone wrong today, I can't stand having you mad at me. Please call." She looked at her watch. It was 12:30 p.m. "Make it soon," she added. "Court resumes at 1:00, and I'll have to turn off my phone."

She spent the next half hour in agony. Her phone didn't ring, there were no messages from Josh, and she felt like crying. All too soon, the bailiff arrived to escort them back.

When the judge called the court to order, Mary Ellen took the witness chair, and Geneva got up to question her. "Can you explain what happened on January 21st of last year?"

As she began, Mary Ellen's voice was shaky. "It was around 10:30 on a school night. I'd been studying and was getting sleepy. I had a lot more work, so I decided to get some fresh air. I planned to take a ten-minute walk, then come back and study. It was nice out, and there was a full moon. I should have circled the building and gone back to my room, like I'd planned, but instead I headed down the hill toward the ocean. That's when I noticed a bunch of students sitting on the beach across the highway. I normally wouldn't hang out with people I don't know, but somehow, that night..." she paused and looked at Geneva.

Geneva nodded encouragingly. "Go on."

"When I got there, I saw they were, like, drinking beer. I don't drink, but one of the guys offered me lemonade, so I sat down and had some. Actually, I had, like, two glasses. I didn't really talk to anybody, and I should have left. But—" she paused and looked over at the jury. "—I think they'd, like, put something in my lemonade—liquor or I don't know what. I fell asleep right there on the sand. That's not like me at all.

"When I woke up, most of the others were gone. The only ones left were these guys from the football team. It made me nervous. They have a reputation—you know, with girls. Doshan saw I was awake, and he came over. He said he'd walk me back to my dorm."

"How did you feel about that?"

"Well, I didn't really know him that well, but he was polite and seemed concerned, so I said 'Okay.'"

"You said you didn't know him that well. Had you met him before that night?"

"Yes. He came to Bible study a couple of times."

"What did you talk about when he walked you home?"

"Bible study. He said he was really interested but couldn't come much because of football practice. Then he told me about his grandmother's rosary. She'd left it to him when she died. He told me how much it meant to him and that he kept it locked in his desk. When we passed his dorm, he asked if I'd like to go up to his room and see the rosary. I was feeling more comfortable with him by then, so I said yes. When we got to his room, he closed the door and locked it. I asked about the rosary, and he just laughed. I said I wanted to leave, but he threw me on the bed and got on top of me."

As Mary Ellen was saying this, Nicole glanced at Doshan. He was looking down, shaking his head. His lawyer reached over and gripped his shoulder, as if to steady him.

"He put his leg between my knees …" She began to cry and put her hands over her face.

Geneva's voice was gentle. "I know this is hard for you to talk about," she said. "But you'll have to say what happened next."

"He forced himself on me."

"Can you be more specific? What do you mean by 'forced himself?'"

Mary Ellen was still crying, her shoulders shaking. She dropped her hands, and her face was wet with tears. She drew in a ragged breath and mumbled something.

"You have to speak up, Mary Ellen," Geneva said. "We can't hear you."

Mary Ellen pulled a tissue out of her pocket, wiped her face, and blew her nose. Her eyes flickered briefly to the back row of the room, where the two athletes were still sitting. Then she said, quite clearly, "He pulled down my underwear and raped me."

"Is the person you know as Doshan in the courtroom today? Can you point him out?"

Hesitantly, Mary Ellen lifted her hand and pointed at Doshan.

For a brief moment, their eyes locked. Doshan's jaw was tight; he was clearly angry.

"Did you scream or call out?" Geneva said.

"No, I was too scared. I couldn't believe what was happening. It was like a bad dream, like you're paralyzed and can't even scream."

Geneva bowed her head for a long moment, as if contemplating her next question. Finally, she said, "But you didn't report this to the university right away."

"No."

"Did you tell your friends or anyone else about it?"

"No."

"Why not?"

By now Mary Ellen had somewhat regained her composure. "I was too embarrassed and ashamed. I felt it was my own fault. I shouldn't have been out there with kids who were drinking. I shouldn't have gone to his room. Later, the counselor at WAR told me a lot of girls blame themselves. When I said 'no' he should have respected that. He should have stopped."

"Thank you, Mary Ellen. That's all we need for now." With that, Geneva returned to her seat.

Doshan's lawyer, George Goodman, stood up and walked over to Mary Ellen.

"Now, Mary Ellen." His voice was kind, sympathetic. "Everyone in this courtroom understands how difficult it must be for you to talk about what happened. I hear that you're an observant Christian. Is that true?"

"Yes, sir." She looked confused and was studying his face, as if trying to figure out whose side he was on.

"And you believe that it's a sin to bear false witness," Goodman went on.

Mary Ellen blinked and looked away. "Yes, sir."

"Especially when that lie could ruin another person's life," he added.

Tears had begun to leak down her cheeks. "I'm not ly-lying," She choked on the word.

"Maybe you're just confused. I want you to think back about what really happened." He paused, as if expecting her to search her memory and come up with a different story. "Isn't it true that it was you who asked Doshan to walk you back to your dorm?"

She shook her head. She was crying in earnest now, covering her face with her hands.

Nicole noticed that Geneva had tensed as if she were about to stand up. Sue reached over, grasped Geneva's arm, and shook her head. Geneva pulled away. She looked annoyed but sat back in her seat.

"You need to answer the question 'yes' or 'no,'" Goodman prompted. "For the record."

She dropped her hands. "No! That's not—" She gulped back a sob. "That didn't happen."

He kept talking in the same calm tone, "You were thrilled Mr. Williams had noticed you and invited you to his room, weren't you? He asked if you were willing to have sex, and you said yes. Isn't that true? The encounter was consensual."

"No!" she said. "It wasn't like that. I vowed in church to save myself for marriage."

"All right, let me ask you this: You let—" He consulted his notes before he went on, "two whole months pass before you went to the authorities. Why did you wait so long?"

"I already said. I was ashamed. I was—" She broke down again, and her next words were unintelligible. She wilted against the railing in front of her and began to sob.

Geneva stood up. "Your honor—"

"Yes, yes," said the judge. "The witness appears too distraught to continue." He consulted his watch. "We'll take a forty-five-minute recess and be back here at 3:30."

Mary Ellen got up from the witness chair and stumbled over to the table where her lawyers and Nicole were sitting. The girl put her head on the table and continued crying. Nicole took her by the hand and led her to the waiting room. Sue, Geneva, and Alise were close behind.

"She's exhausted," Nicole told the women. "She didn't sleep last night."

"Do you think you can calm her down?" Sue said.

"I'll try," said Nicole, "but it would be easier on my own, if you don't mind."

After they were gone, Nicole said, "The worst is almost over, Mary Ellen. I know you can pull yourself together and finish the cross-examination. Otherwise, you'll just have to come back tomorrow and answer Mr. Goodman's questions."

The girl blew her nose and said in a shaky voice. "I'll try. Can you get me a glass of water?" Nicole remembered seeing a restroom sign in the short passage they'd used to get there from the courtroom. Lunch had been cleared away, but an unused plastic cup had been left on the table. She took the cup and went to get some water.

Moments later Nicole returned to an empty room. She could hear some kind of commotion from behind the room's other door, which led to the main corridor. The door opened, and a very pale Mary Ellen stumbled backward into the room. Reporters and paparazzi were crowded around her, shouting questions and shoving microphones in her face. With the help of the guard stationed outside, Nicole and the girl managed to shut and lock the door.

"Where were you going?" Nicole said. "You weren't trying to leave, were you?"

"No, ma'am. I needed the lady's room." The girl flushed and looked away. *She's lying*, Nicole thought. *She had every intention of leaving.*

"The women's room is back here." Nicole led Mary Ellen to the facility and waited outside until she was done. As sorry as she felt for the girl, who did seem genuinely distraught, Nicole reminded herself that Mary Ellen couldn't be trusted. Back in the waiting room, they sat for the next fifteen minutes without speaking. Nicole checked her messages again, but there was still no word from Josh. At last the bailiff opened the door and announced that the trial was about to resume.

Nicole linked arms with the girl and led her back. She was pale and her expression unreadable, but she did seem calmer.

Once Mary Ellen was back in the witness chair, Goodman resumed his questions.

"Before the break, you said you didn't report the alleged rape for two months because you were ashamed and afraid no one would believe you. Is that right?"

"Yes."

"When did you first contact the Women Against Rape organization?"

Mary Ellen looked confused. "I don't remember exactly."

"Was it before or after you filed your complaint against Mr. Williams?"

"Before. I called them for advice after I saw something about them on TV. Like how they help campus rape victims. They had me talk to a counselor. She said I should report Doshan to the university."

"Did she help you work out what you were going to say?"

Mary Ellen was quiet a moment. "No. I mean, I can't remember what she said because I was so upset. It was the first time I'd told anybody."

"I understand you're staying in a suite in a boutique hotel near the beach," Goodman said. "That's a pretty fancy place, isn't it?"

Geneva Ford stood up. "Objection. Argumentative."

"I withdraw the question," Goodman said. "Who is paying for the suite you're staying in?"

"WAR. I mean Women Against Rape."

"You also have a paid companion, a limousine to drive you, and what appears to be a new outfit. Who is paying for all this?"

Geneva stood up again. "Objection. How is this relevant?"

"I'm just trying to establish that Women Against Rape, which is an advocacy group, may have had undue influence over a naïve young woman and convinced her that she was raped when she, in fact, agreed to the encounter."

"Your honor!" Geneva said in an aggrieved tone.

"Mr. Goodman," the judge said. "Please limit your questions to establishing facts and stop fishing for admissions to back up theories about what might or might not have happened."

Without missing a beat, Goodman was ready with the next question. "Let's go back to the night of the alleged incident," he said. "Did you have anything to drink or any drugs?"

"I don't do drugs," Mary Ellen said. "And I don't drink alcohol. I just had some lemonade."

"Did the lemonade make you feel funny?"

"I guess. I mean, I got sleepy all of a sudden."

"What time did you wake up?" he said.

"After midnight. I checked my watch."

"What happened next?" he said.

Mary Ellen repeated what she'd told the court earlier.

"So you found yourself alone with those young men. Is that when you asked Doshan to walk with you?"

"No. He came over and asked me if I wanted him to take me back."

"What did you say?"

"I told him I'd appreciate it if he would do that," she said.

"Was that true? Did you appreciate his offer?"

"At the time I did. He was polite and seemed concerned."

The lawyer was quiet for a few moments, studying the floor as if considering what to ask next. When he looked up at her, his eyes slightly narrowed. "Now think back to when Doshan invited you up to his room. You went willingly, knowing you were going to have sex with him, didn't you?"

"No!" she said. "He said he wanted to show me his

grandmother's rosary. But when we got to his room, he locked the door and attacked me. You saw those bruises. That was from when he grabbed me and threw me on the floor."

"Floor?" Goodman looked at his notes. "Earlier you said it was the bed."

"Yes. I meant the bed."

"At any point did you tell him to stop?"

"I did! When he started putting his hands on me, but he wouldn't listen."

"What happened next?"

"He raped me."

"There must have been others on that floor of the dorm. Did you scream or call for help?"

"No. I was too frightened. I couldn't believe what was happening."

"After the incident you described, what happened next?"

"I got up, unlocked the door, and ran back to my dorm."

"Did the alleged assailant follow you?"

"How would I know?" For the first time, Mary Ellen sounded exasperated. "I didn't hear anybody running after me. It's not like I'd stop and look around to see."

"Can you tell us again why you didn't tell your roommate what happened?"

She drew a long, impatient breath. "I was ashamed, like it was my fault for being there. And I was afraid no one would believe me because Doshan is a big deal on campus. Everybody thinks he's such a great guy, and me—I'm just nobody. But the people at WAR told me that didn't matter. I was a victim of a crime; I'm suffering, and I want justice. People who say 'Well, it's a he-said, she-said' are just plain wrong. They're siding with guys, who will always deny being rapists."

Goodman regarded her for a long moment. "Have you ever seen a demonstration staged by the WAR organization?"

"No."

"Have you read any of their literature?"

"After I talked to the counselor, she sent me some of WAR's brochures. I looked through them."

"Do you realize you've just repeated, practically verbatim, some of the slogans that appear on placards carried by WAR demonstrators."

"No. That's not—" Mary Ellen was starting to cry again.

Goodman turned away. "Thank you, Ms. Barnes. That will be all."

By now it was 4:30. The judge adjourned for the day. Once again, the women filed into the waiting room to confer before going home for the night.

Nicole had one order of business in mind. "Sue, remember I told you that Mary Ellen couldn't sleep last night? I think that's one reason she fell apart on the stand. Can we arrange for her to see a doctor and get some sleeping pills?"

"We'll take care of it," said Sue. "I know someone who'll prescribe by phone. But, since it's a sleeping pill, it will have to be picked up in person. I'll tell the doctor to make it out to Alise so she can sign for it and bring it to you at the Windward."

They agreed to meet at 8:45 the next morning to strategize before court. They left by a back delivery door to escape the building without encountering the media.

FIVE

IT WAS SEVERAL HOURS BEFORE ALISE ARRIVED at the suite to drop off a small white pharmacy bag containing two bottles. One was labeled Valium, the other some kind of generic sleeping pill. Sue had already texted Nicole instructions: "Have Mary Ellen take one Valium right away, another half in the a.m. The sleeping pill is for bedtime. Keep the pills on your person at all times. Don't let her get her hands on them."

After Alise left, Mary Ellen came out of her room, flushed, puffy-eyed, and disheveled. Nicole handed her a single Valium. "Do you want water?" she said.

Listlessly, Mary Ellen shook her head. She popped the pill in her mouth and swallowed.

Nicole checked her watch. It was almost 8:00 p.m. "I'm going to order from room service. What do you want?"

"A burger and a Coke, I guess," Mary Ellen said. "I'm really not hungry." She got up from the couch and disappeared into the bathroom.

Nicole ordered Moroccan lamb with a side of spinach for

herself, the burger and Coke for Mary Ellen. It wasn't long before a young woman arrived with a serving cart carrying their orders. She unloaded two dome-covered plates and the beverages onto the dining table, parked the cart next to the door, and left.

Nicole sat down, waiting for Mary Ellen to join her. After a good ten minutes, she decided to find out what was taking so long. She was about to knock on the bathroom door when the girl came out.

Mary Ellen—her face now washed, her hair combed—was looking marginally better. But, as soon as she sat down at the table, she put her hands over her face and began to cry.

"What's wrong?" Nicole said. "You did really well today."

"I'm in so much trouble," Mary Ellen said. "I don't know what to do."

"What do you mean?"

"What Doshan's attorney said? About it being a sin to bear false witness? He's right, and I—I — " By now Mary Ellen was crying so hard it was impossible to understand her. She put her head on the table, shoulders shaking. After a while she looked up and met Nicole's eyes. "It was all a lie—everything I said in court. It wasn't rape."

Nicole was stunned, hardly able to take this in.

"It was just like his lawyer said," Mary Ellen went on. "I asked Doshan to walk me home. I'd met him before. He came to Bible study a few times. I liked him a lot, and he was really nice to me. He doesn't deserve any of this.

"That night, we were passing his dorm on the way to mine. He stopped and asked me up to his room. I knew what was going to happen, and I was scared, but I wanted him. I really did. I was sick of being the meek little girl who never had any fun. When we got there, he asked my consent, and I said yes. It took two months for me to work up the courage to go to the school health center and tell them he'd raped me." She started crying again.

"But why?" Nicole said. "Why would you do that?"

"Because someone has something on me, you know, a video of me and Doshan having—" She broke off, unable to finish the sentence. "I don't know how he got it. He said he'd post it online unless I told the school that Doshan had raped me. I kept putting him off. But finally he said time had run out, and he was putting it up that night unless I did what he said. I didn't have any choice.

"The guy who was blackmailing me?" Mary Ellen went on. "I met him on the beach when I snuck out night before last. I told him I couldn't go through with it and begged him to delete the video. When that didn't work, I said I'd tell the police he was blackmailing me. He just laughed."

"Who is he, Mary Ellen? What's his name?"

"I can't tell you."

"Why would he want Doshan charged with rape?"

Mary Ellen ignored the question. "I messed up so bad!" she said. "I lied in court, and I'll go to jail if I admit it. But bearing false witness is a sin against God. And if I don't confess what I've done, it will wreck Doshan's life." Her head was on the table again, her sobs interrupted by hiccups.

Finally, she looked up at Nicole. "I don't know what to do," she croaked.

"You have to tell the truth," Nicole said. "Or you'll never be able to live with yourself."

"But if that video comes out, it will ruin me. I'll never be able to go back to school and face people. My parents will disown me for having premarital sex. And think of how ashamed they'll be if they see that video." She took a ragged breath before going on. "Knowing their friends and neighbors can see it, too. My minister will never speak to me again." She began to sob. "I hate my life! I wish I was dead!" With this, Mary Ellen broke down completely. Nicole got up from the table and went over to put her arms around the girl.

"It's going to be all right," Nicole said. "We'll call Sue. She's really smart, and she'll know just what to do. Everything is going to be okay." Even as Nicole said this, she didn't think it was going to be okay at all. Perjury was a felony. In a case like this—entirely based on perjured testimony—did that mean jail time? It was unthinkable, but Mary Ellen had done a terrible thing.

By the time Nicole got out her phone, the girl had stopped crying and stood up. "I'm going to bed. Can I have the sleeping pills?"

Nicole took the bottle out of her pocket and placed a pill in the girl's hand.

"Why don't I take the bottle?" Mary Ellen said. "I might wake up in the night and not be able to go back to sleep."

Nicole studied the girl's tear-streaked face. Sue had been right. Mary Ellen was too distraught to be trusted with a bottle of sleeping pills, especially when she'd just said she wished she was dead.

"This prescription is really strong," Nicole said. "It's going to knock you out. If it doesn't last the night, wake me up. We'll see what time it is and decide whether you should take another one. Okay?"

After Mary Ellen went to her room, Nicole immediately dialed Sue's home number. There was no answer. She tried the cell phone and, after four rings, Sue picked up.

"Mary Ellen just told me she lied about everything," Nicole said. "Doshan Williams didn't rape her. It was consensual. I thought I should tell you right away."

"Mother of God!" Sue said. "Wait 'til Geneva hears this. She'll throw a fit. Tell me exactly what Mary Ellen said."

Nicole repeated the girl's words as closely as she could remember.

"Shit," Sue said. "The best we can hope is that she made up the blackmail story so she wouldn't have to face another day in court."

"Don't count on it," Nicole said. "She was very emotional. I'm certain she's telling the truth. Now she's terrified about what's going to happen to her."

"I'll be there in thirty-five or forty minutes. I want to hear it for myself and ask her some questions."

"Uh-oh," Nicole said. "I just gave her a sleeping pill, and it will probably knock her out. I don't know that you're going to get much out of her."

"We'll order a big pot of coffee. We'll pour enough down her to get her talking."

"Do you want to call Geneva and have her come, too?"

"Good heavens, no. She'll scare Mary Ellen to death. We might as well waterboard her. You can't begin to imagine how angry Geneva will be if this case goes south. It will reflect badly on her that she didn't vet the girl thoroughly enough, and there may be repercussions. We'll talk about that later. Okay, I'm ready. I just have to pack an outfit for court, and I'm on my way."

Nicole paced the living room. Neither she nor Mary Ellen had eaten, and the food looked cold and unappetizing. Nicole loaded the plates back onto the cart and pushed it into the hall. She made another attempt to call Josh. He didn't pick up, and his failure to do so made her stomach knot. He'd never behaved like this before.

Nicole grabbed her jacket and went out to the balcony, hoping the view of the bay would calm her. Slightly north of the hotel, the pier was closed for the day. The Ferris wheel was at rest, no longer displaying its hypnotic pattern of swirling colored lights. The pier was dimly lit, casting a hazy pink, green, and yellow halo against the black sky. Only the area immediately surrounding the pier was illuminated. The rest of the beach was shrouded in darkness.

She thought about Mary Ellen's predicament. Maybe a good lawyer could plea bargain the perjury charge into probation since Mary Ellen was a blackmail victim. But Mary Ellen's legal troubles were only part of her problem. If the video went up on the web, the tabloids would make sure it went viral. Once that happened, it would be pretty hard for Mary Ellen to return to the university or resume small-town life in Georgia. Where would she go? What would she do?

Nicole heard a sound and came in from the balcony in time to see Mary Ellen, now fully dressed, slip out the front door. Nicole ran after her. She couldn't allow the girl to run off after what she'd said about the hopelessness of her predicament. By the time Nicole got to the elevator bank, it was empty. The girl was already on her way down.

Nicole couldn't take the stairs; she was on the tenth floor. But the elevator bank had four cars, and luck was with her. Moments later, the door to another elevator opened. When she reached the lobby, she caught sight of Mary Ellen through the window. She had just left the building and was jaywalking across Ocean Avenue toward the beach.

Nicole rushed after her. The wind was picking up, blowing through her jacket. She was halfway across the street, when a car heading south skidded to a stop a few feet away. The driver leaned on his horn and opened his window to scream at her. She ignored him, trying to keep Mary Ellen in sight. The girl seemed to be headed toward the shoreline. When Nicole reached the sand, she started running. She was in good shape, but running on the beach was completely different from a morning jog around the neighborhood. Her shoes sank into the soft surface, making it impossible to gain momentum. Meanwhile, sand leaked into her shoes, chafing her sockless feet.

The beach near the waterline was dark, and Mary Ellen was no longer in sight. Nicole looked desperately around, trying to figure out which way the girl had gone. All at once she stumbled over something lying in her path. As she hit the sand, the figure she'd tripped over slowly sat up, like a zombie in a horror film.

Nicole lay there a moment, heart beating in her throat. Even though the sand was relatively soft, her hands and elbows stung from skidding to a stop. A flashlight clicked on. The beam was trained on her face, blinding her. She thought of the pepper spray in her purse. Now, when she really needed it, she'd left it in her room.

"Oh, my god," a voice said. "You're a woman. I thought it was one of those drunks sniffing around for a quick fuck." The figure turned off the flashlight and stood up. Despite the hulking shape, it was clearly a woman. She appeared to be swaddled in an assortment of sweaters and coats. "Lucky I didn't hit you with this." She waved her oversized flashlight in the air. "I use it to keep them off me. Are you hurt?"

"I don't think so," Nicole said.

Nicole, still hurting from the fall, forced herself to get up. She ran over to where the waves were lapping at the sand and stared out at the water. It was dark, and there was nothing to be seen. Then she turned her head and looked in both directions for any sign of Mary Ellen. Finally, she gave up and headed back.

The homeless woman had gathered her things up but was waiting in the same place. "Can you spare some change?" she said in a loud whisper. "I haven't eaten since yesterday."

Nicole reached into the pocket of her jeans and found her hotel key card and a dollar bill, or maybe it was a five. It was too dark to see. "Here," she said, handing it to the woman.

"God bless you." The woman was interrupted by a sound from farther down the beach, a peal of slightly manic male laughter. "This place is a jungle," she said. "I can protect myself, but you're on your own. Go home before something bad happens to you."

Nicole paused once again to see if there was any trace of Mary Ellen. The palm trees, backlit from the street, cast eerie shadows on the sand, and the place appeared deserted. Nicole began trudging across the sand toward the relative safety of the street.

When she got back to the suite, the first thing she did was go into Mary Ellen's room. Even though she knew it was impossible, she hoped the girl had somehow returned and was tucked up in bed. Her heart gave a little leap when she saw the shape of a body huddled under the covers.

Nicole went to the bed and put her hand on Mary Ellen's shoulder. It felt wrong, too light and insubstantial. She pulled. The form under the comforter turned out to be three pillows. Before leaving, the girl had put them there in case Nicole checked on her during the night.

She went into the living room for her purse and pulled out her phone. Her hands were shaking as she called Mary Ellen's number. She'd gotten it from her office before she met the girl at the airport. Instead of ringing, the phone went immediately to voicemail. She tried again with the same result. She tried Sue's cell. This, too, went to voicemail. Sue probably wasn't picking up because she was driving, on her way to the hotel.

Nicole looked at the clock. It was 11:00 p.m. The trial would resume at 9:00 tomorrow morning—if Mary Ellen came back. Somehow Nicole doubted it. The girl was probably too panicked at the prospect of going back to court, admitting she'd lied, and paying the penalty, whatever that might be.

Nicole tried Sue again. This time Sue picked up. "I'm ten minutes away," she said. "I ran into an accident in the Sepulveda Pass."

"Mary Ellen is gone. She left the hotel. I tried to follow, but she had a good head start and disappeared. She was out of her head, and I'm afraid she might try to kill herself."

"My god!" Sue said. "Now we'll have to get the police involved."

"Do you think she'll come to her senses and turn up before court?" Nicole said.

"Considering her state of mind, we can't afford to wait," Sue said. "Call the police. Explain Mary Ellen's role in the trial and that she's gone missing."

"But she left of her own volition. Do I say that? I mean, do they bother looking for people who choose to leave?"

"Tell them about her mental state and that she ran onto the beach in the dark. Say you think she's a danger to herself. You don't have to go into detail unless they ask."

"God, I wish I'd—I mean, if only I'd—" Nicole paused, trying to imagine how she might have prevented the girl from escaping.

"Don't blame yourself, Nicole," Sue said. "You did everything you could. Call the police right now. I'll be there shortly."

After they hung up, Nicole dialed 911. A woman's voice answered. "What is your emergency?"

She explained to the operator, who asked a few questions and then said she was sending out a patrol car. She suggested Nicole meet the car in front of the hotel.

The response was almost immediate. Nicole was still in the suite, emptying the sand out of her shoes, when she heard the wail of a siren. She slipped her shoes on and dashed for the elevator, reaching the ground floor as two policemen walked in the front entrance. Young and fresh faced, they looked as if they'd just stepped out of a recruitment poster.

Nicole introduced herself and, feeling panicky, suggested they talk outside so the officers could start searching for Mary Ellen immediately.

The taller of the two, who introduced himself as Officer Brad Garlich, said, "First we need some basic information. Let's take a seat in here." He gestured toward the empty lobby, with its clusters of couches and easy chairs. Nicole followed the two men in, and they all sat down. Only now did Nicole realize that she was actually shaking.

Just then, Sue walked into the lobby, spotted Nicole with the police, and joined them. She introduced herself and took a seat next to Nicole.

Garlich asked for Mary Ellen's full name, age, and occupation. Sue explained about the trial, the girl's pivotal role as plaintiff, and her extreme distress after a difficult day testifying. She turned to Nicole and said, "Tell them what happened with the pills."

"She tried to get me to give her a bottle of prescription sleeping pills," Nicole explained. "I wouldn't do it because I was afraid she'd overdose. She was that upset."

"Okay," Garlich said. "Let's back up. How did she disappear? Is it possible she was kidnapped?"

"No. I saw her leave the suite," Nicole said. "I followed her to the beach, but I lost her. I don't know which way she was headed."

"Okay, so let me understand this. You're telling us she's—" he consulted his notes "—nineteen and left the hotel of her own free will."

"You don't understand!" Nicole glanced at her watch. Ten minutes had elapsed since the police arrived, ten minutes they could have spent looking for Mary Ellen. "She wasn't in her right mind. She was having an emotional breakdown. She told me she might as well be dead. Those were her exact words. I'm afraid she might hurt herself. Besides, a lot of dangerous people hang around the beach at night."

"Mary Ellen Barnes," Sue said. "Surely you've heard of her. She's the principal in a civil trial underway in Superior Court in Santa Monica. It's all over the news."

The cops looked at each other. "Yeah," Garlich said. "The girl who was raped by the quarterback." He stood up and turned to his partner, who got up as well. "We'd better get out there and take a look." He turned back to the women. "Does either of you have a photo?"

Nicole produced her phone, searched the web, and pulled up a photo of Mary Ellen from XHN. "Here she is. I'll have the desk clerk print out copies for you."

It took another ten minutes for the desk clerk to figure out how to print copies of the photo. Finally, the policemen left the hotel. Nicole was profoundly frustrated by the long delay before they started searching for the girl. But she and Sue had done everything they could. All that was left was to go back to the suite and wait.

Once more, Nicole asked if they should call Geneva. "No sense creating a crisis at this hour," Sue said, pointing to her watch. It was almost 2:00 a.m. "I'll call her in the morning and ask her to meet us in court at 8:30. Then we'll break the news. The best thing to do now is get some rest and hope Mary Ellen returns."

Nicole turned her bedroom over to Sue. Nicole, herself, was too wired to sleep. She went to the closet where bedding for the sleeper-couch was stored, grabbed a comforter, and went out to the balcony. She wrapped the comforter around her and spread out on a chaise lounge. The beach was completely dark, except for the pier. All she could see were the shapes of a few palm trees and some glowing patches where the water caught the reflection of a skinny, crescent moon. She waited, hoping for Mary Ellen's knock at the door.

When she opened her eyes, it was daylight, and she was freezing. She stumbled inside and closed the door to the balcony. The clock on the end table said 6:45 a.m.

Nicole knocked on Sue's door. "I'm up," Sue said, opening the door. She was already dressed, her hair done, her makeup flawless.

Outside, the day was brightening as the sun began to burn off the morning fog. Nicole called Mary Ellen's phone again; there was still no answer, not even a voicemail response. After hanging up, she thought of Josh and stopped to send him a text. It was her fifth attempt to reach him since he'd gone silent: "Something terrible has happened," she typed, "Please answer."

His reply was almost instant. "Call me."

"Can't. Phone might be hacked."

"What happened?"

"Can't text. Same reason."

"Are you at the hotel? I'll come."

"No." She texted back. "Leaving for court soon. Glad you answered. I love you."

"Love you, too. Sorry about yesterday. I was upset. Let me know if you want me to come."

Nicole went into the bathroom to take a quick shower and get dressed. When she was ready, she made coffee in the one-cup machine that sat on a small table outside the bathroom, serving Sue first, then brewing a second cup for herself. At 8:15, she called for the driver to pick them up. As they drove to the courthouse, Nicole felt sick with worry.

The media was even more aggressive than on the previous day. "Hey, where's Mary Ellen?" "Are you two setting up a diversion so she can sneak in another way?" and, finally, "Did something happen to her?" Nicole could see they were hoping for bad news.

The women ignored the questions, walking as fast as they could into the courthouse. The place was jammed, and a crowd was waiting for the elevator. Nicole followed Sue up the stairs. The staircase was packed; they had to push their way up. A guard was stationed by the unmarked door Nicole and Mary Ellen had used the day before. The women had to show their IDs. Except for a court reporter and the bailiff, the courtroom was empty.

They went into the private waiting room and found that Geneva hadn't yet arrived. The two of them took seats. Sue seemed calm, but Nicole was trembling with nervous energy.

After a very long ten minutes, Geneva walked in, and Sue told her what had happened.

Geneva's face turned red. She looked at Nicole and fairly shouted, "You were supposed to be watching her. That was the one thing you were hired to do! And I don't believe for a minute she was serious about recanting. We vetted that girl and her story thoroughly. She's just upset about going back to court."

Geneva stopped and checked her watch. "We have to be there now. You wait here. I want to hear the whole story when we get back."

As Sue and Geneva left, Sue turned around to give a sympathetic smile. She mouthed what Nicole herself was thinking. "What a bitch!"

Nicole sat down to wait but couldn't sit for long. She got up and paced. Then sat again, head in hands.

It wasn't long before Geneva and Sue returned. Sue took a seat next to Nicole, while Geneva paced. "Tell me exactly what Mary Ellen said to you," Geneva said. Her voice was low and accusatory.

Nicole repeated their conversation.

"Any idea who this alleged blackmailer might be?" Geneva said. "Or his motive?"

Nicole shook her head. "I asked, but she wouldn't say. I feel terrible about this."

"Look, you gave it your best," Sue said. "I don't think Geneva or I would have had the courage to follow her onto the beach in the dark." She glanced at Geneva, who'd taken a seat at the table and was tapping her foot impatiently.

"You can't blame yourself if Mary Ellen chose to leave," Sue went on. "Sometimes witnesses flake out. Sometimes they fail to show up. And if Mary Ellen was determined to bolt, you had no authority to stop her. Geneva and I are going to my office. We'll make some calls and try to track her down. We'd like you to go back and wait in the hotel suite in case she returns. If she does, give us a call. Otherwise, wait there until you hear from us."

After the attorneys had gone, Nicole pulled out her phone and asked the limo driver to come back. Before long, she got a message that he was waiting outside.

Leaving the courthouse, she had to face the media again. Once more, cameras were trained on her as she walked to the limo. She did her best to look calm and unrattled. Questions were hurled at her, mostly about Mary Ellen's whereabouts. Apparently, word had already leaked from the courtroom that she was missing. Nicole didn't respond.

She climbed into the limo and closed the door. They started up, followed by a small fleet of paparazzi. The limo driver headed north, away from their destination, zipping into the parking entrance of a large office building. He circled up one floor and then down and out an exit that led to a back alley. The ease with which he did this indicated he'd used the route before, perhaps many times. It occurred to Nicole that this particular skill would be handy for anyone who made a living driving celebrities. The maneuver lost their pursuers and, before long, Nicole was back at the Windward.

As soon as she reached the suite, she texted Josh. "I'm at the hotel. Room 1018. Come ASAP."

Within minutes, she got a message that he was on his way. She turned to her iPad to check the tabloids. The story of the girl's disappearance was already there, along with a video of Nicole walking from the courthouse to the car. Despite the effort she'd made to appear calm, she looked pale and stricken. The accompanying stories had some fairly wild speculation about what had become of Mary Ellen Barnes. On XHN, there was a sidebar about Nicole herself with a recap of the murder and inheritance that had landed her in the tabloids the previous year. To her annoyance, it also revealed that she was now working at Colbert and Smith Investigations.

It was more than an hour before the doorbell rang. After checking through the peephole, she opened the door.

Josh put his arms around her, and they held each other before she pulled him into the suite. Once they were seated on the couch, she told him about Mary Ellen's flight. "I'm afraid of what she might do to herself. But she'd taken a sleeping pill, and I really thought it had knocked her out."

"Well," he said, resting his face against her hair. "Consider this. Maybe she only pretended to take the pill. Maybe she had a plan, like catching the next plane home or hiding out with a friend."

Just then, the phone rang. It was Sue, wondering if Mary Ellen had turned up. "We've made some calls, but nothing panned out," Sue said. "She hasn't contacted her mother. We also got in touch with Mary Ellen's roommate, but she hasn't heard from her either. I gather they weren't close. The police are making the search a priority since she's a trial witness.

"And, Nicole, do not blame yourself. If she wanted to leave, that was her decision. You have no authority over her, nor do we."

"Right," said Nicole, but somehow this failed to make her feel better.

"Why don't you stay put while we contact the police?" Sue said. "I'm sure they'll want to call you and arrange to take a look at the suite. I'll talk to you later."

After they hung up, Nicole told Josh what Sue had said.

"She's right. If that kid wanted to run off, there was nothing more you could do," he said. "I'm sure Mary Ellen will turn up. But I worry—" He broke off.

"Yes?"

He swallowed and took a long look at her. "Don't take this the wrong way. I love you no matter what. But I'm afraid you're some kind of excitement junky and on some level—conscious or subconscious—can't resist getting sucked into these crazy, fucked-up situations. And here's the thing. I'm afraid for you. I'm afraid of losing you. You have to stop doing this."

"I know," she murmured. "You're right." But looking back at the events of the last couple of days, she wondered what she could have done differently, other than turn down the assignment in the first place. If she'd done that, none of this would have happened, at least on her watch. The rest—offering support the girl needed in the courtroom, following her onto the beach—she'd do again.

Josh kissed her, and they relaxed back onto the couch, listening for a call from the police, then forgetting to listen. They both jumped when it finally rang.

"This is Detective Martinez of the Santa Monica Police Department." It was a woman's voice. "I've got your room number. It's the Windward, right?" Then, after Nicole confirmed it, the detective said she'd be right there.

About ten minutes later, there was a knock at the door. The detective was in her forties, substantially built but not unattractive. She wore her dark hair pulled back in a bun. "I'm Detective Anna Martinez," she said. "You must be Nicole Graves."

Nicole invited her in, introduced Martinez to Josh, and went to sit next to him. The detective took a chair facing them and looked around, "Nice place," she said. Then she pulled out her phone and placed it on the coffee table. "Do you mind if I record this? It's easier than taking notes."

She asked for Nicole's address and phone number, then moved on to questions about Mary Ellen.

Nicole repeated what had happened, starting with the girl's determination to recant her testimony and ending with her disappearance. The detective asked for a timeline: What time had the girl confessed? When did she go to bed? When did she leave the hotel? She asked if Mary Ellen had revealed the name of the blackmailer or what he had on her. Finally, she said. "Do you have any idea whatsoever—even a hunch—about where she might have gone, what might have happened to her?"

"Not a clue. I'm just worried she might try to kill herself. She was that distraught," Nicole said.

Martinez stood up. "Thank you. If I have any more questions, I'll give you a call."

After the detective left, Nicole looked around to find Josh staring out the window. He turned to her. "Beautiful day," he said.

"Is it? I've been dying to get out of here, and now I'm actually free to go. I know! Let's have lunch at The Lobster and go for a walk on the beach."

"That would be great. But here's the thing," he said, turning back to the window. "There's a bunch of paparazzi and a couple of TV vans in front of the hotel. I'm just trying to figure out how to get you home without being followed."

SIX

AS SOON AS THEY WALKED INTO THE HOUSE, Nicole felt less shaky. It was well past 1:00 p.m. She'd had nothing to eat since lunch the day before. Without a word, the two of them headed for the kitchen.

"Why don't you have a seat while I put lunch together?" Josh gestured toward the small breakfast table in a sunny corner of the kitchen. No sooner had Nicole sat down when her phone began to ring. She pulled it from her purse and checked caller ID, half hoping, half dreading it was Sue with news of Mary Ellen. She didn't recognize the name or number, so she put the phone down without answering. It stopped ringing only to start up again. Caller ID displayed another unfamiliar name. After the third call, she turned the ringer off but left the phone on vibrate, glancing over each time it buzzed to see who was calling.

Josh pulled some dishes out of the fridge and turned to look at her. "What's up with those calls you're not answering?"

"People I don't know," she said. "Probably the tabloids. They would have found me by now."

Josh said "Huh" in a tone that Nicole interpreted as "I told you so," but he wisely withheld comment. He busied himself constructing tuna melts. He'd buttered the outsides and put them in a pan when their home phone began to ring. Nicole got up to answer, but once again the caller ID displayed a stranger's name. She turned off the ringtone and set the phone on the table next to her cell.

When the sandwiches were ready, Josh brought them to the table along with glasses of iced tea. He went into the living room and immediately returned. "They've found you all right. I counted eight out front."

"Let's pretend they're not there, okay?" she said. "I'm not central to this story, and I'm certainly not going out there. Eventually, they'll give up and go away." This might have been a bit optimistic, but Nicole understood how the paparazzi worked. The instant a more forthcoming source or (better yet) a bigger story materialized, they'd be gone.

Josh raised his eyebrows, as if about to say something. Then he seemed to change his mind. They chatted while they ate, avoiding any mention of Mary Ellen or the cameras outside. Josh was his old, amiable self again. Nicole checked her phone each time it vibrated to be sure it wasn't Sue. By the time they were done eating, it was a little after 2:00 p.m.

Josh got up and cleared their plates. "I have to get back to the office," he said.

The thought of spending the afternoon alone made Nicole want to cry. "I wish you didn't have to go."

"I'll be back by 5:30, 6:00 at the latest. We can go out for din—" He stopped, gave a rueful smile, and said, "Oh, yeah, I forgot. We'll have dinner delivered."

Nicole followed him to the front door. She put everything she had into their goodbye kiss, hoping to change his mind about leaving. But he pulled away, gave a crooked smile, and kissed her on the forehead. "Later," he said. "Lock up after me."

She watched through the small window in the front door as he walked down the front path. There was a spring to his step, and he completely ignored the paparazzi. When he reached the sidewalk and turned in the direction of his office, they didn't follow.

She returned to the kitchen, did the dishes, and wiped off the table and counters. Once this was accomplished, she put her cell phone in her pocket and paced around, not knowing what to do with herself. She walked through the house, looking out the windows at their small, neat garden. Josh owned four houses in the valley. He'd bought them as fixer-uppers and refurbished them, doing some of the work himself and subcontracting the rest.

The other three houses were rented out. This one had been redone in California-craftsman style with a large, modern kitchen. But the house itself was small, two bedrooms and a single bath, a tight fit for two people, each used to having a study. After their wedding, they planned to buy a larger place, one that would someday accommodate a family.

She was in the living room, staring out the window, when her cell buzzed again. A familiar name popped up: Greg Albee. This time she answered.

"Hey, Nicole," Greg said. "I'm hoping you've got something for me."

"Would you mind calling back on our home phone?" she said. "I have to keep this line open." She gave him the number, and the phone rang a few seconds later.

"So, what have you got?" he said.

"Off the record," she said. "You can't mention my name."

"Agreed," he said.

"Okay. I don't know much, but here's where we are. We have no idea what's happened to her. We've notified the police she's missing. They're working on it, but as far as I know, they haven't found her. I'm waiting for news. That's why I didn't want to tie up my cell."

"I gather you were assigned to look after Barnes by that outfit you work for," he said. "How'd you lose track of her? What happened?"

"I can't comment," she said. "Sorry."

She thought of Mary Ellen's plan to recant her accusation of rape and clear Doshan. This revelation would have been in the news by now if Mary Ellen hadn't disappeared.

"Nicole?" Albee said. "You there?"

"Listen, Greg, I have to go. If something comes up that I can tell you, I'll call. Okay?"

"My deadline is 6:00," he said. "I'll be waiting."

"Bye, Greg," she said.

She rang off and stood there with the phone in hand, debating what to do. Almost without thinking, she tapped in Sue's number.

"Any news?" Nicole said.

"Nothing, I'm afraid," said Sue. "This long silence is extremely worrisome."

"What she told me?" Nicole said. "You know, that thing I can't mention on the phone? Do you think I should tell anyone else—like Doshan's lawyer?"

"That isn't a good idea," Sue said. "What if she turns up and decides to change her story again? It's possible Geneva was right, and Mary Ellen just made up an excuse to avoid going back to court."

"I'm sure she was telling the truth," Nicole said. "She was genuinely sorry for the trouble she's caused Doshan."

"But keep it to yourself until we find Mary Ellen and see what she has to say."

"You're right," Nicole said. "Absolutely. When she turns up, she'll speak for herself." But she had the feeling that something had happened to Mary Ellen, and she'd never have the chance to tell her story.

That night, Nicole was wide awake, reading the *New Yorker* on her iPad long after Josh had dropped off to sleep. She'd figured out how to stop the incessant buzzing of her smart phone, setting it to allow calls only from Sue, Josh, her sister, and Detective Martinez. Once in a while, she checked the tabloids, but there were no new developments.

It wasn't until dawn was starting to light the sky that she dropped off to sleep. When she awoke, it was 9:30, and Josh had already left for work. She immediately called her office. It wasn't until dawn was starting to light the sky that she dropped off to sleep. When she awoke, it was 9:30, and Josh had already left for work. She immediately called her office. Her boss answered.

"I overslept," Nicole said. "I'm going to be late."

"Have they located the Barnes girl?" Jerry said

"Not as far as I know."

"I've been trying to call, but your phone goes right to voicemail," he said. "I want you to take a few days R&R. You've earned it."

"I'm still pretty upset, and I couldn't sleep," Nicole said. "I'll take the day and see how I feel tomorrow. Thanks."

"It's the least I can do after all you've been through," he said. "What a mess."

Nicole stayed in bed, half dozing until almost 11:00. When she finally got up, she checked her phone for messages. There were dozens, none from anyone she knew. As she got busy deleting them, she looked out the bedroom window to see if any paparazzi were hanging around. To her relief, the street was empty. After getting dressed, she went out to get the paper and then made herself breakfast. While she ate, she looked at the news. The top story on the front page of the *L.A. Times* bore Greg's byline. It went into detail about Mary Ellen's disappearance but was mainly a recap of what she already knew. The same was true of the tabloids, except that XHN was now running a list of places where Mary Ellen Barnes allegedly had been seen, which pretty much covered all western states plus Georgia, New York, and New Jersey.

Just then her phone rang. It was Sue. "Terrible news, I'm afraid," she said. "I just got a call from Detective Martinez. They found Mary Ellen this morning: She's dead. They've already taken her to the morgue."

"She's dead," Nicole repeated dully, as a wave of shock went through her. "Was it suicide?"

"They don't think so. Her neck was broken. They know that much. Someone buried her in the sand under the pier, and the tide had partially uncovered her. They'll have to do an autopsy to get a full picture of what happened."

For a moment, Nicole thought she was going to be sick.

"Nicole?" Sue said. "Are you okay?"

"She was murdered?"

"That's what it looks like."

"It's just so hard to take in," Nicole said. "How do they know it's Mary Ellen?"

"That's the thing," Sue said. "They don't have positive identification. They recovered her purse, but there was no wallet, no photo ID, no phone. She doesn't have fingerprints on file. Apparently she'd never applied for a driver's license. Detective Martinez wants someone who knew Mary Ellen to go to the morgue and officially identify her. I'd do it, but I have to go back to court with Geneva to hash out what we're going to do with the civil suit."

"You mean WAR still wants to pursue it?"

"More than ever. This makes their case a real headline grabber," Sue said. "I hate to ask. I know how you must be feeling right now. But could you possibly meet Detective Martinez at the morgue and see if it really is Mary Ellen?"

Nicole swallowed, remembering a visit she'd made to the morgue when she was in high school. Her advanced-placement government class had done a unit on the criminal justice system. For her class paper, she'd chosen to write about the coroner's office. What had she been thinking? That it would be a lark? That it would earn her some kind of bragging rights? That it would prove how tough she was?

Instead, the experience had traumatized her in a way she'd never forgotten. The deputy coroner had taken her on a tour of the morgue, and the rank odor of decay stayed with her for weeks. She still had a clear memory of disorganized rows of gurneys holding sheet-covered bodies. One had his hand raised, as if hailing a cab. While the deputy coroner was talking to her, he'd suddenly pointed behind her and said, "Don't look." Instinctively, she'd turned in the direction he was pointing. Through a doorway she could see an autopsy underway. The subject's intestines were being pulled out, an unbelievably copious heap of grayish entrails tinged with blood. She'd almost fainted.

Nicole shivered. "Of course I will," she said.

Next, Nicole called Detective Martinez. They agreed to meet at the morgue in an hour. Nicole brushed her teeth, washed her face, and dabbed on some lipstick. Once she was in the car, she headed for the Hollywood Freeway, which would take her to East L.A. and Boyle Heights, where the morgue was located. She prayed that it was a mistake, that this body wasn't Mary Ellen.

The coroner's office had moved since Nicole's visit years before. It was now housed in a grim, three-story building that loomed over several smaller wooden structures in the same complex. Nicole had read somewhere that the main building had once been Los Angeles General Hospital. With its brick façade, dingy gingerbread trim, and cupola-topped entry, it looked like a nineteenth-century madhouse.

She got out of the car and climbed the stairs to the entrance. She told a man at the front desk that she was meeting Detective Martinez, and he asked her to take a seat. The lobby was enormous, dimly lit, and filled with rows of wooden benches. They reminded her of the seating in a church, and she wondered if services had once been held here. More likely, it served as the old hospital's waiting room. She perched on one of the benches;

it was hard and cold. A notice on the wall said that the use of mobile devices was prohibited, and she dutifully turned off her phone.

The building was cool, and, to Nicole's relief, the only discernable smell was a mixture of disinfectant and floor wax. It made her wonder where they kept the bodies—perhaps in one of the out buildings. The huge, gloomy room gave her a sense of unreality. This couldn't have happened. Mary Ellen couldn't possibly be lying in cold storage somewhere nearby.

A few minutes later, the detective arrived, had a brief conversation with reception, and joined Nicole on the wooden bench. They greeted one another, their voices creating an eerie echo in the vast lobby. After that, the two sat in silence until a rosy cheeked young man in a dark suit and tie appeared and introduced himself as Deputy Coroner John Ortega. He ushered them into an elevator and took them up to the second floor. Nicole felt herself trembling as Ortega led them to a small interview room.

Nicole looked around. "Aren't we going to view the body?"

"That only happens on TV," Ortega said. "In real life, we use photographs." He placed a manila folder on the table and sat down across from them. "Okay," he said. "If you're ready, I'll take the photos out so you can see them. She doesn't look too bad. I'd warn you if she did."

Nicole's stomach lurched as he laid out the photos in front of them. There were only three, all of a girl's head, the front view and each side. Nicole gave them a quick look, covered her face with her hands, and started to cry. "Oh, God," she said. "It is her. It's Mary Ellen."

She wiped her eyes and forced herself to take another look. The girl's appearance, as the deputy had said, wasn't that bad, but she looked decidedly dead. Her wide-eyed stare and blank expression were deeply disturbing. She had red blotches beneath her eyes and on her neck. Her face was slightly bloated, possibly from the time she'd spent under wet sand when the tide was in.

As Ortega picked up the photos and slipped them back into the folder, Nicole felt chilled. It was impossible to believe this was the girl she'd been with less than two days before, the girl she was supposed to keep safe.

They were making their way down in the elevator when Martinez said, "The police want to notify next of kin before they release news of Ms. Barnes' death. So, I have to ask you not to tell anyone."

"Of course." Nicole's voice was thick with emotion.

They passed through the big reception hall without speaking, their footsteps echoing against the high ceiling. They left the building and headed for the parking lot. As Nicole started to turn down the row where she'd left her car, Martinez put a hand out to stop her. "You seem a little shaky," the detective said. "Are you sure you're up to driving? We can get you a ride, or maybe you have someone who can pick you up."

"No, I'm okay. Really."

Nicole retrieved her car from the lot and started home. She'd only gone a few blocks when she remembered the tabloids and their relentless pursuit of the next scoop. They'd have the news of Mary Ellen's death soon, if they didn't already. She wouldn't be surprised if they had informants in the coroner's office. The tabloids, she knew, wouldn't have any scruples about waiting for Mary Ellen's family to hear the news before going public.

Here was something she could do for Albee. He'd helped her in the past, and she owed him. She pulled over to the curb and made the call.

"What's up?" he said.

"I wanted to let you know—" she said, "Oh, this is off the record. You can't use my name."

"Understood."

"We were asked to keep this under wraps until the next of kin is notified, but with the tabloids involved, that's not going to happen. Mary Ellen Barnes is dead." The words came out in a rush, and her voice broke. It took a moment before she could go on. "She had a broken neck, and they don't know what happened. Her body may have been buried in the sand under the Santa Monica Pier, but that hasn't been verified. That's all I know."

"Thanks so much, Nicole," Albee said. "I owe you big time."

After they hung up, she pulled a tissue out of her purse to wipe away her tears. She blew her nose, then started the engine; a long line of cars had to pass before she could pull into the flow of traffic. Her emotions were in turmoil, making it hard to focus on driving. She kept replaying the night Mary Ellen disappeared. If only she could go back in time and come up with a different outcome. But how? Staying up all night or sleeping across the threshold of the suite? Even then, Mary Ellen still could have run off. The outcome would have been the same. But there were things Nicole still could do: make sure that Doshan's name was cleared, as Mary Ellen had wished, and that whoever killed her was caught and punished.

Nicole was at the signal on Mulholland, at the crest of the hill between L.A. and the valley, when the cars behind her started honking. Only then did she notice the light had turned green.

Josh met her at the door and pulled her into his arms. "Thank God you're all right. When you didn't answer your phone, I called your office, your sister, everybody I could think of. No one had heard from you. I've been going out of my mind."

"Oh, Josh," she said. "I have the most awful news." Her voice broke again. "Mary Ellen is dead. She may have been murdered. I was just at the morgue to identify her."

"That's terrible," he said. "Why didn't you call and ask me to come with you?"

"I had to turn my phone off inside the building, and I was just focused on getting through it," she said. "I'm sorry. I should have let you know."

"I'm with you in this," he said. "You know that, right?"

"Of course." But she remembered how he'd chided her for accompanying Mary Ellen to court, how he'd said he was afraid she was an excitement junkie.

"So let me in," he was saying. "I know how traumatic this must be, but you don't have to deal with it by yourself. I'm here for you."

"I know you are," she said. She could see that he meant what he was saying, yet she'd never felt so alone. The chill that had come over her when she saw those photos had reached into her bones. She shivered.

"Are you cold?" he said. He reached into the hall closet, pulled out one of his zippered sweatshirts, and held it up while she put it on. "Come on," he said, "let's get you a drink."

Nicole told Josh about what had happened at the morgue. After dinner, he lit a fire in the fireplace. Still cold, she wrapped a knit throw around herself, and the two of them curled up on the couch to watch TV. Still, she couldn't rid herself of the deep chill she'd carried home with her.

Once in bed, she lay awake again while Josh slept. He'd spooned himself against her, his arms wrapped around her. She gently pried herself loose and sat up; he didn't move. His mouth was slightly open, his wavy hair flopped over his forehead.

As if aware she was looking at him, he lifted his head and gave her a bleary look. "What's wrong?" he said.

"Nothing. I'm just getting up for a drink of water."

He relaxed against the pillow and closed his eyes. She put on her robe and slippers, wondering if the room was really that cold or if the chill inside her had become a permanent condition.

Nicole went into the study they shared and turned on her computer to find the latest news about Mary Ellen's death. On the front page of the L.A. Times, the lead story described a press conference that the Santa Monica Police Department had held late the previous night. The police chief had announced that Mary Ellen Barnes was murdered, and detectives were now searching for the person or persons responsible.

XHN was having a field day. "Rape Victim Murdered on Trial Day 2," was the main headline. They'd done everything they could to sensationalize the story. It said that Mary Ellen (incorrectly described as five-feet tall and less than a hundred pounds) was brutally raped by a six-foot-five quarterback. They characterized her as a devout Christian and a straight-A student. XHN also pointed out that she was a divorced couple's only child, the one great hope of an impoverished and broken family, the first to make it to college.

At the same time, they'd begun to demolish Doshan's character. One of the stories on XHN quoted a "close friend of the quarterback who asked that his name be withheld." According to this source, Doshan, on first learning about the rape charge, had said: "I get all the pussy I want. Why would I rape anyone, especially an ugly cunt like her?" Nicole noticed the way XHN freely quoted vulgar language that would usually be prohibited in a daily newspaper.

Nicole finally looked at the *L.A. Times'* website. Here was a detailed description of the body's discovery, which Albee must have gotten from a source in the coroner's office. The piece also had an item the tabloids had missed: Doshan Williams had been asked to appear at police headquarters for questioning first thing this morning.

Questioning? She wondered if that was all they had in mind. Since Mary Ellen had charged him with rape, he'd be their prime suspect. If they arrested him, Nicole would have to come forward with Mary Ellen's confession and appear as a witness. She could imagine Josh's reaction to that. But what choice did she have? Mary Ellen's last wish had been to clear Doshan of rape, and she had no one else to speak for her. Nicole was certain Doshan hadn't killed Mary Ellen; it must have been whoever was blackmailing her. Once again, Nicole promised herself she'd see justice done.

As for Doshan, she hoped that either the D.A. lacked enough evidence to charge him or that he had an airtight alibi.

SEVEN

Josh got up at his usual 5:45 a.m., surprised to find Nicole already at the breakfast table, drinking coffee. "I couldn't sleep," she said. "My job was to keep her safe, and now she's dead." She grew quiet, wondering once again how she could have saved Mary Ellen.

Josh put his arms around her, and she leaned against him. "You did everything you could," he murmured into her hair. "She chose to leave. There was nothing you could do." He was silent for a bit, then added, "Why don't we take a run? Maybe that will make you feel better."

"Maybe it would," she said, "but I'm too wiped out."

Josh fixed breakfast, and they sat at the table without their usual morning banter. A toxic mix of emotions—guilt, grief, and regret—churned in Nicole's stomach, making it impossible to eat. She kept seeing the photos of Mary Ellen: her dull, staring eyes, the blank expression death had left on her face.

Josh seemed to understand. He cleared up the dishes while Nicole sipped her coffee and stared out the window. "Why don't I stay home?" he said. "We could go for a drive and take your mind off what happened."

"It's sweet of you to offer," she said, "but I know how much work you have. I'll be all right."

"Are you sure?"

"Positive."

The moment Josh left, Nicole's feelings of grief and guilt came rushing back. She decided that keeping busy was the only way to get through the day. She started in on her email, which she hadn't looked at since the night of Mary Ellen's disappearance. Her inbox was filled with what looked like hundreds of new messages. Aside from the usual junk mail, messages had come in from friends and acquaintances who'd seen Nicole in the news and expressed either sympathy or curiosity or both. These she read without answering. *Maybe later*, she thought. There was an even larger number of messages from people she didn't know. She guessed they were reporters or curiosity seekers who'd found her email address on her company's website. These she deleted.

She was about to turn off her computer when a new message arrived. It was from Veronica Smith, yet another person she didn't know. Her cursor was hovering over the delete button when she noticed the email address. It ended with *Oceanside.edu*, which meant it had come from someone at the university. She opened it and read:

> "You don't know me, but I was Mary Ellen Barnes's roommate. I saw that item about you in the news and know you spent time with her before she died. I need to talk to you. Please call me at 424-462-8906.
>
> Veronica"

It was early, not quite 7:00 a.m. But the message had just come in, which meant the sender was awake. Nicole tapped in the number. A young woman answered with an upbeat "Veronica here."

"It's Nicole Graves."

"Nicole! Thanks for getting back to me. How soon can we meet? I'll come to your office, if you like."

"Can you tell me what it's about?" Nicole said.

"Not on the phone. But it's really important. I promise."

Nicole thought about it. This Veronica could be a reporter or someone else trying to set her up. But the Oceanside email gave her a certain amount of credibility. "Okay," Nicole said. "I'm off work today. Why don't I come out to the campus and meet you there?"

"That would be great," said Veronica. "I'll be in the main room of the student center, say about 1:00?"

"Sure," Nicole said. "How will I recognize you?"

"I have curly red hair in a ponytail. I'm wearing a black-and-white striped tunic with ripped jeans. You can't miss me. Besides, I saw your photo on XHN. I know what you look like."

After they hung up, Nicole checked Veronica on the company database. Her parents lived within the posh confines of the Malibu Colony, their house valued at a cool six million dollars. From Veronica's social media pages, Nicole gathered that the girl had gone to one of the most expensive private high schools in L.A. She'd had no brushes with the law, at least none that were public record.

With this information in hand, Nicole felt reassured that Veronica was who she said she was. The rest of the morning was spent on household chores. The prospect of driving to Malibu had refocused her thoughts. What did this young woman have to tell her? Before leaving, she called Josh to let him know she'd be out. She didn't want him getting upset if he couldn't reach her at the house. He didn't pick up, so she left a message explaining she was going for a drive, and he'd be able to reach her on her cell. She didn't say where she was going, much less why. He didn't want her involved in the case—but why did he even have to know?

She had plenty of time, so she took the scenic route, heading south, then onto the freeway to where it ended in downtown Santa Monica. She had to fight her way through city streets clogged by construction projects and road work. Once she turned onto Pacific Coast Highway, however, traffic was light, and she lowered her car window. The ocean breeze was invigorating. The road wound its way along the coast. On her left was the water, reflecting the blue, cloudless sky; to her right, the stratified cliffs of Pacific Palisades. The water looked calm, although wind was ruffling the fronds of the palm trees along the beach.

Eventually, the cliffs gave way to rolling green hills, and Oceanside University came into view. The campus sprawled along the crest of a hill overlooking the highway and the ocean. The university featured a picturesque series of white stucco buildings with red tile roofs. From the highway, it resembled a Greek hilltop village, a vivid contrast to UCLA with its high rises and mashup of architectural styles.

Nicole turned onto the road leading up to the school. Before entering the campus, she stopped at a guard station, where a young man gave her a pass to display in her window. When she explained she was headed for the student center, he told her how to get there, marked "X" on a map, and handed it to her.

She found a spot in the parking lot and was getting out of her car when she heard loud male voices punctuated with laughter that marked the approach of a group of young men, students by the look of them. Most were big and muscular and their demeanor gave the impression they'd been drinking, even though it was only midday. She locked her car door and stood next to it, waiting for them to pass. As they drew level with her, one of them caught sight of her. "Hey, you," he said, "Smile!"

It was a command she was familiar with, a way for men (usually young) to intimidate or harass women in public places. She looked around the parking lot. There was no one else in sight—just her and these muscle-bound specimens of raging hormones. She wasn't afraid of them, not exactly, but she decided the best course was to remain silent and stand her ground.

A second young man chimed in. "Yeah. Give us a little smile, baby. No need to look all sour like that." A third veered in her direction. "I know how to get a smile out of her," he said. He paused at a spot near her car and leered at her. Finally, he turned and hurried to catch up with his cohorts, who'd moved on between the rows of cars. "Did you catch that look on her face?" he said. Whether they had or not, they seemed to find this highly amusing, laughing as they stumbled along. Nicole waited until they were out of sight before making her way uphill to the campus.

Close up, the buildings were much larger than they appeared from the highway. Students were everywhere, walking to and from classes. They were homogeneously clean-cut; most were white or Asian, she noticed, although she did see a few Latinos and one African American who looked big enough to be a football player. She made her way to the student center. Once inside, she didn't see anyone who matched the description Veronica had given her. She sat down to wait.

The main room of the student center was large and high-ceilinged, furnished with clusters of red-and-orange upholstered couches, as well as white tables and chairs. Sunlight streamed in through floor-to-ceiling banks of windows. Those facing west offered a view of the ocean. The room was bright, cheerful, and inviting. Most of the seats were taken by students reading, working on laptops, or socializing.

When Veronica walked in, Nicole spotted her instantly. Veronica was beautiful, slender, and stylish. Her "tunic," as she'd described it, looked expensive, and the "ripped" jeans had come by way of a high-priced designer. Her curly red hair was tied in a side pony tail with a black ribbon. She wore bright red lipstick and a generous amount of eye makeup. On someone else, the getup might have looked ridiculous, but Veronica had the panache to pull it off.

"Hi," the girl said. "I'm Veronica. You're Nicole Graves. I'd know you anywhere. I followed that murder case you were involved in. Pretty sensational stuff!" She paused to smile, then added. "Your photo was all over the tabloids." Veronica's voice was low and throaty, with an edge of sarcasm that might have been intended as humor. Her tone seemed to say, "Yes, I may sound like I'm being snarky, but it's all in fun."

Nicole had known girls like this in school, queen bees with a sense of entitlement and uncanny talent for dominating their peers. A girl like Veronica would always be the center of attention, and her followers would do her bidding, afraid of falling out of favor. Nicole could never figure out this social dynamic, how it worked or why.

"Let's go somewhere we can talk," Veronica said. "It's too crowded in here."

Veronica led Nicole to a bench in a patio just outside the building. It was deserted, perhaps because it was in the path of a frigid breeze.

"I have some things of Mary Ellen's," Veronica said. "A journal she kept and a Bible she made notes in. I found them a couple of nights ago—they'd fallen between her bed and a bookcase. The journal might have something important, you know, like a clue to the murder. I couldn't make out her writing in the Bible. You'll see what I mean.

"Anyway, I called the sheriff's office. I thought they'd want it, but they never called back. When I saw your name in the paper, I remembered you from that murder case awhile back. I figured you'd know who to give them to."

"The sheriff isn't involved," Nicole explained. "Mary Ellen was killed in Santa Monica, so the Santa Monica police are in charge."

"No wonder I never heard back," Veronica said. "Can you take her stuff and turn it over to the right person?"

"Of course."

Veronica got up. "I forgot to bring them. They're in my room.

Do you mind walking over there? It's a bit of a hike."

Her curiosity buzzing, Nicole followed the girl up and down several of the rolling, grassy hills. Veronica walked effortlessly, her long legs keeping her well ahead. Nicole scurried to keep up. By the time they reached Richardson Hall, she was sweating. This building, like the rest of the campus, was white stucco with a tile roof. Inside, it was much nicer than Nicole's dorm at UCLA. Veronica's room had a black-and-white motif that looked like the work of a decorator: Matching black-and-white print spreads covered the twin beds, each adorned with artfully arranged pillows. The room was beyond neat, not a book out of place, not a closet door open.

"What a lovely room!" Nicole said.

Veronica smiled. "Decorating is one of my things." She pointed at the bed against the wall. "That's—I mean, that was Mary Ellen's. When she first moved in, she wanted to use an old, faded quilt as a spread. It looked ridiculous. I offered to buy her one like mine. She said she preferred the quilt because her granny made it. I had to insist."

Veronica gestured toward a striped loveseat, and the two of them sat down. For a long moment, Veronica was quiet, staring at her lap, as if pondering what to say. When she looked up, her expression was somber. "You know, we weren't a good fit, Mary Ellen and me. Now, after everything that's happened, I feel really bad about the way I treated her. I should have been nicer."

"Don't beat yourself up," Nicole said. "When someone you know dies suddenly, it's natural to feel responsible or wonder if you should have done more. I was supposed to keep Mary Ellen safe. She was my responsibility, and she died. Imagine how that makes me feel."

"You don't understand. I was really unfriendly to Mary Ellen; I barely spoke to her. Sometimes I was downright mean. She seemed like—" Veronica paused, searching for the right words. "I'm going to be brutally honest here. She came off like a clueless hick. Her cornpone accent got on my nerves. And—get this—right from the start she was trying to convert me. Me!" Veronica let out a snort of laughter. "Can you picture me as a born-again Christian? I mean, a person can only put up with so much. We'd only been roommates a few days before I told her to zip it about the religious stuff.

"I shouldn't have been such a bitch," Veronica went on. "I could have, you know, helped her fit in. Taken her under my wing. Given her a makeover or something."

Poor Mary Ellen, Nicole thought. Veronica had reason to feel guilty.

"Well, none of us can rewrite history," Nicole said, "but we can try to do better in the future."

"You're right. I'm going to be a better person. For one thing, I'll request a freshman for my roommate next semester. I'll make her my project."

"That's an idea," Nicole said. She wondered if Veronica would really be doing her next roommate a favor. What if she took a perfectly nice girl and turned her into a copy of herself? But there was no point in thinking about it. Her only thought was to get a look at Mary Ellen's journal. "Those books you mentioned?"

Veronica got up and opened a glass bookcase under the window. She pulled out a hefty black volume and a notebook with a marbled black-and-white cover. Nicole took a moment to examine them. The Bible was a handsome leather-bound copy of the King James version with Mary Ellen's name stamped in gold on the front cover. The book's margins were covered with tiny, penciled notes that were almost illegible. In the notebook, which Mary Ellen appeared to have used as a journal, her writing was messy, but not as hard to make out. Turning to Veronica, now seated beside her, Nicole said, "Tell me what you know about Mary Ellen. Did she have friends? Boyfriends? Living with her, you must have picked up on what she did with her time."

"Boyfriends? That's hard to picture, but I wouldn't know. We hardly ever talked. She didn't have much to say, especially after I yelled at her for trying to convert me. Later, when news of the rape got out, I was sorry to hear what she'd been going through. I wish I'd known, but ..." Her voice trailed off.

"I understand," Nicole said. "She told me she was being blackmailed. Someone had a video that she was terrified would be posted online. Did you hear anything about it?"

"Mary Ellen?" Veronica shook her head. "That's hard to imagine." She paused and thought a bit. "Wait a minute. I just remembered. She'd been going to Bible study meetings the last few months. It's in the student center, a room reserved for nerdy campus clubs. You know, stamp collectors, anime fans, astronomy freaks, that kind of thing."

Veronica was silent, tapping her cherry-red lips with a matching, cherry-red fingernail. "The guy who runs Bible sessions is Jonathan Lyons, the school chaplain. He's super hot. I mean, he's the reason all those girls are dying to take up the Bible. And there've been rumors—" By now Veronica was grinning, as if she was telling a joke and about to deliver the punch line.

"Like what?" Nicole said.

"He has an office in the student center where he counsels students." Veronica made air quotes with her fingers when she said *counsels*. "Word has it that this counseling goes way beyond spiritual matters, if you get my meaning."

"Has anyone reported him?"

"Not that I know of. He's also declared war on Oceanside's athletic program, especially the football team, which he says leads to 'idolatry,' whatever that means. And he says sporting events condone violence and team members lead immoral lives. Translation: He hates minorities, who make up most of the football team."

"Wow," Nicole said. "He sounds like a real piece of work." She flashed back to her own student days. Blackmail, murder, a randy, racist chaplain—if things like this went on, she'd never heard about them. Oceanside, tiny by comparison, seemed a hotbed of scandal and a much more hazardous place for young people to get an education.

Veronica wasn't finished. By now she was almost gleeful. "I almost forgot," she said. "I don't know if he was a boyfriend, but Mary Ellen definitely had a crush on somebody."

"Was it the chaplain?"

"No idea. She left her journal open one time when she left the room. I got a look at what she'd written: It was about how thrilled she was because some hot guy had chatted her up."

Veronica took the journal from Nicole's lap and leafed through it until she found what she was looking for. "Here it is: 'All the girls are crazy about him. I never thought he'd even look at me. But today he came over to say hi, and we talked a bit. I was so freaked I could hardly speak."

Nicole took the notebook and glanced at the passage. "But you don't know who this was."

"No. Mary Ellen came back and caught me with her journal. After that, she hid it. I never saw it again."

Nicole stood up. "Well, thanks for calling me. I'll make sure the police get these. If you remember anything else, let me know."

"Will do," Veronica said. "Here. I'll give you something to carry them in." She reached into the closet and pulled a striped book bag from a hook.

"Thanks," Nicole said. "I'll mail it back to you."

"No need. I've got tons. I'll show you where Lyons's office is. I have to go back to the student center anyway."

While they walked, Veronica kept up a steady chatter about her extracurricular activities. Besides cheerleading, she was involved in fencing, model senate, debate team, and the women's rowing team. By the time they reached their destination, Nicole, who usually wanted to know all about the people she met, felt as if she knew a little too much about Veronica.

Once they were in the student center, Veronica pointed to

a staircase. "Lyons's office is up the stairs and to your left. Nice meeting you!" She gave a wave and headed toward a group of similarly well-dressed girls. At the sight of Veronica, several of them screeched with delight, or a good imitation of it. Nicole found herself remembering high school and thinking that some things never changed.

When Nicole got to the second floor, she took a left and looked for Lyons's office. Each door had the occupant's name and position painted on the frosted glass window. JONATHAN LYONS, CHAPLAIN, was at the end of the hall.

Nicole knocked. There was no response, but she could hear the low murmur of voices inside. She waited patiently until a girl came out. Her face was flushed, and she looked as if she'd been crying. She wiped her eyes with a tissue while she held the door open for Nicole.

"Come in, come in," Lyons said. He was seated at his desk and didn't get up. He was indeed handsome in a square jawed, old-fashioned, movie-star kind of way. She guessed he was in his mid-forties. His voice was deep and resonant. "Welcome," he said. "Close the door and have a seat." He paused while she did this, then went on, "How can I help you?"

Nicole introduced herself and explained why she was there. Lyons listened attentively, but there was something about him that made her uncomfortable. Perhaps it was his aggressive use of eye contact. It was as if he was trying to draw her in and, if such a thing were possible, hypnotize her. She found herself having to look away once in a while.

"Mary Ellen Barnes, that poor young woman," he said. "Such a tragedy. Such a terrible thing for her family and for our community of young people."

"I understand Mary Ellen came to your Bible sessions."

"Yes, indeed. She was a very dedicated student."

"I wonder if you could tell me anything about her. Maybe she asked you for advice about a problem she was having?"

"I'm sorry, but I can't discuss my counseling sessions with

an outside party. I can't even say whether or not she sought counseling. These communications are confidential."

He paused before continuing, "But what about you? Why are you really here? I sense that you're troubled in your own life. That you're searching for something you haven't yet found. Am I right?"

Nicole was taken aback. Where was he getting this? "You're mistaken," she said. "I'm just trying to figure out what happened to Mary Ellen."

"It all goes back to God's plan, doesn't it?" Lyons said. "As they say, He works in mysterious ways. Just look at how He led you into my office this afternoon."

Nicole was getting goosebumps. This guy wasn't hot, as Veronica had put it. He was creepy. She stood up. "I gather you won't be telling me anything about Mary Ellen then. Thanks for your time." When she reached the door, she turned back. "Do you want me to leave it open?"

Once again his eyes locked on hers. "My door is always open. When you decide you want help, I'll be waiting."

She left the door ajar and walked quickly away. The girl who was in his office earlier had come out crying. Nicole wondered why. She couldn't understand how anyone would be taken in by Lyons's Svengali stare and mind-reading act. As for her, she couldn't wait to get away.

As she left the student center and walked down the hill to the parking lot, something occurred to her. Was it possible Lyons was the killer? According to Veronica, he'd declared war on the school's athletic department, and Doshan was its biggest star. But would a man like him commit murder to discredit a member of the football team? It seemed preposterous. She was letting her imagination run wild.

Reaching the row of the parking lot where she'd left her car, she was surprised to see a young man kneeling next to her rear tire. He was running his hand around the edge, as if he were feeling for something.

"Hey!" she shouted, hurrying toward him. "What are you doing? That's my car."

Startled, the young man jumped to his feet. She didn't recognize him as one of the group she'd run into earlier. He had a baby face and looked as if he should be in high school. She could tell by his expression that he'd been caught doing something he shouldn't.

She repeated her question, softening her tone. "What were you doing?"

"Uh," his eyes were darting about, as if he were trying to come up with an answer. "I was checking your tire."

"Checking my tire?"

"I thought you, like, had a flat." He was visibly sweating and looked as if he wished he were anywhere else.

"A flat? Let me see." Nicole studied the tire and then checked the front tire for comparison. "It looks fine to me."

"Yeah," he agreed. "It's fine."

Only then did it occur to her that he might have been about to let the air out of her tire. But why? She didn't know him. Still, his guilty look told her he'd been up to something. Maybe it was fraternity hazing. Perhaps some frat boys had ordered this kid to let the air out of tires in the public lot during broad daylight, figuring he might be caught and get in trouble.

She pulled out her keys. "All right, then," she said. "Thanks for checking my tire." He swallowed hard, bobbed his head, and walked quickly away.

She'd started the car before she noticed a piece of paper tucked under her windshield wiper. She turned off the engine and got out to retrieve it. It was a sheet of paper folded into a square. She unfolded it. In large, hand-printed block letters, it said:

IF YOU KNOW WHAT'S GOOD FOR YOU, YOU'LL MIND YOUR OWN BUSINESS.

She read it over several times. The threat was vague and could have been directed at anyone, but she had the feeling it was meant for her. She stepped back from the car and looked around. The young man had disappeared.

When Nicole left the campus, she headed in the opposite direction she'd come. No one left the parking lot after her. She drove a mile or so. Then she took a left into one of the beach parking lots, turned the car around, and headed home. She was watchful all the way, but as far as she could tell, no one was following her. Still, the note troubled her, giving her the feeling she was being watched.

§

Once she was safely in the house, Nicole leaned against the front door and thought about her last glimpse of Mary Ellen as she ran away and disappeared into the darkness. Nicole put her hands over her face and gulped back tears. *She was never going to get over this*, she thought. Mary Ellen's ghost would always be with her.

At last she went into the bathroom and splashed her face with cold water. Then she got the Bible and notebook from where she'd left them on the hall table. She settled on the couch with the Bible in her lap and checked her watch. It was after three, and Josh wouldn't be home before 5:30 or 6:00. She had plenty of time.

She started with Mary Ellen's scribblings in the margins of the Bible. As Veronica had pointed out, they were hard to decipher. Mary Ellen had penciled in tiny notations to fit in the margins. Nicole read some notes at the beginning of Genesis, then flipped through the book, reading comments at random. From what she could make out, they all seemed to be about the scriptures, questions about the meaning of certain passages, and brief exclamations of agreement. Mary Ellen had noted things like, "For Bible Study," and "Have L explain." There didn't seem to be anything of a personal nature.

Next, she picked up the journal. Here, in much more readable form, was the sad story of Mary Ellen's life in the months leading up to her death. The girl's mother was working two jobs, barely managing to support herself. She was divorced from Mary Ellen's father, but he regularly stopped by the house drunk, looking for a fight that often turned physical. Mary Ellen complained about her overwhelming load of homework and the fact that her grades were so low she was in danger of losing her scholarship. She also fretted about her run-ins with Veronica and her failure to find friends at the university.

After her first finals, Mary Ellen wrote that she'd barely passed. She started off the next quarter with the news that she'd joined the Bible studies group. Soon after, she wrote, "I saw him close up for the first time. He is so handsome I could die. My parents would have a fit if I had anything to do with this guy. But I don't care. As my roommate would put it, I 'have the hots' for him. I've always been the goody-goody who never gives in to her feelings. I took that stupid oath about saving myself for marriage, but now I'm taking it back. Why can't I let go of those stupid rules and have fun like everybody else. "

Nicole wondered if the unnamed crush had been Doshan. Mary Ellen had said she'd met him in Bible study. The journal entry went on to list her strategies for attracting his notice. It sounded like she was all but stalking him.

Her last long entry was mid-January, about five weeks before her sexual encounter with Doshan. After that, there were only a few entries. Mary Ellen seemed to have lost interest in keeping the journal. For the next few weeks, she just noted events and times, but nothing of a personal nature. The rest of the book was blank.

Nicole glanced at her watch. It was almost 5:30 p.m., and Josh could be home any time now. She took the books upstairs and put them on her night table. She'd call Detective Martinez in the morning.

She thought of the note she'd found on her car telling her to mind her own business. It was a moot point—she had no intention of poking into the murder investigation again. She was leaving it to the police this time. But what if she had to testify? *One step at a time*, she told herself.

Nicole tried to focus on the evening ahead with Josh, but she couldn't shake off her sense of regret and dread. She had the feeling that, while this tragedy had all but crushed her, something else was about to happen, something bad.

EIGHT

WHEN SHE WOKE UP THE NEXT MORNING, Josh was standing by her night table. He was just out of the shower, dressed only in his underwear. She smiled, taking in his muscular legs, the trail of dark blond hair leading from the top of his briefs to his navel. Her eyes moved up, and she saw he was reading Mary Ellen's journal. Only now did it occur to her that she should have put it in her night table drawer instead of on top, where he was likely to see it.

Josh sensed her attention and gave her a puzzled look. "What's this?" he said.

She felt herself flush. Reluctantly, she admitted that the reason for her outing the day before was Veronica's message and the drive to Oceanside University.

"Hey!" he said. "Why didn't you tell me?"

"It wasn't that big a deal. I was going crazy in the house. Then Veronica contacted me, and I said I'd drive out there and meet with her."

"Okay," he said. "But I'm still wondering why you didn't tell me."

"Because you've made it clear you don't want me involved in this case."

"I don't. You should have put this Veronica in touch with the cops. What really worries me is that you felt you couldn't tell me. We've discussed this, remember? No secrets." He tossed the journal back on the nightstand. "Do everybody a favor. Get this into the proper hands, and leave the investigation to the authorities. Next time you're tempted to get involved—and I hope there isn't a next time—just don't. Okay?"

There it was. He was doing it again. "I don't want to keep things from you," she said, "but I don't like the way you assume you can make decisions for me, and I don't like your tone."

"Sorry." He flushed, as if just realizing he was talking down to her. "But when did I ever try to make decisions for you?" His voice was softer now, more conciliatory.

"Let's see," she said, "how about just now? And when I told you I was going for my P.I. license, you objected. I got stuck babysitting Mary Ellen, and you threw a fit. I don't like being told what I can or can't do."

"I'm not—" He paused, formulating his words. "All I'm asking is that you let me know what's going on, okay?"

She gave a noncommittal nod, then got up to go downstairs and call Detective Martinez. The case was no doubt in the hands of a murder squad by now, but Martinez would know who to contact. She didn't answer, so Nicole left a message.

Still perturbed, she sliced a couple of bagels, got out cream cheese and jam, and set the table. She was drinking coffee and reading the paper when Josh, now dressed for work, walked into the kitchen. Noticing the sliced bagels, he popped them in the toaster and sat down across from her. "Are you going in to work today?"

"Might as well," she said, gazing at him over the paper. "Staying home doesn't seem to be helping."

"Good," he said. "It will get your mind off things." He lifted one eyebrow and tilted his head in half-joking disapproval. "And keep you out of trouble."

§

Nicole was digging into a pile of reports when her boss walked into her office. "Mary Ellen's lawyers want us to handle arrangements for her body," Jerry said. "Can you get the ball rolling on that? Start with the coroner's office. Find out when they plan to release it. Then contact the girl's mother and see what she wants done."

She put in a call to Deputy Coroner Ortega. He told her it would be at least another few days, perhaps as long as a week, before the body could be released. Next, she called Mary Ellen's mother, Linda Barnes, and expressed her condolences.

"Thank you," Linda sniffled.

"Do you know what you want done with Mary Ellen's remains?" Nicole paused a beat, regretting the word *remains*. "Do you want her cremated or shipped home for burial? You can have a service either way."

"Look," Linda said, "I don't have that kind of money. No way I can pay for this." She sounded aggrieved, even a little angry.

There was a silence while Nicole considered this. "Maybe the Women Against Rape organization will cover the expense. I'll get in touch with them and call you back."

She was put right through to the organization's director, Maddy Corrigan. "Of course we'll take care of it. Sorry I didn't think to offer. We'll also pay for a memorial service. Several of our board members will want to speak, especially Geneva Ford. Aside from being Mary Ellen's attorney, Geneva felt very close to her."

Nicole fought the urge to say, "You've got to be kidding." Geneva had shown no interest in Mary Ellen other than making sure she appeared in court and testified in a way that didn't blow the case.

"Ask Mrs. Barnes what she wants," Maddy added. "It would be

good if you can go to Georgia and help with the arrangements. We'll pay for that, too."

After the trauma of the last few days, Nicole shrank from the prospect of having to comfort Mary Ellen's mother and make funeral arrangements. "I'm afraid I have other commitments," she said. "But I think one of my associates might be available. I'll have her call you."

While they were talking, Nicole had seen Joanne walk into her cubicle. Once off the phone, Nicole got up from her desk and made her way over. Joanne didn't look well at all; her nose was red, and she was coughing. "Hey," she said in a hoarse whisper, "I finally managed to drag myself out of bed."

"Welcome back," Nicole said. "But are you sure you should be here? You sound like you're still sick."

"It's been five days, and I feel better than I sound. Besides I'm no good at staying home."

"Can you take over the Barnes case? WAR wants someone to go to Georgia and help Mary Ellen's mother with the arrangements."

"I'd love to go," Joanne said. "I've never been out of California."

"Great," said Nicole. "There's nothing I need less right now than an out-of-town trip."

"Right. You want to get on with your wedding arrangements. Do you have a date yet?"

Nicole shook her head. Now, with tension growing between Josh and her, she didn't want to think about the wedding. "The venues we wanted are booked through the summer," she said. "So we're still trying to figure out a date."

It must have been Nicole's tone, for Joanne was giving her an odd look. "Are things okay with you two?"

Nicole managed a smile. "Of course. Everything's fine. I'll let Jerry know I'm handing over the assignment."

After conferring with Jerry, she wrote a memo of instructions and contact numbers for Joanne. Then she went back to clearing her accumulated backlog.

Around 4:00 p.m., her sister called. "Have you seen what XHN is saying?"

"Wait. I'll take a look," said Nicole, as she typed XHN.com into her browser. There it was—the headline she'd been dreading: "Doshan Williams Charged in Murder of Mary Ellen Barnes."

"Thanks for the tip, Steph," Nicole said. "I've got to go." She immediately called Sue and told her about Doshan's arrest.

"Really?" Sue said. "Where did you hear that?"

"It's on XHN. If he has a defense lawyer, I need to tell him about Mary Ellen's confession. Can you find out who it is?"

"First of all, let's make sure he's actually been arrested," said Sue. "The tabloids don't always get the story straight. I'll make a few calls to verify the arrest and see if he has legal representation. I'll call you back."

While Nicole was waiting, she pulled up another news site. One of the top stories showed a photo of Doshan in his football uniform. A video featured Geneva Ford in the dark, shiny wig she'd worn in court. Nicole clicked on the link, and the video clip began. In contrast to her calm demeanor in court, Geneva was shrill and angry. "The perpetrator has been arrested and will be tried for this terrible crime. But justice has yet to be served. If Oceanside University had done its job—if the school had gone after rapists to keep coeds safe, Mary Ellen Barnes would be alive today. That's why WAR is continuing its civil suit against the university. The criminal courts will take care of Doshan Williams.

"The authorities need to listen when a woman reports a sexual assault, even in these so-called he-said, she-said cases," she went on. "Studies show that ninety-five percent of all rape charges are valid. Many women don't even report attacks because they don't have the strength to fight a system that is stacked against them. If you aren't familiar with the epidemic of campus rapes, I invite you to view the public service video posted on WAR.org."

Nicole did just that. The WAR video included interviews of campus rape victims, and she was struck by how Mary Ellen's behavior differed from that of the young women who appeared in the short video.

Nicole could see these women had been severely traumatized in ways that Mary Ellen did not appear to be. Several expressed fear their assailants would hunt them down, rape them again, and perhaps kill them. This was a recurring theme. Such fear had driven a number of victims to withdraw from school. Some even refused to leave their homes.

Nicole searched the web, curious about Geneva's ninety-five percent figure. What she learned, after reading several articles, was that the percentage of false rape charges was unknown and unknowable. Estimates of false claims ranged from two percent to forty percent, depending on the source. But according to all estimates, most of the victims were telling the truth.

She ran across another statistic that was more disturbing. According to the Federal Bureau of Labor Statistics, sixty-five percent of all sexual assaults went unreported. She thought about it. If they were unreported, how could anyone come up with a percentage? Through public surveys? Maybe.

She thought Mary Ellen's case must be highly unusual. How likely was it that a woman would be blackmailed into making a false rape accusation? Another question was how Mary Ellen had so completely bamboozled WAR. They'd spent time drilling her on her story. She must have put on a pretty good performance to get them to take her case. By the time Nicole met her, Mary Ellen was a basket case. She never could have stood up to tough vetting like that.

Suddenly weary, Nicole turned her chair to face her office window and stared out, watching the clogged lanes of traffic along Wilshire Boulevard. The ringing of the phone startled her, and she swung around to pick up.

It was Sue. "He's in custody but he hasn't been formally charged. They're processing him now. Once the D.A.'s office brings charges, if it does, there will be an arraignment. As I understand it, several Oceanside alums have arranged for David

Sperantza of Jones, Elston & Sperantza to represent him. I know David, and they couldn't have made a better choice. He has lots of experience and a good track record. I'll give you his number."

"Wait," Nicole said as a thought struck her. "If Doshan is charged with murder, and I'm on the witness list, will my name be made public? As soon as the tabloids see it, they'll be after me again. I don't know if I can take it. I know Josh can't."

"The prosecution and defense must provide a list of witnesses to each other," Sue said, "and that list is public record. There is a way to keep a name off the list under certain circumstances. You'll have to discuss this with David. But once you testify, your name will be out there, and you will get hits from the media."

Sue was silent for a moment. "Now that I think about it, I don't know if David can use your testimony. It would probably be considered hearsay, which is inadmissible."

"Right, I guess it would be hearsay since I didn't actually witness anything. But I did get it directly from Mary Ellen, who was the victim," Nicole said. "Now she's dead and can't speak for herself."

"Talk it over with David. Maybe he can figure out how to get around the hearsay rule. But, look, you don't have to testify. There's no legal requirement. If it's going to cause problems, you should think it over very carefully."

"I have thought it over. If it would help Doshan, I want to do it. And I want to do it for Mary Ellen."

Nicole wrote down Sperantza's number and, as soon as she and Sue hung up, called his office. She was transferred several times before she reached his secretary.

"This is Michelle." The woman was brusque, clearly annoyed. "How can I help you?"

"My name is Nicole Graves. I'd like to speak to Mr. Sperantza, please."

"May I ask what this is about?"

"I have information bearing on the Doshan Williams case,

which I understand Mr. Sperantza is handling."

"You have to give me more than that," the woman said. "The phone has been ringing all morning. Dozens of people want to talk to Mr. Sperantza, and they all say they have vital information."

"I can't talk about it with anyone but Mr. Sperantza. Just take my name and number and tell him I have information that could significantly impact his case."

"Fine. What's your number?" The woman was highly impatient, her words clipped.

Nicole gave her name, spelled it out, then her number. As soon as she was done, the woman said "Goodbye," and the line went dead. Nicole wondered if the secretary had actually taken her information or had simply pretended. Would the attorney even get the message? The afternoon seemed to confirm her suspicion when Sperantza failed to return her call.

Before dinner, Nicole and Josh settled in the living room for their usual glass of wine. Josh seemed to have forgotten about their morning spat and was brimming with good cheer. He had three new clients coming in for consultations. "If I get even one of these jobs, I'll have to hire another assistant." All at once, he noticed her expression and stopped. "Hey," he said, "you're upset, aren't you? Is it Mary Ellen, or are you still mad about what I said this morning? I'm sorry if I was too pushy—"

"It's not that," she said. "Doshan Williams has been arrested for Mary Ellen's murder. I have to tell his lawyer about her confession—if he thinks it will help, I'm going to offer to testify."

Josh gave her an incredulous look. "Nicole, I thought we had an understanding. You're going to avoid anything that might attract the media's attention."

"You're right. After the fallout from Robert Blair's murder, I said I'd try to avoid those situations. This is different. I have information no one else has. It might help prove Doshan's innocence, which was Mary Ellen's last wish. How can I keep it to myself? I've already called Doshan's attorney, but he hasn't gotten back to me."

"That's probably because he's getting a call from every crank in Los Angeles."

"Crank!" she said. "For God's sake!"

"That came out wrong. I'm sorry. But there are a lot of reasons why you shouldn't, well, rush into anything."

"I'm not *rushing* into anything. I'm just going to talk to his attorney and see what he has to say. Then I'll decide what to do."

"Okay," Josh said. "Can you calm down and listen for a few minutes?"

"Of course." Nicole was annoyed. Why was he telling her to calm down when he was the one who was so excited? She took a deep breath and tried to hold onto her patience.

"Mary Ellen's decision to take back her accusation of rape doesn't clear Doshan of murder," Josh said. "After all, he didn't know she was going to recant, so he still had a motive to kill her."

"That's true, but—"

He held up his hand. "I'm not done. Please, just listen. Mary Ellen was, and I'm putting this kindly, an unreliable witness. She lied to you about leaving the hotel. And either she lied in court about the rape or she lied to you in recanting it. Don't you think the prosecutor is going use that to discredit what she told you? I'm sorry to say it, but she was a liar."

"But—"

He put his finger up to silence her. "Let me finish. If you do this, you'll be subjecting yourself to all that nasty publicity again. The tabloids will dredge up last year's headlines when everyone's just about forgotten them. And for what? Your testimony isn't going to clear Doshan."

"Josh, really, what harm would it do for me to talk to his lawyer? If he doesn't think my testimony would be helpful, he won't use it. But if he thinks it might help, I have to do it. Can't you see that?"

"So, you're determined to go ahead with this?

"I am."

His jaw was tight, his face flushed, and he was clearly angry. Nicole was shocked. She'd never seen this side of him. They rarely argued, and never like this. If only she could make him understand.

"I don't think you realize how bad I feel about Mary Ellen's death," she said. "I should have kept a closer eye on her. That was my job. And after what she told me, I honestly believe Doshan is innocent. That means whoever killed her is still out there. Don't you see the position I'm in? I couldn't live with myself if the real killer got away, and an innocent man went to jail."

"Oh, I get it, all right," he said. "You feel guilty, and you think that becoming a witness will make you feel better. Let me ask you this: What about this other guy, the one you think is the killer? If you're right, then you'll be putting yourself in danger by appearing as a witness."

"There are ways around that. If there's good reason, they can leave my name off the witness list so no one will know I'm going to testify."

"Okay, but what happens after you appear in court?" he said. "Or did you imagine they'll put you on the witness stand under an assumed name, sitting behind a curtain?

"Look," he went on, "you say you don't like the attention these situations generate, but you keep getting into them." He held up a finger. "First there was that episode in England you told me about. You almost got yourself killed. Just thinking about it makes me feel sick."

He held up a second finger. "Next, there was the murder of the law firm's investigator. The media went crazy with that one, and, once again, you almost got killed."

She stared at him, stunned by his sarcasm. And the finger counting was especially irritating. He'd never done that before.

He went on to his third point, three fingers up. "Then there was Mary Ellen's civil trial, which you could have avoided. Instead, you jumped right in and got into the news again." Four fingers.

"Next you drove out to Oceanside University on an errand you should have turned over to the police."

"Hang on," she said. "When Veronica said she wanted to talk, I had no idea what it was about."

"Fine," he said. "Lucky no one saw you there." His fifth finger went up. "Now you plan to go public with what may be another of Mary Ellen's lies. It probably won't do any good, but here you are, putting yourself in the spotlight again."

He paused and seemed to be studying her. "These things don't happen to other people. I'm afraid for you, and I'm beginning to think there's something in your personality that makes you seek this stuff out, like you have some kind of martyr complex."

Nicole lost her patience. "Martyr complex? Last time we talked about this, you said I was an excitement junkie. Which is it?"

Josh bowed his head slightly, as if considering what to say next. At last he looked at her. "How about this? I'll go with you when you talk to Doshan's lawyer. Can I at least do that?"

She was silent. After listening to his harangue, she didn't want him to come with her. He'd get the attorney to talk about the down side of appearing as a witness. But she already knew what the fallout might be, and this was her decision.

"I take that for 'no.'" Josh stood up. "Fine. See him on your own, if that's what you want."

He went to the front hall closet and pulled out a jacket. "I'm not going to discuss this anymore because I'm afraid I'll say something I'll regret. Don't wait up."

A moment later, he was gone, the door slamming behind him.

NINE

NICOLE WAITED UP UNTIL MIDNIGHT, hoping Josh would return so they could talk things out. She was still awake an hour later when her phone dinged with a message: "Spending the night at Dirk and Denise's. Need to think." There was no "Love, Josh," no sign-off at all.

It was a jolt when morning came and she woke up alone. She started to give him a call, then reconsidered. Best let him cool off. When he thought it over, she told herself, he'd realize he was being unreasonable. The Josh she knew was kind, loving, and bore no resemblance to the stranger who used his fingers to count off her shortcomings.

As soon as she got to her office, she put in another call to Doshan's lawyer. This time the receptionist refused to connect her with Sperantza's secretary or even take a message. Since Nicole had left a message the day before, the woman told her, there was no point in leaving another. Someone would get back to her.

She was getting the runaround. The office was probably inundated with calls that no one was going to return. All at once she remembered Sue mentioning that she knew Sperantza. She called Sue and asked if she'd intervene. As always, Sue was willing to help.

When Nicole's phone rang a few minutes later, it was Sperantza's secretary. She sounded rushed, but not unfriendly. "Mr. Sperantza has a busy day in court. But he can meet you for a quick lunch at City Tavern. It's downtown on Figueroa. You want the address?"

"I know the place," Nicole said. "What time?"

"12:15."

"I'll be there. Thanks."

She looked up David Sperantza on his lawfirm's website, on Google, and on her own firm's database, searching for background and a photo so she'd recognize him. He was a nice-looking man with wavy brown hair and piercing blue eyes. His expression was solemn and a little grim. She found his professional affiliations. He'd served as president of the Association of Southern California Defense Counsel. He volunteered at the Loyola Law School Project for the Innocent, an affiliate of the Innocence Project. She also learned that he had a good credit rating and no liens, arrests, or convictions. He was 38, divorced, the father of three.

Traffic was bad, and Nicole arrived at City Tavern five minutes late. The place was large and decorated in minimalist style. She was familiar with this stark design concept, which had reached the height of popularity a decade before. A bank of windows produced glare while failing to provide much light inside the restaurant. With its dark-wood paneling, wood floors, high ceiling, and lack of acoustical tiles, the place seemed designed to magnify sound. Background music, some kind of rap, was pumped up to full volume, making it hard to think. Nicole had read about marketing studies that showed people felt they were having a good time if a restaurant was noisy, even if they had to shout to make themselves heard.

Sperantza was already there, seated at a table near a long, faux-antique bar. He seemed to recognize her and waved her over. As she reached the table, he stood. They shook hands and sat down.

"Sorry I couldn't do this in my office," he said, handing her a menu. "I'm between court appearances. We'd better order. I've only got forty minutes." He raised his arm to summon a waiter while Nicole gave the menu a quick look. Sperantza ordered a burger and an iced tea.

"I'll have the grilled veggie salad and a Coke," she said. After the waiter was gone, Nicole told Sperantza about Mary Ellen's decision to recant.

When she was done, she could see that he was stunned. For a long moment, he didn't speak, as if he was mulling over the impact of this development on the case.

"This could be a real game changer," he finally said. "On the other hand, there are certain aspects that are problematic. The most serious is that your testimony is hearsay.

"I know that, but Sue thought you might find a way around it," Nicole said. "Mary Ellen herself told me she was going to recant. She was the plaintiff in the case. Now she's dead and can't speak for herself."

"True, but in Mary Ellen's case, it's further complicated by the fact that she'd already testified under oath that Doshan did rape her. Say we're able to get around that, there's another issue," he went on. "It's been reported that the girl was extremely upset under cross-examination. The prosecution could say she was just looking for an excuse to get out of returning to court. And finally, as you probably realize, Doshan didn't know she was going to recant, so he still would have had a motive."

"Mary Ellen said she wasn't raped," Nicole said. "Doshan knew he was innocent, so why would he kill her? He'd have reason to think the trial would clear him. Besides, he'd have to be monumentally stupid to murder someone when he'd be the prime suspect."

"True, true. Actually, this is the best news we've had so far,"

Sperantza said. "But here's the bad news. When Doshan was brought in, he let the police question him without a lawyer present. I can't go into what he said, but it's hard to tell a story the same way twice, especially when you're being questioned by the police, who do their best to trip you up. By agreeing to talk, Doshan made things worse for himself. If you're ever in that position, don't say a word without a lawyer present."

"Good advice," she said. "Oh, I just remembered. Before Doshan was charged, Mary Ellen's roommate gave me a journal Mary Ellen was keeping. I turned it over to the Santa Monica police. The journal stops about a month before the alleged rape, so it may not help, but I thought you'd want to take a look at it."

Sperantza pulled a notebook out of his jacket and wrote in it. "I'll get my hands on it. Even if it doesn't have anything pertaining to the rape charge, it might provide us with the names of people we can talk to."

"About Doshan," Nicole said. "I really do believe he's innocent, and I want to testify if it might help."

"It just might. I can't tell you how much I appreciate your coming forward. It gives us more to work with." Just then the busboy arrived with their food. Sperantza glanced at his watch, doused his burger with a good amount of ketchup, and took a bite.

"If I testify," Nicole said, "I'd like a favor."

"What's that?" he said.

"I want my name withheld from the witness list. I'm concerned about being held hostage by paparazzi and the tabloids. That happened to me before when—"

"I know," he said. "I followed that story in the news. It was, when? A year ago? What a nightmare!"

"Truly."

"Well, as for keeping your name confidential, we can ask. But the judge has to approve it."

"How likely is that?"

"Have you received any threats?" he said.

"Actually, I have." She took the note from her purse and handed it to him. "I meant to give this to you." She also told him about the young man who'd been fiddling with her tires in Oceanside's parking lot just before she discovered the note.

Sperantza read it. "How do you suppose they knew which car was yours?"

"A bunch of students passed my car when I first arrived. They noticed me and gave me a bit of harassment. You know, the way young men sometimes do, imagining they're being funny. I can only guess that one of them recognized me from the news. Maybe he's mixed up in this, or maybe he just did it for the fun of it."

"Whatever the case, I need to turn this over to the police," Sperantza paused to put the note in his pocket. "This kind of threat is illegal. And it's something tangible to help ensure the judge allows your name to be left off the witness list—especially since Miss Barnes's statement to you suggests someone else had reason to kill her. But if there's a chance the real killer is still out there, I'd suggest you give it serious consideration before you agree to testify."

"I've already done that," she said. "When will the trial take place?"

"Doshan wants it as soon as possible, so he can go back to playing ball. He'll probably be getting out on bail. The alumni are offering to cover it. They believe he's innocent and want him in shape and back on the team when the season begins in September. I don't know if that's possible—we have a lot of preparation to do. I can't predict when we'll be ready. I'll be in touch. What's the best way to reach you?"

She got out her card, jotted her cell number on the back, and handed it to him.

After another glance at his watch, Sperantza placed his napkin next to his plate and stood up. "I have to leave. Thanks again. You've given us another direction to explore. You'll be hearing from us. Meanwhile, why don't you write down what you remember of Ms. Barnes's confession. As time passes, these memories fade, and we want to be as precise as we can." He put some bills on the table to cover the meal.

"I'll pay for mine," Nicole protested.

"No worries. The firm is paying. You've done us a huge favor."

As Nicole walked back to her car, she thought of Josh. Remembering how angry he'd been, she felt sick. She loved him so much; she'd do almost anything for him. But he couldn't expect her to keep quiet about this. It wasn't in her to stand by and do nothing when she had the power to help someone in trouble.

At 6:00 that night, Josh arrived home. When he saw her, he pulled her into his arms. They held each other a while without speaking. Finally, he said, "I really hate to see you putting yourself out there. But I respect your right to make your own decision. Just promise one thing: This will be the end to it. You're not going to get involved in any other way."

Nicole nodded, almost dizzy with relief. "Once I testify, that will be it. I promise." And at that moment, she really did mean it.

§

While Nicole appreciated a return to normality—for the most part—she was still uneasy about Josh's attitude toward the trial. Whenever news of it came up on TV or in conversation, Josh would clam up or fiddle with his phone. It was like he was putting his fingers in his ears, pretending not to hear.

Sometimes she caught him studying her, as if she were a puzzle he was trying to work out. One night, when they were reading in the living room, she noticed Josh had closed his book and was staring at her. Finding it hard to concentrate, she said, "Why do you keep looking at me that way? It makes me feel like you're deciding whether I'm worth the trouble."

He moved over closer and put his arms around her. "What trouble?" he laughed, kissing the top of her head. "Of course you're worth it. Everything's fine." But she could tell it wasn't fine. He was still bothered by the impending trial.

It was several weeks before she heard from Speranza again. The call came from Michelle, his secretary. "Mr. Speranza wants to speak to you."

After a click, Speranza himself came on. "Hi, Nicole. There are a couple of things I'd like to tell you. First of all, Doshan has been released on bail, and he'd like to thank you in person for offering to testify. Let's set up that meeting first."

For a moment, Nicole was too surprised to answer. She hadn't expected gratitude; she was only doing her duty. But she was curious about Doshan and more than willing to meet with him.

Speranza went on, "We also need to set up another meeting so we can go over exactly what Ms. Barnes said about recanting. I'll prep you on what the prosecutor might ask in cross-examination."

"Then I am going to appear?"

"It looks like it, unless we can prevent Ms. Barnes's testimony from the civil trial from being introduced. That doesn't seem likely."

"I don't understand. Why would you want to prevent it?"

"If her testimony is thrown out, it would greatly weaken the prosecution's case. But I don't think the judge will rule in our favor on this. I'm pretty sure you'll be testifying."

They set up the meeting with Doshan for Monday of the following week. Later Nicole told Josh about it. He nodded and looked away without comment.

When Nicole arrived at Speranza's office, she was asked to sit in the waiting room, which was large and almost as posh as the reception room of the law firm where she'd once worked. She waited only a few minutes before a woman in a fitted beige sheath came out and called her name. The woman had light-brown curly hair, rosy cheeks, and a warm smile.

"I'm Michelle, Mr. Speranza's secretary. I think I spoke to you on the phone a while ago. Sorry if I blew you off, but the phones were going crazy."

"I completely understand," Nicole said.

"Just follow me." Michelle led Nicole through a long corridor and turned right. Through a doorway, she could see a large corner office. "They're waiting for you. Go on in."

Three men stood when Nicole walked in. She recognized Doshan, who immediately reached out to take her hand. He shook it very gently while she gazed up at him. His height was the first thing she noticed. The second was his big, friendly smile. It emanated such warmth that it was impossible not to smile back. She'd seen him in the courtroom, of course, but he hadn't been smiling then, just staring straight ahead. Now she could see the charisma she'd read about in the papers.

"Nicole," he began. "Can I call you that?" When she nodded, he went on, "I want to thank you for what you're doing. Before you spoke up nobody really believed I was innocent. Not even my family. I don't think David here really believed me. So I wanted a chance to meet you face-to-face and tell you how grateful I am."

He released her hand and gestured toward the young man standing next to him. "This is my buddy, Andy Drummond. He's one of my character witnesses and is here to go over his testimony with David."

Drummond was almost as big as Doshan. He was fair-haired with a flat-topped marine-style haircut. He looked familiar, and as Nicole shook his hand, she recognized the snake's head tattoo peeking out from under his collar. He was the guy she'd seen in the spectator section the day she attended Mary Ellen's civil trial. He was the one who'd winked at her.

"Good to meet you," Drummond smiled. He seemed friendly enough, but her glance was drawn back to Doshan. *With his amazing charisma*, Nicole thought, *he must be the center of any gathering.* Did that mean he'd have to be "on" all the time? She wondered what that would be like—ego-gratifying or exhausting.

Sperantza came around his desk to shake hands next. "Thanks for coming in," he said. "You three sit, and I'll have Michelle bring in some coffee. Oh, and I'd like you to meet my investigator. At some point, he'll want a sit-down with Nicole to go over his own questions." Sperantza went to the door of his office and said a few words to his secretary, then returned to his desk where he picked up the phone and dialed an extension.

While he was busy, Nicole turned to Doshan. "I'm glad you got bail."

"Thank God," Doshan said. "Conditions in the Twin Towers jail are unimaginable. I had no idea. They throw so many people in there just because they're mentally ill. That's the real crime. I'm thinking of switching my major so I can help people like them—social welfare, maybe, or even law school."

"Aren't you planning to play professional football?"

"If I'm lucky enough to get chosen, yes. But that career is only good for a decade at best. Once you're past your prime, you have to figure out what to do with the rest of your life."

"Have you been going to classes?" Nicole said.

"Yes. I don't want to get behind, and I'm working with a personal trainer to keep in shape, so that's all good. Want to be ready for fall." He was silent for a long moment, and a corner of his mouth twitched downward, as if he were thinking about something unpleasant. "When people heard I was a suspect in the murder, I had to move out of the dorm. I couldn't take the disrespect. Not that anyone said anything." He looked at Drummond. "My friend here spoke up for me when I wasn't around. I couldn't stand the way people looked at me, like they believed I was guilty. Some of the women acted like they were afraid of me. Me! I'd never hurt a woman. Fortunately, one of the alums is letting me use the apartment over his garage. It's not far from campus."

At this point, a heavyset man walked into the office. He had a ruddy complexion and was wearing khakis and a baggy, gray T-shirt. "Nicole," said Sperantza, "this is Don Slater, our investigator."

Slater's steel-rimmed glasses had slipped down his nose. He pushed them back before he reached out to shake Nicole's hand. "How ya doin'," he said, barely glancing at her. Without waiting for an answer, he turned to the two young men. Slater nodded at Drummond and clapped Doshan on the back. "There's the man," Slater said. "See they got you out of the joint."

The joke—if it was a joke—fell flat. Doshan gave Slater a polite smile and a nod. "Good to see you, Don," he said.

Greetings apparently over, Slater looked at Sperantza. "Well, back to work," he said. He left the office without another a word to Nicole.

"Excuse his manners," Sperantza said. "He's not much on charm, but he's a good investigator. He'll be giving you a call in a few days."

By now Michelle was back with a tray that held three mugs of coffee, cream and sugar, and an assortment of cookies. Nicole took one, while Doshan and Drummond heaped up their plates.

They sat and made small talk for a while. Then Doshan turned to Nicole and said, "So Mary Ellen told you she'd been lying."

"That's right. She felt terrible about it. She told me someone blackmailed her into accusing you."

Doshan turned to Drummond and they exchanged a look. It made Nicole wonder if these two knew more than they were saying. After a moment, Doshan turned back to her. "Yeah," he went on. "David here told me about that. But she didn't say who the blackmailer was or what he had on her, did she?"

"She didn't say who, but she said he had a video, the kind you wouldn't want posted on the web. Mary Ellen said it would ruin her with everyone, especially her parents and her minister. In the end, she couldn't live with her lie. No matter what the consequences, she was determined to recant." Nicole was quiet a moment before she went on. "But she never got the chance."

She looked at Sperantza. "How's the case going?"

"It's early days. I have Slater looking for people at Oceanside who Ms. Barnes might have told about the blackmail, but it appears she only confided in you."

"She said she didn't have many friends there," Nicole said. "That's not surprising with her Southern manners and all that excessive politeness. According to her roommate, she was also given to proselytizing, which didn't fly too well with her classmates."

Sperantza frowned. "Isn't it a religiously affiliated university?"

"Interdenominational Christian," Nicole said. "But in reality, it's a party school. What do you think those kids were doing on the beach in the middle of a school night? They were drinking, smoking weed, and God knows what else. The school's security didn't even bother to patrol the area. The campus police are supposed to monitor that strip of beach, since it's directly across from the entrance to the campus."

Both Doshan and Drummond nodded in agreement. "She's right," Drummond said. "It's a party school. Malibu—that's what attracts kids. Most of them aren't looking for religion."

Nicole glanced at her watch and stood. "I have to get back to the office."

Doshan got up. "Thank you again, from the bottom of my heart."

"You're very welcome. Good luck. I really do think you're going to beat this." She shook hands all around and turned to leave.

"Oh," Sperantza said, as she headed for the door, "I'd like to meet with you so we can go over exactly what Mary Ellen said. I'd appreciate it if you'd take a minute to make an appointment with Michelle on your way out."

§

Two days later, Nicole was back. This time Sperantza came out to reception to welcome her and lead her into a conference room. A young woman—plump and androgynous with a helmet of short, dark hair—was already sitting in the room. "This is

Tammy, one of our paralegals. She's going to record the session. We're just waiting for one of our junior associates. He's new to the firm, and I wanted him to sit in on this. And here he is."

A pale young man with very curly red hair joined them in the conference room. Sperantza said, "Nicole, this is Kevin Volk; Kevin, Nicole." Kevin wasn't much taller than Nicole. He was slightly built with a beaky nose and wire-rimmed glasses that gave him the look of a highly intelligent lizard. He reached out to shake Nicole's hand and then took a seat on the other side of Sperantza.

They went over what Mary Ellen had told Nicole. She'd written it down after her first meeting with Sperantza. It hadn't been easy remembering the girl's exact words. After the attorney was done recording Nicole's proposed testimony, he said he was going to ask her a number of questions. "Some may sound hostile, but I'm just preparing you for what the prosecution might ask."

The questions were indeed unfriendly and answering them took a fair amount of thought. Most involved the issue of whether Mary Ellen was telling the truth in court—when she was under oath—or later in the hotel suite when she said her courtroom testimony had been a lie. Had Nicole herself seen or heard anything that would confirm the girl's story? And so it went, with several of the same questions asked in different ways.

Finally, Sperantza said, "I think that will do."

"Wait!" Nicole said. "Aren't you going to help me make my testimony more credible?"

"No. I want you to tell the truth, exactly the way you did now."

"But it will be a snap for the prosecution to discredit what I say," Nicole said. "All it seems to show is that Mary Ellen was a liar. I'm wondering if my testimony will be of any value at all."

"I'm having Slater, my investigator, look into possible corroborating evidence. But even if he doesn't find any, your evidence introduces an element of reasonable doubt, the idea that someone other than the defendant is the guilty party," Sperantza said. "What we call the SODDI defense."

"Saudi?" she repeated, "as in Saudi Arabia?"

"No," he laughed. "It's an acronym. S.O.D.D.I. It stands for 'Some other dude did it.' But we do need more evidence to corroborate this as an alternate theory. I guess that's all for now. Thanks for coming in."

As Nicole stood up to leave, Sperantza said, "Slater will be in touch with you. Meanwhile, think about your time with Mary Ellen. Maybe you'll remember something else she said or did that will help us."

TEN

TEN DAYS WENT BY, and Nicole still hadn't heard from Slater about the follow-up interview. She was wondering if he'd uncovered any evidence that would make her testimony more credible. Finally, she decided to take the initiative and contact him herself. It took several messages before Slater returned her call. Even then she had to explain who she was and why she was calling. He seemed to have forgotten all about her.

"Oh, yeah," he said. "You're the one that Barnes kid confided in. I've been meaning to come up with some questions for you. Let me get back to you."

By the following Friday, when she still hadn't heard from him, Nicole considered going over Slater's head and contacting Sperantza. Then she decided against it; no sense alienating members of his staff. She called Slater again. This time he answered.

"Sorry," he said, "I've been meaning to get back to you. I listened to your recorded interview, and it pretty much covers everything. No need for you to come in."

"How's it going?" Nicole said.

"Oh, you know. It's coming along."

"Any word when the trial will be?"

"Nope."

"Have you found anything that will make my testimony more credible?"

"We're, uh, still looking," Slater said. Something about the casualness of his tone suggested the opposite was true. He hadn't been looking at all.

Nicole immediately put in a call to Sperantza. As usual, he was in a rush.

"I'm hoping you've found some corroborating evidence to bolster my testimony," she said.

"Sorry," he said. "Nothing's turned up yet."

"What about a court date?"

"We still have a lot of work to do. I'd say October, but it could be sooner than that or even later. We'll let you know."

§

Another five weeks went by, and it was early August before Nicole got a call from Sperantza. "The trial is set to begin September 15th," he said.

"Six more weeks? I thought Doshan wanted a speedy trial."

"Six months—that is a speedy trial," he said. "We're really pushing it."

"Is it certain I'm going to appear as a witness?"

"Indeed it is. We're counting on you."

"Do you have any idea when I'll appear in court?"

"The trial will probably last six weeks, give or take. The prosecution goes first," he said. "So you'd be somewhere in the last half of the trial, week four or five. That would be the second or third week of October."

"There's something else I've been wondering—" Nicole began.

Sperantza interrupted. "I'm really sorry, but I'm late for a hearing. Can I call you later today? No, why don't we meet for a drink after work. How about the Wilde Wine Bar on La Brea near Third. Six o'clock OK with you?'

Nicole only hesitated a moment before she agreed. After they hung up, she called Josh to let him know she'd be late for dinner. She decided it would be prudent not to mention she was meeting Doshan's lawyer for a drink. "I just got handed a stack of names to look up," she said. "Jerry needs the results right away. I think I can finish and be home by 7:30 or 8:00."

"I'll hold dinner. Love you."

"I love you, too." She felt guilty about lying to Josh yet again. But she'd promised him that—other than appearing as a witness— she'd stay away from the case. And here she was meeting with the defense attorney to discuss it. If she told Josh, he'd be upset, and she didn't want to deal with that.

Sperantza was already at the bar, nursing a glass of whiskey. Once she'd ordered a glass of wine, he said, "So what's up? You had a question."

"It's about Doshan's teammates. Has your investigator taken a look at them? It seems to me that if he's being framed, whoever is doing it must hope to gain something. Maybe it's a teammate, hoping to get Doshan's position as quarterback."

"Yeah, I thought of that. I had Slater take a look, but he couldn't find anything."

"I also wonder about the chaplain at Oceanside. Mary Ellen went to his Bible study sessions, and she may have seen him for counseling. He's at war with the school's athletic department. It's a long shot, but he might merit checking out. His name's Jonathan Lyons."

Sperantza pulled the small notebook from his pocket and wrote in it. "I'll give this to Slater and have him take a look." He paused to put the notebook away and sip his drink before he went on. "We do have a number of character witnesses, like Andy Drummond, who you met. He and several others are willing to testify that Doshan is mild tempered, and they've never seen him become violent off the field."

"What are his chances?"

"It's hard to say," he said. "The prosecution doesn't have a strong case. It's all circumstantial. On the other hand, we don't have a very strong defense. Doshan doesn't have an alibi. He talked to the police, which was a terrible mistake, and in doing so, he changed his story. If nothing else turns up, I'll have to consider putting him on the stand to see if the jury buys his version of what happened that night."

Nicole looked up. The waitress was approaching with her wine. When she was gone, Sperantza said, "Tell me about yourself. You're planning to become an investigator, is that right? What made you decide to go into that line of work?"

"I was office manager at Nichols, Rice, Smith & Di Angelo," she said. "Sometimes I helped the in-house investigator when I had time, and I really enjoyed the work. You said you followed the Robert Blair murder case, so you know the rest of the story. After that, the law firm went under. Office management wasn't my thing anyway, so here I am."

The next twenty minutes or so were taken up by the attorney's accounts of trials he'd handled for celebrity clients. He was a good storyteller, and Nicole was entertained. When she finished her drink, she pulled the valet ticket out of her purse and started to get up.

Sperantza put his hand over hers. "Don't go," he said. "Stay and have dinner with me."

"Sorry, David. My fiancé's waiting at home. But thanks for the drink and the update. Let me know if you find out anything."

She left the bar somewhat puzzled by Sperantza's dinner invitation. She was wearing a sizeable diamond on her finger. Hadn't he noticed, or was it that he didn't care? She was no stranger to attention from men, but he was the first since she'd started wearing an engagement ring.

Nicole's thoughts turned to the upcoming trial. Somehow she doubted Slater had devoted much time to investigating Doshan's teammates. Why not do some digging of her own? She had the resources, and she was good at it. Maybe she could uncover something.

She started using her lunch breaks at the office to troll the company's databases for information. It was slow going. She couldn't get much done within the limits of her time, but she didn't want to work at home because of the risk that Josh might find out. Each day, she'd buy lunch from a woman named Charlotte who came around selling food she made and packaged herself. Her sandwiches were excellent and her brownies in a class by themselves. She carried her goods in a basket with a red-and-white gingham cover; it reminded Nicole of the basket Red Riding Hood had been carrying when she encountered the big bad wolf. This became a running joke between her and Charlotte.

Nicole started her research with the chaplain. One look at his records seemed to show an exemplary life. He was married with five children. He'd never been arrested or involved in a scandal, at least any that showed up in the records. His credit was excellent. His college degrees checked out. He'd never even had a traffic ticket. This, of course, didn't mean he wasn't fooling around with coeds, as Veronica implied. Still, as far as the records went, he was clean.

She looked at the team roster on the Oceanside Sharks' website. She was surprised by how many players there were—more than sixty, with five quarterbacks. Doshan's name wasn't there. He was working with a trainer, but he was no longer on the team because of the criminal charges against him. Andrew Drummond's name did appear. He was now one of the quarterbacks, although it looked as if he was simply a replacement in the lineup who played other positions as well.

She started searching the players on the firm's databases and on her browser. Two weeks went by without turning up a single bit of useful information.

September 15th finally arrived. The trial was beginning, and she still had nothing.

Nicole would have given anything to be in the courtroom and watch the proceedings first hand. But, even if she hadn't been working, she was banned from attending because she was going to testify as a witness. She had to satisfy her curiosity by reading the paper and checking the tabloids.

§

While Nicole was stuck reading about the trial, Doshan was living it. As his limo approached the criminal courts building in downtown Los Angeles, Doshan was struck by how different it was from the Santa Monica Courthouse, which looked more like a high school than a legal institution. The downtown court, where his trial was about to begin, was a high-rise on a busy downtown thoroughfare. The building's façade resembled a honeycomb, suggesting it was filled with busy worker bees.

The broad sidewalk and steps leading into the building offered the only space where reporters, television crews, paparazzi, and spectators could wait for a glimpse of Doshan arriving for his first public appearance since he was arrested.

At 8:30 a.m., the limo pulled up to the curb. The crowd parted as the entourage pushed its way into the building. Reporters hurled questions at Doshan. He ignored them, squaring his shoulders and taking long, unhurried strides. His lawyers scurried to keep up.

He hadn't slept the previous night and felt numb. In the car Sperantza had coached him on how to conduct himself. "Look serious and confident," the lawyer had said. "There will be press outside asking questions. Ignore them. If anything needs to be said, leave that to me. The same goes for your appearance in court today. Keep your cool—and keep your mouth shut."

Doshan and his lawyers entered the building, boarded an

elevator, and rode up to the ninth floor, where L.A.'s high-profile criminal trials took place.

Judge John Lloyd, white-haired and gaunt as death, appeared at the stroke of 9:00 a.m. to call the court to order. Sperantza had told Doshan that Lloyd was strict in matters of courtroom procedure, but he was also known to occasionally cut a break for the defense.

"Lloyd used to be a deputy D.A." Sperantza had said, "a very tough prosecutor who usually got convictions. Then a couple of years ago—it was after he'd been appointed to the bench—the Innocence Project cleared two men he'd had convicted of murder. One was on death row. You can bet that shook him up. He's been a different man ever since, much more inclined to give the defense leeway to introduce evidence and witnesses."

Once they were in session, Deputy District Attorney Frank Kendell began presenting the prosecution's case. Kendell was wearing the uniform of his profession, a dark blue suit, light-blue shirt, and red-striped tie. In his fifties, he had close-cropped, graying hair and was twenty pounds overweight, most of it through his middle. His demeanor was cool and professional, betrayed only by his tendency to raise an eyebrow and smirk when he felt he'd made his point.

A forensics investigator from the police department was up first to present the prosecution's evidence. Exhibit A was Doshan's billed cap, grimy from exposure to the elements. It bore the aqua logo for Oceanside's football team, featuring the face of a shark, teeth bared in a sinister smile. The investigator said the cap had been found at the murder scene. It was hanging from a fishing line that had been snagged on a pier support beam. Not surprisingly, Doshan's DNA was found on the cap.

Doshan passed a note to Sperantza, "What about any DNA they found on the body?" it said. "Are they going to talk about that?"

Sperantza jotted at the bottom of the note, "Don't worry. We'll ask on cross. And we have our DNA experts with their own findings."

The forensics investigator went into detail about the spot under the Santa Monica Pier where Mary Ellen's body had been found. He explained that Mary Ellen had been moved from wherever she'd been killed. He said evidence showed that she'd been dragged under the pier, probably by her feet, judging by the way her top and jacket were pulled up, exposing part of her bra and a shoulder. From the condition of the body, she appeared to have been half buried in the sand for at least twenty-four hours before the tide uncovered her. On a video screen, he showed photos, first of her body and another of her face, red-splotched neck, and blank stare. Some of the jurors took a quick look and averted their eyes. Others studied the photos closely, as if they might reveal the identity of the killer.

When Kendall was done with his questions, it was Sperantza's turn. "Tell me this," he said, "was any other DNA found at the crime scene besides on the hat."

"Yes. But it was a small amount, and ..."

Sperantza interrupted. "Just answer the question, please. Where was the other DNA found?"

"Some skin was found under the victim's fingernails," the investigator said.

"Where is the report on that DNA?"

"We couldn't analyze it. The victim had been buried in wet sand and covered with salt water when the tide was in. Exposure to the elements degraded the DNA, making it useless."

"Thank you," Sperantza said. "That will be all for now, but I would like to reserve the right to question this witness again if the need arises."

The next witness was Detective Gregory Morse, one of the team who'd questioned Doshan after he was taken into custody. He confirmed that he'd interviewed Doshan that day and said he was now going to play an audio recording of the interview. There was a click, and the detective's voice came on, giving both his name and Doshan's, as well as the date and time of the interview.

Morse: "Where were you the night of March 23rd of this year?"

Doshan: "I was home in my apartment over the garage at Joe Connelly's house in Malibu. He's an alum of Oceanside and is letting me stay there."

Morse: "Did anyone see you there? Mr. Connelly? Anyone in his family?"

Doshan: "They were away. So, nobody saw me."

Morse: "Okay. I'm going to show you a video. It's from a webcam at the Santa Monica Pier. It's dated March 23, 2017, 12:00 a.m."

There was a click, and the detective's voice said, "I'm running the video now. It shows Mr. Williams walking past the entrance to the Santa Monica pier, turning right and heading in the direction of the water."

Doshan came on, sounding rattled: "Oh, right. Sorry, I got mixed up. I stayed in my apartment the first night of the trial. It was the second night that I went to Santa Monica beach. I couldn't sleep and thought a walk on the beach might help relax me."

Morse: "Why did you drive all the way to Santa Monica? There's a beach just across the road from the university."

Doshan: "Wait. Shouldn't I talk to my lawyer before I answer any more questions?"

Morse: "That's totally up to you. But I want to make this clear. This is your only opportunity to tell us your side of the story. Once you call for a lawyer, we can't talk to you anymore, and you lose that opportunity."

At this point, Morse leaned over and turned off the recorder. "That's where the recording ends."

Listening to it, Doshan once again regretted talking to the police. The night before the police interview, he'd been too keyed up to sleep. He understood he'd be the primary suspect in the girl's murder, and the prospect of being questioned terrified him. Yet he'd felt he had no choice. An innocent man wouldn't refuse to answer questions, and he was innocent. He'd gone to bed and lay there, listening to his heart pounding in his ears. Around 1:00 a.m., he got up, found a bottle of tequila, downed five or six shots, then a few more, hoping this would help him sleep.

The liquor had done the opposite. Not only had he not slept, but when he arrived at the police station in the morning, he'd been hung over and still a little drunk. His brain wasn't working. Only after he'd screwed up his story did he realize he shouldn't have told the cops anything.

The next witness was Deputy County Coroner John Ortega. Once again, photos of Mary Ellen's corpse appeared on the screen. Ortega zoomed in on her, using the red beam of a laser pointer to direct attention to the marks on her neck. "These are finger marks," Ortega said. "They indicate the killer had large hands with a wide span. I'd say this man was bigger than average."

"Can you tell us how tall that person might be?" asked Kendell.

"Not with any accuracy. I'm guessing well over six feet."

"Like six-foot-five?"

Doshan noticed Sperantza tense up, as if he were about to stand and object, but he seemed to change his mind.

"As I said, I don't know," Ortega said. He projected another photo of Mary Ellen on the screen. This was a shot of the back of her head, her hair matted with blood. In the next photo, her hair was parted to show a long, jagged wound on her scalp. "She was struck on the head with a blunt instrument," Ortega said. "From the extent of that wound, I would say she was probably unconscious when her neck was broken."

The coroner said the approximate time of death was 3:00 a.m. and then began describing in numbing detail the fine points of the physical evidence. Doshan started dozing off, only to be woken when Sperantza gently shook his arm.

§

As the trial progressed, and Nicole realized she had to narrow her search. She found Doshan on several social media sites. His pages were well put together and appeared professionally designed. They were also similar to other players' social media pages. This made her think the university set them up for its star athletes. Doshan's held quite a few photos, most with a group he seemed to pal around with. Drummond was one of them. The rest looked like football players as well. She checked the names and found they were indeed fellow Sharks.

Her targets were now pared down to the five quarterbacks, their close friends online, as well as Doshan's buddies who appeared most often on his social media pages. Still, the thought of doing background checks on all of them was daunting. She sat for a while, drumming her fingers on her desk while she tried to think of a better approach. Before too long, she came up with a plan.

She wrote down the names of a dozen players who appeared to be closest to Doshan. Then she called Veronica Smith, Mary Ellen's old roommate.

"Whazzup," Veronica said. Listening to her snarky tone, Nicole could picture the young woman with her inflated sense of entitlement.

"I need a favor."

"Just name it," Veronica said.

"Do you have access to some kind of student phone directory? I need the phone numbers of some Oceanside students."

"Sure. They'll be on the school's database. Who do you want?"

Nicole read them off, and Veronica found the numbers and read them back. When they finished, Veronica said, "Hey, these guys are all on the football team."

"Right," Nicole said. "Thanks so much, Veronica. This is a huge help."

"So, what's this for? I mean, are you still trying to get Doshan off?"

Nicole wasn't going to share her plans with a gossip like Veronica. "This isn't related to the case. It's just for our records. Thanks again, Veronica. I really appreciate it." With that, she rang off.

Nicole spent the next half hour calling the numbers. Most didn't pick up, so she left messages. Of the remainder, two seemed flummoxed by her call and asked if she was with the police. When she said she wasn't, they refused to talk to her. Another said that he was too busy and hung up.

Nicole's next call was to a receiver named Johnny Austin. To her surprise, he said, "Sure, I'd be glad to talk to you. We're done training for the afternoon. I'm hungry for some Mexican food, so I'm heading over to Santa Monica in a bit. How about meeting me at El Cholo at about 3:00?"

Nicole thought of a witness she was supposed to interview in the next few days. She could set that up for 4:00 and leave the office early to meet with Johnny first.

"Sure," she said. "El Cholo at 3:00. See you there."

Since she'd looked up his photo on the team roster, Nicole recognized Johnnie right away. He was a tall, well-muscled redhead with freckles. He looked like a Mid-Western farm boy, although he was born and raised in L.A. He was seated in the main dining room next to a cooking station where one of the cooks was making fresh tortillas. She seemed to have taken a shine to Austin, for as Nicole approached, the woman flipped a hot tortilla onto his plate.

Nicole sat down, and a waiter scurried over to get her order. "Just coffee," she said.

Johnny didn't seem curious about why Nicole wanted to talk, nor did he ask if she was with the police. She had the feeling he knew who she was. "What do you want to know?" he said.

"It's about Doshan Williams. Was there anyone on the team who was jealous enough of him to frame him for murder?"

There was a long moment while Johnny finished chewing an enormous bite of his burrito. "Everybody on the team was jealous of Doshan. He was my friend, and I was jealous. I would have made a great quarterback, but he had more talent, and he got the gig. I'd never have done anything to fuck him over, much less frame him for murder. But I can't speak for the others. There are people who would stop at nothing to be a star."

"Have you got anyone in mind?"

"Not really. But you ought to take a look at those guys with the snake tattoos. The tatts cover their chests and run up their necks. When they're dressed, all you can see is the snakehead poking out from under their shirt."

"What makes them worth a close look?"

"I've overheard them talking about Doshan. They hate him and would do just about anything to get him. They don't make a secret of it."

"Andy Drummond has a tattoo like that, and he's Doshan's best friend."

"Right. And there are two others with the same tattoo. The three of them hang out when Doshan's not around. There's something going on with them, like they're up to something."

"Who are they? Can you give me their names?" Nicole was pulling her notebook out of her purse.

"Cody Marshall and Joe Sabatella."

"Thanks," she said. Jotting down the information.

"Can I buy you a meal? This is delicious."

"Thanks, but I have another appointment."

"I hope Doshan gets off, Nicole. I really do."

§

By mid afternoon, the trial had stalled on a legal point, the significance of which had gone over Doshan's head. The prosecutor, Sperantza, and Judge Lloyd had disappeared into the judge's chambers; the jury was on a break. In the lull, Doshan was thinking about how this nightmare began. It started with a bet he'd made with his roommate—a stupid bet that could ruin his life. He'd thought little of it at the time. Now it ate at him. If only he could take it back.

The bet had been not just monumentally stupid, but also cruel. Maybe he hadn't raped Mary Ellen Barnes, but he had taken advantage of her naiveté, and he hated himself for it. He'd spent his life building a reputation as the good guy—kind, generous, and responsible. That was how he wanted people to see him. But what he'd done to Mary Ellen hadn't been good at all. In a way, it was his fault she was dead.

He was so ashamed of what he'd done that he hadn't told anyone about the bet, not his lawyer in the rape case nor Sperantza. Besides, it wasn't as if it would help his case; it would only make him look bad.

It all began when he and Andy were sitting around drinking beer one night. Andy was complaining that he never could hook up with the girls he really wanted. "There's this one—we met at a party and I made a move on her. She got all weird about it and left with some other dude."

Doshan decided to hand out some advice. "Your problem is you're in too much of a hurry. If she's not that into you, you gotta have some patience. Make an effort to run into her; you know, hang out a few times. Be friendly, but pretend sex is the last thing on your mind. A peck on the cheek when you say goodbye—if it feels right. By then, she'll be begging for it." At this point, Doshan hadn't been able to resist bragging. "Once I figured that out, I haven't had a single girl turn me down. I could bag any girl on this campus. No lie."

"Oh yeah?" Andy had said. "I bet I can find one who won't put out for you."

"Bring her on," Doshan had said.

"One condition," Andy said. "You'll have to bring her up to our room. Get her up here, and I'll know you've scored."

"No problem," Doshan said. They shook hands on a $100 bet. A week later, Andy had chosen his candidate: Mary Ellen Barnes. His criteria had been her modest, unfashionable clothes; lack of makeup; outsider status; and membership in the school's Bible studies club. She looked like one of those girls who had taken the vow to save herself for marriage.

Once given his "mark," Doshan had attended a couple of Bible study meetings, sat next to Mary Ellen, and chatted with her. After the second meeting, he'd offered to walk her to her dorm. She'd stopped him before they'd emerged from the trees beside the building. He interpreted that to mean she didn't want to be seen with a black guy. This offended him, but he pretended not to notice. They'd had three dates—walks in the woods east of campus. This had been her choice, a place where no one would see them. They'd exchanged a few chaste kisses.

He'd been planning to invite Mary Ellen up to his room on their next date. Before that happened, he'd run into her on the beach one night. He'd offered to walk her home, then asked her to his room. He told her he wanted to show her his grandmother's rosary, which meant so much to him that he kept it locked in his desk. He wasn't surprised when Mary Ellen accepted. Once she was in his room with the door closed, it had been easy to coax her out of her clothes and into bed. The rosary was never mentioned. He didn't even have to take it out of his desk.

After Doshan collected the $100 bet, Andy had gestured toward a small black teardrop-shaped device from their shared bookcase.

"What the hell is that?" Doshan said.

"You'll see," Drummond said, sniggering. "Boy will you see! It's a nannycam. The guy who invented this was a genius." He got the device from the shelf and pressed a button. There in full-living color were Doshan and Mary Ellen, going at it on Doshan's bed. They still had most of their clothing on, but it was clear what they were doing.

"For fuck sake, Drummond!" Doshan said. "You're really disgusting. Delete that. Delete it this minute."

"All right, all right," Drummond had said, choosing a drop down menu and pressing delete. "You don't have to get so mad. I thought it was funny."

"Well, it wasn't."

Doshan was so angry that he didn't speak to Drummond for several days.

Other than that, he hadn't given much thought to Mary Ellen. She'd been a virgin, but he had asked her permission, and he'd been gentle. He hadn't gone to Bible study again, nor had he called her, as he'd promised. The following week she'd showed up at practice a few times to watch from the bleachers, and he could tell from the way she stared at him that she had a crush on him. He'd nodded in greeting, but that was all. Then she stopped coming. He'd actually forgotten her until he was called into the dean's office and was told she'd accused him of rape.

Doshan had been stunned. He wondered if this was her way of getting revenge because he'd dropped her. Not for the first time, Doshan thought about what Nicole Graves had said. That Mary Ellen was being blackmailed by someone who had a compromising video. It couldn't it be the one Andy had taken because Doshan himself had seen Andy delete it. That is, unless someone else had found out about it and made a copy. Who would have done that and why?

Just then they called the next witness for the prosecution: Cody Marshall, one of Doshan's teammates. Marshall was a belligerent-looking Nordic giant with a sumo-wrestler topknot just behind his hairline. He had the same snakehead tattoo rising from his collar as Drummond. Doshan and Marshall had never gotten along. Doshan wasn't too surprised that Marshall would jump at the chance to testify against him, although he couldn't imagine what that testimony might be.

Kendell asked Marshall if Doshan ever discussed women with

him. "Oh, yeah," Marshall said. "That's his favorite topic. He's always talking about who he hooked up with the night before and bragging about how he could have any girl on campus."

"Objection," Sperantza said. "Bragging about sexual conquests may be in bad taste, but it has no relevance to rape."

"Sustained," the judge said.

Then began a new assault on Doshan's character. "How would you describe your teammate Doshan Williams?" the prosecutor asked. "Is he laid-back and easy-going or does he have a violent, hair-trigger temper?"

Sperantza stood up. "Objection. Leading the witness."

"I withdraw the question, your honor," the prosecutor said. Turning back to Marshall, he went on, "Can you tell us what happened on or about January 15th of this year between you and Doshan Williams?"

"Yes, sir," said Marshall. "It was after practice that day. He saw me outside the student center and started yelling at me. He said I'd deliberately tripped him on the field. I told him he'd tripped over his own two feet, which was the truth. Next thing I know, I'm on the ground, and he's choking me. I'm big, but he's got fifty pounds on me. I thought I was dead. Lucky for me some dudes came by and pulled him off."

Doshan was instantly on his feet. "Liar!" he shouted. "I never touched you!"

The judge banged his gavel three times. "Sit down and be quiet, Mr. Williams. If I hear another word from you, I'll remand bail, and you'll find yourself in a cell until this trial is concluded." Doshan sat down. He took out his pen and wrote a note, which he slid over to Sperantza. "We argued, but I never laid a hand on him," it said.

Kendell pressed on. "Did you see him behave in a violent way toward other members of the team?"

"Yeah, one time I saw him take a punch at a teammate because the guy bumped into him in the locker room. Another time he attacked a guy for dissing him. Knocked him to the ground and kicked him."

On cross-examination, Sperantza said, "Isn't it true you've exaggerated what happened between you and Mr. Williams? There were words between you, but he did not attack you physically."

"He did, too. He jumped on me and tried to choke me."

"You said there were witnesses, students who separated the two of you. Can you give us their names?"

"I never saw them before," Marshall said. "After they broke us up, they left. I never got their names."

"Were there other witnesses?"

"Not that I remember."

"You mentioned someone else who you claimed Doshan knocked to the ground and kicked," Sperantza said. "Who was this person and what was the provocation?"

Marshall seemed to be thinking. "Sorry. I don't remember. It was a while back."

The prosecution's next witness was yet another team member, Joe Sabatella.

Watching Sabatella walk to the witness chair, Doshan was puzzled. He'd never had much to do with Sabatella. What did this guy have against him?

Once Sabatella was seated and the right side of his face was visible from the defense table, Doshan did a double take. Sabatella's right eye was black and almost swollen shut. Doshan also noted Sabatella had the same snake tattoo on his neck. It made him wonder if this was a new fad for Coastline's football players. But why a snake when the team's mascot was a shark?

After establishing the witness's identity and the fact that he was Doshan's teammate, Kendell asked him what had happened to his eye.

"Doshan punched me. But it was all my fault. I was messing with him, and I went too far."

Doshan stiffened in his seat and was about to stand and call

Sabatella a liar when Sperantza grabbed his shoulder. Doshan sat back, picked up a pen and dashed off a note, which he passed to the lawyer: "This never happened. He made it up."

"What did you say to him?" Kendell asked.

Sabatella seemed unwilling to get to the point. "Most of the time Dosh is a nice guy, but he does have a temper. Most football players are violence prone. It's a known fact."

The judge banged his gavel. "Answer the question, Mr. Sabatella."

Sabatella turned to look at Doshan and gave a slight, apologetic shrug, as if to indicate that he couldn't help what he was about to say. He turned back to Kendell. "Well, yeah. We'd been joking around. I said I wondered how he'd do in jail. Like, would he end up being someone's wife or would he be so much bigger than the other cons that he'd get to choose his own wife.

"When I said that, Doshan completely lost it. He grabbed me by the neck and punched me in the eye."

"Was this typical of Mr. Williams's behavior?"

"Sometimes. I've seen him use his fists when he gets riled up."

"With other teammates?"

"Yeah. You see, a football team isn't a band of brothers. There's a lot of competition and jealousy. Most people think Doshan's a super nice guy, but with some of his teammates, not so much. But we all get into dustups once in a while."

"You're not answering the question, Mr. Sabatella," Kendell said. "Did Mr. Williams turn violent when he lost his temper?"

Sabatella hesitated, with another quick glance at Doshan. He grimaced, as if it pained him to answer. "I'd have to say 'yes' to that."

ELEVEN

THE PROSECUTION WAS WINDING UP its final week, and things weren't looking good for Doshan. As for Nicole, she was overwhelmed with work assignments. Colbert and Smith was inundated with new cases, and two staffers were out sick. This had completely stalled her research into Doshan's case.

At breakfast on Wednesday she leafed through the *L.A. Times* for the latest on the trial. Today the story had dropped to page three of the California section. It went into testimony of the previous day's witnesses, who claimed Doshan was prone to violence. Their names were the ones Johnny Austin had given her.

She had yet to follow up on these guys. This was on her mind the whole time she was getting ready for work and saying goodbye to Josh when they left the house. She was halfway to the office when she decided to turn around and drive back home. Only a few days remained before the defense presented its case, and this research couldn't wait. She pulled over to the curb, got out her phone, and called the office.

No one was there yet. The firm didn't open until 9:00 a.m. and it was only 8:40. She left a message: "I think I'm coming down with the bug that's going around the office. I'm going to work from home today."

As she drove, she reflected on her latest lie. She'd lost track of how many she'd told in the past couple of weeks. When this case was over, she promised herself, this was going to stop. She hated lying; it made her feel guilty. Even worse, it was frightening to discover how good a liar she was and how readily people believed her.

Once in the house, she went directly to her computer and resumed her research. She took another look at the football team's lineup on Oceanside's website. Cody Marshall and Joe Sabatella were on the list. Along with other information, the site provided the players' high schools and the position each had played on his high school team. Here was something intriguing. Not only were Joe and Cody from the same high school, so was Andy Drummond. All three had attended Hemet High; all had played for the Hemet High Bulldogs. All three had the snake tattoo. It seemed unlikely to be connected to their football team, whose mascot was a bulldog. Was it a gang thing?

Nicole knew a little about Hemet. Once, on the way to Palm Springs, she decided to take a longer, more scenic route. It had taken her through Hemet, where she stopped for lunch to break up the trip. Hemet was a down-at-the heels community filled with working poor. Many Southern Californians lived in outlying towns like Hemet because they couldn't afford to buy or rent in L.A. If they worked in the city, they had to make a long, bumper-to-bumper commute to work. Nicole's impression was that any young person who could get out of Hemet probably would.

The *Valley Chronicle* and the *Press Enterprise* covered Hemet, along with the rest of the "Inland Empire" burbs that sprawled across the arid land east of Los Angeles. Nicole began looking at high school sports coverage in both papers starting with

September two years prior, the beginning of Andy, Cody, and Joe's senior year. She went through several months of stories, scanning each day's news and sports sections.

She made several discoveries and was so absorbed in her work that she jumped when she heard the front door close. She checked her watch. It was a little after noon. Josh's office was a short walk from the house, and he sometimes came home for lunch. *Damn it.* Now she'd have to tell another lie to explain why she was home in the middle of the day. She turned off her computer and went downstairs.

She gave Josh a hug and explained she hadn't been feeling well, so she'd come home. "I took some ibuprofen, and I'm feeling better now."

"Are you going in this afternoon?"

Was she? She thought about what she'd just learned. She'd worked her way to mid-October, and Drummond hadn't yet shifted to quarterback. He was still a receiver. She'd also found the name of the quarterback at the time, Alejandro Rojas. She was itching with curiosity. *When had Drummond become quarterback and what had happened to Rojas?*

"Nicole?" Josh said. "I asked if you're going to work this afternoon."

"Oh, sorry. I don't feel up to facing all that traffic. I think I'll telecommute."

Although she wasn't remotely hungry, she sat down to have lunch with Josh. She had to force herself to eat slowly and focus on Josh's latest fight with the city department in charge of building permits. He called it "the bureau of circumlocution," a phrase coined by Dickens to lampoon slow-moving bureaucracy.

When they were done eating, Josh left for his office, and Nicole hurried back to her computer. She looked at the Hemet team lineup in the third week of October. Rojas was no longer on the team's roster.

Just then, a message arrived from Joanne at work, asking

if Nicole was feeling up to completing a report on a case she'd been working on; they needed it right away. If not, Joanne asked, would she send in the case file, so someone else could complete it? Nicole abandoned what she was doing and got to work on the report. It was well after 5:00 before she was done.

She was itching to find what had become of Rojas. Once the report was dispatched, she went back to her research, focusing on the news pages from the beginning of the fall term. It wasn't long before she found it. On October 10, a news article appeared in the *Press Enterprise* about a rape accusation at Hemet High. A student had been suspended from school, pending the outcome of an investigation. The girl's name wasn't given, since she was underage, but the boy was 18. It was Alejandro Rojas, the Bulldog's quarterback. Checking the sports pages over the next few days, she discovered something she'd missed before. A high school sports brief mentioned that the new quarterback for the Bulldogs was Andrew Drummond. *Bingo!* she thought. *There it is.*

Nicole checked her watch. It was 5:45 p.m., and Josh would be home soon. She'd have to stop for the day. If she really was under the weather, it wouldn't make sense that she'd work until bedtime. As soon as she heard his car pull in, she reluctantly turned off the computer.

After dinner, she and Josh cuddled on the couch, watching two detective shows in a row. Nicole was thinking about the Hemet rape charge that resulted in the quarterback being kicked out of school. It was just like what had happened to Doshan. And there was more. Three Hemet Bulldogs had ended up on the Oceanside team, and two had testified against Doshan. The third Hemet grad was Andy Drummond, now a second-string quarterback at Oceanside. How was that for coincidence?

She wondered if there a way to reach Rojas and get his story. And what about Andy Drummond? In high school, he'd directly benefitted from Rojas' expulsion. Was it possible Andy had been behind that rape charge? What if he'd set up some poor girl at Hemet High to accuse Rojas? Even if that couldn't be proved, the information she'd found showed a pattern that could point to Andy Drummond as a possible suspect in Mary Ellen's murder. If it could be proved, it could change the course of the trial.

In the morning, Nicole told Josh she still wasn't feeling well and lingered in bed while he got dressed. He went downstairs and, after a few minutes, returned with a breakfast tray complete with a rose in a vase.

"Oh, Josh, you didn't have to do that," she said, feeling even guiltier. She waited for him to leave for work before she got up, pulled on jeans and a T-shirt, and went back to her computer. It only took minutes to find Rojas on the firm's database. He was still in Hemet, and a phone number was listed. She pulled out her cell phone and called.

"Hola?" a woman said. In halting Spanish, Nicole tried to explain that she wanted to speak to Alejandro. The woman interrupted, switching to slightly accented English. "He's at work. You want his cell phone?"

Nicole took the number and thanked the woman profusely. As soon as she hung up, she called Alejandro. No one picked up, so Nicole left her name and number, briefly explaining that she wanted to talk about Andrew Drummond.

It wasn't more than ten minutes before her phone rang.

"This is Alejandro Rojas. You called about Drummond. That right?"

"I need to talk to you about what happened at Hemet High. Do you have time?"

After a long moment, he said, "You a cop or a reporter or something?"

Nicole explained, and he hesitated again. Then he said, "Give me your name so I can check you out. I'll call you back."

Her phone rang a few minutes later. "Okay," he said. "But I can't talk about it on the phone, and I don't have wheels. I'll tell you what I know, but you'll have to come to me."

They agreed to meet the next day. After they hung up, Nicole looked at the clock. It was 9:30 a.m. She considered going in to work but decided against it. If she was going to meet Alejandro tomorrow, she'd need yet another excuse to get off work. It would be easier to say she wasn't up to coming in today and work from home. Tomorrow she'd feign a relapse. *Lies, lies, lies,* she thought. But it couldn't be helped.

She decided that she was going to own up to Josh about her trip to Hemet. She couldn't keep this from him any longer. She was in too deep, and the meeting in Hemet could have significant implications. She considered what to say. Was there any way of telling him without starting a row?

Josh arrived home loaded with grocery bags. When she told him she was feeling better, his face lit up. He unpacked his groceries and got busy making her favorite dinner, chicken tagine with couscous. He had the music turned up and was humming to himself as he worked. She tiptoed up behind him and gave him a hug. He turned to her, planting a kiss in the middle of her forehead before happily turning back to the stove.

Oh, God, she thought. *How can I spoil this? I'll wait 'til later.* But there never seemed to be the right moment. Finally, when they climbed into bed, she turned to him and said, "There's something I have to tell you—"

He put his face against hers so that, from her perspective, his two eyes merged into one. This always made her laugh. "It can wait until later," he said. Then he was kissing her, and the moment had passed. Afterward, she lay awake for a long time, hating herself for being such a coward.

In the morning, she overslept, then had to rush to get ready for the day ahead. It was too late; she couldn't tell him now because there wouldn't be time to discuss it. When they both left the house at 8:30, Josh was still in his upbeat, affectionate mood, which made her feel even worse.

Recalling the incident in Oceanside's parking lot, Nicole took steps to make sure she wasn't followed. She'd reserved a rental car and took a circuitous route through side streets before heading to the auto agency. She left her car and drove out in a generic, white compact.

She routed the journey on the car's GPS, which told her it would involve three freeway changes and over two hours to get to Hemet, if traffic was clear. She was supposed to meet Alejandro at noon at a coffee shop near his work and figured she'd probably arrive at least an hour early. But traffic was stop-and-go for much of the 102-mile drive. She arrived just a few minutes before noon. The diner where he'd asked her to meet was on the outer fringe of town in an industrial area. The place looked like a shack from the outside, but the interior was decent enough. It had a U-shaped counter and half-dozen tables against the wall. Except for two men at the counter who looked like day laborers, the place was empty. She chose a table and sat down.

She spotted him as soon as he walked in, a tall Latino in his late teens or early twenties. He'd undergone a radical change since the photo of him she'd found on a newspaper website. It had been taken before he was expelled. Now, only two years later, he looked as if life had defeated him. Much of his muscle had gone to fat. His face was bloated. He had dark circles under his eyes, and he looked hungover. She gave him a wave and he sat down opposite her. They shook hands across the table.

Alejandro's first words were spoken with heavy sarcasm: "So what's with my old pal Andy? Got himself in some trouble?" Nicole could smell alcohol on his breath.

"Not yet," she said. "At least not that anybody knows. He's to be a witness in the trial of Doshan Williams."

"Yeah, I heard about that Williams guy. He's on trial for murder."

"Tell me what happened at Hemet High when you left the football team."

Just then, a waitress appeared. They ordered drinks—a Coke for Nicole, a beer for Alejandro.

After the waitress was gone, he said, "You know, even after all this time I'm still steamed every time I think about it. I was kicked off the team, thrown out of school, and I'd done nothing wrong. Nothing. I was out with my bros one night drinking beer. Some girls drove up and started to joke around. This girl I barely knew came onto me. She led me into the women's room, locked the door, and what happened happened. She wasn't even my type, but I wasn't about to say no. The next day she went to the principal's office and said I'd raped her. It was her word against mine, and the school chose to believe her.

"The police investigated and decided there wasn't enough evidence to charge me. It was, like, you know, he-said, she-said. But the school wouldn't take me back. I had to finish senior year at continuation high, you know, where the screw-ups and gangbangers get their diplomas. So that was the end of any hope for college. Losing my place on the team meant I couldn't get an athletic scholarship. My parents couldn't help. They're barely making it as it is."

"There are grants and work-study programs for students who can't afford school," Nicole said. "Can't you apply for one of those?"

"Nah. I got incompletes in my college prep classes. I'd have to make those up."

"What about community college?"

"I'd be thirty before I got out of school. I'm working two jobs. Full time at the auto repair where my dad works and three nights as a security guard. I'm saving so I can get my own pad. I'm still living at home. Which is hard, you know. My family's pretty disappointed in me."

"What's the name of the girl who accused you?"

"Kayla Jones."

"Do you have any idea why Kayla would have made a false accusation?"

"I think Drummond put her up to it so he'd get quarterback. He was always telling people he was better than me, and how he should have been picked. After the rape thing came out, I remembered I'd seen Kayla with him in his car and wondered about it. She's not the hot, cheerleader type he usually went for. Maybe he conned her into thinking she was his girlfriend and talked her into setting a trap for me. A couple of weeks later some porno shots of her got posted on the web. After that, she dropped out of school."

"Do you know where she is now?"

"Sure," he said. "She's a waitress at a place in town—Harry's Waffle House."

"Did she ever take back her accusation?"

"Nope. Hemet's a pretty small town. I run into her once in a while. She won't even look at me. She acts like—I don't know—like we both know she lied. She's not about to own up, and she's ashamed."

They ordered lunch. While they ate, he told her in depressing detail what it was like to be a blue-collar worker in a small, dead-end town. She noticed that, despite his youth, he already had what looked like permanent frown lines. He didn't seem interested in anything except the bum deal life had handed him. When they were done, she picked up the check.

As they were leaving the restaurant, Alejandro said. "If you're planning to go into town and talk to Kayla, be careful. Drummond's family lives in Hemet, and he still has a brother and a lot of close friends out here. Besides that, the cops love him. He's like a hometown hero, big college man and all. People will notice if you go around asking questions about him."

"Thanks for the advice. What does Kayla look like? I don't want to have to ask for her when I get to Harry's."

He shrugged. "I dunno. She's got blonde hair. Kinda chubby." He thought a moment. "She usually wears glasses, big round ones with black frames. Look, if you're determined to talk to her, keep it short and get out of town. Andy's friends are not nice guys."

"I'll be fine."

Nicole stopped by her car to get her hat out of the trunk and put it on, along with her sunglasses. She was pretty sure no one had followed her.

She pulled out her cell phone to see if she had any messages, but the phone was dead. This was the second time this had happened, and it made her suspect her battery needed replacing. She plugged it into her portable charger and waited a few minutes. It still showed the icon of an empty battery. This meant it was going to take a while to charge. She put it back in her purse and used the car's GPS to find her way to Harry's Waffle House. On the way, she monitored her surroundings to be sure she wasn't being followed.

Harry's looked like its days were numbered—the place needed paint inside and out. The faux-wood floor was grimy, as were the red upholstered booths, which were frayed and ripped in places. At 12:45 p.m., the place was barely half full.

Nicole stood near the door, pretending to read the posted menu. She took a quick glance around. A middle-aged brunette was working as cashier, and there only seemed to be one waitress, an older woman with gray hair flattened by a hairnet. She was dressed in what looked like the establishment's uniform, a brown blouse with a logo on the pocket, brown slacks, and a red-and-white half apron. She was pitifully thin and looked well past retirement age.

Where was Kayla?

Just then, the double doors to the kitchen flew open, and a young woman carrying a loaded tray hustled out. Her outfit matched that of the older waitress. But any resemblance ended there. This girl had rosy cheeks and a substantial build. She wore round, oversized glasses, and her blonde hair was pulled into a topknot with a pencil stuck through it. She hoisted her tray and headed for the booths to the left of the cashier. Nicole followed, picking a booth next to the one Kayla was serving.

The girl pulled out her order pad as she stopped at Nicole's table. "Can I get you something to drink?"

"Sure," Nicole said. "Coffee. And I wonder if I could talk to you about something. Maybe you have a break coming up?"

Kayla stared at Nicole a moment before she broke out in a big smile. "Hey! I know you. You were all over the news when that guy got murdered. I saw you on TV. Wow!" She seemed genuinely impressed.

Nicole smiled. Usually she denied any connection with the case, but she could see that Kayla was thrilled to meet someone who'd actually been on TV. "Right," she said. "Nicole Graves. Pleased to meet you. I'm hoping you can find a minute to talk to me about Andy Drummond."

Outside there was a loud roar of motorcycles; it sounded like Harry's was being invaded by Hell's Angels. The racket stopped just outside, and Kayla's smile disappeared. "I—I can't. I mean— no way. Not here." She looked out the window, then back at Nicole. "I think you'd better go."

"It's really important, Kayla. Someone's life might depend on it."

There was a ding as the front door opened and a group noisily entered the coffee shop. Nicole glanced around. There were seven of them, toughs in their early twenties. They were dressed alike, in black leather jackets, low-slung Levi's, and black boots. They all sported the same tattoo, the snake's head she'd seen on Drummond and the others.

At the sight of them, Kayla uttered a low, "Uh-oh." She turned her back on them and disappeared into the kitchen. Nicole glanced over at the young men. They'd commandeered a booth near the front door and were sitting down.

It wasn't long before Kayla was back with another tray. She walked over to Nicole and put a mug of coffee on the table. She placed a napkin next to it; Nicole could see it had writing on the underside.

When Kayla walked away, Nicole turned the napkin over. A note was written in a hasty scrawl: "Don't look at the guys who just walked in," it said. "When I go back to the kitchen, head for the women's room. I'll meet you there. Leave your sweater at the table like you plan to come back."

With a sidelong glance, Nicole watched Kayla drop off food from her tray and stop at the young men's table to get their orders. As soon as Kayla walked back through the swinging doors, Nicole got up and followed the sign to the restrooms at the back.

Kayla was already in the women's room, waiting. "You've got to get out of here," she said. "One of those guys is Andy's brother. He's sure to have seen the news and recognize you. He'll suspect you're sniffing around for something about Andy."

"Wait," Nicole said, "I need to ask you some questions."

"All right, but make it fast. What's Andy done now?" Kayla didn't bother to conceal her dislike.

"It has to do with the Doshan Williams case. You know—the quarterback who's on trial for murder?"

Kayla nodded.

"Doshan was kicked off his college football team when a young woman charged him with rape," Nicole went on. "She was murdered. Now he's accused of killing her. Can you guess who one of his teammates was?"

"Oh, my God. Was it Andy?"

"It was. And two other former schoolmates of yours are also on the university team, Cody Marshall and Joe Sabatella. Do you know them?"

"Not really," Kayla said. "They hung out with Andy. He was their leader, and they were bullies, just like him and those guys out front. What's this got to do with you, anyway? You're not with the police, are you?"

"No. I'm a witness for the defense. You see, before Mary Ellen was murdered, she told me that she'd lied in court. Someone blackmailed her into accusing Doshan of rape, but she wouldn't tell me who. I think it was Andy. It would help if you told me what happened to you in high school."

Kayla glanced at her watch and bit her lip. "Okay, I'll tell you, but that's it. I won't talk to the cops, and I won't testify in court. Andy said he'd kill me if I ratted him out."

"How did it start?"

"Andy asked me for a date. Then he acted like I was his girlfriend." Kayla was talking so fast that it took all of Nicole's concentration to follow her. "I was sixteen. I'd never even had a boy ask me out. He was a senior and really popular. You can't imagine how thrilled I was. He told me we had to keep our relationship secret. I was so dazzled by him that I never asked why.

"He had it all planned. He'd take me to the woods or a deserted place in the hills to—you know. He had me pose for some pretty raunchy photos. He said he wanted them to look at when he wasn't with me.

"After he got the photos, he changed. He told me I had to seduce Alejandro and then accuse him of rape. I said 'no,' but he said he'd post those photos on the web if I didn't do it. I knew what my parents would do if that happened, so I did what he said."

"Did he say why he wanted you to do that?"

"It's obvious, isn't it? Andy wanted Alejandro kicked off the team so he could be quarterback. After I did it, Andy was supposed to give me the photos, but he wouldn't even return my calls. One day, I waited after school to confront him. He offered to drive me home. Instead, he took me out of town and beat me up. He said if I told anyone, he'd kill me. Then he put the photos online. My folks kicked me out. I had to quit school to support myself."

She put her hands over her eyes and drew in a ragged breath. When she dropped her hands, tears were running down her face. "I feel so guilty about what I did to Alejandro. He didn't do anything wrong." She pulled a napkin out of her pocket, mopped her face with it, and stood up. "We've been here too long. If they get suspicious, they'll come looking for us. There's a back door in the kitchen. You can go out that way. Just follow me."

"Wait," Nicole said, "this time Drummond may have killed a girl, and Doshan could be convicted of the murder. Won't you at least talk to his lawyer? He's really smart. He can figure out how to protect you if you tell your story in court."

"No way," Kayla said. "I mean, why would I? Even if I don't get in trouble for lying to the police, Drummond would kill me."

"I don't think you'd be prosecuted for lying if someone was blackmailing you," Nicole said. "As for Andy, if he's caught and locked up, he won't be any threat to you."

Kayla gave Nicole a disgusted look. "Can you promise me that's really going to happen? That he won't be out in a few days and come after me?"

Nicole didn't answer. Kayla did have a point. It was the same concern Josh had about her own testimony. But she knew there must be a way to protect witnesses who receive death threats.

"I thought so," Kayla said, taking Nicole's silence as confirmation. "Follow me." She turned and went through a side door that led directly into the kitchen. Without a glance back, Kayla hurried through the swinging doors into the restaurant. Nicole found herself in the middle of a cramped, overheated kitchen that smelled of old grease and all the food that had ever been cooked in it. Two men wearing hairnets were working over a grill. Neither looked up. Spotting an open door at the back, Nicole walked out. As she made her way around the building, she thought of the sweater she'd left behind. Briefly, she wondered where it would end up. It was one of her favorites—a robin's-egg-blue knit hoodie.

She walked into the parking lot, then made a dash for her car. Next to it were half a dozen motorcycles, no doubt belonging to the young men inside. She backed out of the space and sped onto the street. In her rearview mirror, she saw Andy's brother and his friends come out of the restaurant and hurry toward the parking lot, presumably on their way to their motorcycles. One of them had her sweater bunched up in his hand. Once she turned the corner, she couldn't see them anymore. She immediately headed for the freeway and, once on it, pushed up her speed.

Nicole was cruising along at seventy miles an hour when she saw a small fleet of motorcycles gaining on her. To her alarm, she noticed that traffic was slowing. At a curve in the road about a mile ahead, the freeway appeared to be a standstill.

It was only a few minutes before the gang was in the next lane, peering into her car. When the car ahead of her advanced a few feet, she took advantage of the space to risk an abrupt turn into the carpool lane, which was moving briskly. A sign on the railing warned: "This lane is limited to vehicles with two or more passengers. Violators will be fined $481." Whether or not the cyclists were willing to follow was a moot point. They were blocked by the bumper-to-bumper lane between them and Nicole.

Luck was with her. The Highway Patrol was nowhere in sight, and she soon left her pursuers behind. She exited the carpool lane just past the bottleneck where an open truck had flipped over, dumping a load of tomatoes across the road.

Only now, as Nicole cruised along, did she realize with both satisfaction and trepidation how vital Kayla's story was to Doshan's defense. As soon as she got home, she'd put in a call to Sperantza and tell him what she'd learned. It would be up to him to figure out how to get Kayla to testify and how to protect her if she did.

TWELVE

NICOLE PULLED INTO THE DRIVEWAY at 5:30. When she started to unlock the front door, Josh opened it, clearly upset. "Where've you been? I couldn't reach you on your cell, so I called your office. Joanne told me you'd taken the day off. I've been out of my head with worry."

Nicole followed Josh into the house, struggling to find something to say. She plopped herself on the couch before she responded. "I'm really sorry. I was going to tell you, but I never found the right moment. Then this morning, we were both in such a rush—" As she said this, she realized how lame this sounded. "And I knew you'd be upset," she added.

"Damned right I'm upset. And you still haven't told me where you were."

"In Hemet. I found some people there who can help Doshan's defense. They wouldn't tell me anything on the phone, so I had to go out there."

"You *had* to go out there? How is this your problem, Nicole?"

"I've told you. Doshan Williams is innocent, and I have

information that can help clear him."

"Let me get this straight," he said. "Aren't you already taking care of that by appearing as a witness?"

Nicole was running out of patience. "I've explained this: Mary Ellen said one thing in court, then she told me something else. The prosecutor can pretty much dismiss my testimony unless there's more evidence to back it up. Doshan's investigator didn't find anything, but I did. Andy Drummond, one of Doshan's teammates, pulled the exact same trick in high school. He blackmailed a girl into falsely accusing the quarterback of rape so that he could get the position himself."

"Look, if this guy is the real killer, then you're putting yourself in danger. And here's what I'm thinking: This isn't the first time you've done this. Are you going to do the same thing when the next 'injustice' catches your eye?" He made finger quotes when he said *injustice*. "Is this going to be your life? Because if it is—"

"If it is? Say it. Then you don't want to marry me?"

"Your words, not mine," he said. His face was flushed, and she could see how angry he was. "But you do have an over-developed sense of moral outrage. You're impulsive, and it's making me crazy. I love you. I want to be with you. But I want a normal, quiet family life. I'm not sure that's what you want."

"Of course it is."

"Then take a look at what you're doing." He glared at her. "You promised you'd leave this case to Doshan's lawyer once you agreed to testify. But you can't stay away from it, can you? You found information that could clear Doshan? Then why in the hell didn't you turn it over to the defense attorney's investigator? It's his job to work this case."

Nicole was barely able to hold on to her temper. "In case you've forgotten, I'm an investigator myself, and Sperantza's investigator is either lazy or incompetent. I told him about things he should be looking into, and he just blew me off."

"You're still a rookie, remember?" Josh was all but shouting. "You need to put in more hours and pass a test before you qualify for your license. So why can't you just stand aside and leave this to the professionals?"

For the first time, it struck Nicole that this was her fault. She'd allowed Josh to think he had the right to tell her what she could and couldn't do. "Maybe you're right," she said quietly. "Maybe I'm not the one for you."

"Quit putting words in my mouth. I love you no matter what. But this thing you did behind my back? It really pisses me off."

"What if I had told you? What would you have said?

"I'd have tried to talk you out of it. But if you wouldn't listen, I'd—I don't know what I'd have done. Here's the bottom line: You can't keep putting yourself in danger. You just can't! Why couldn't you have chosen a normal occupation like becoming a realtor or a teacher? Those are great occupations for a woman raising a family."

Without a word, Nicole walked past him and went upstairs to change. They didn't discuss it again. He barely looked at her during dinner. She made a few attempts at conversation, but after a brief response, he'd lapse into silence.

They went to bed and lay with their backs to each other. Nicole was wide awake, too upset to sleep. Josh's derision of her work had stunned her. It made her realize, for the first time, that he didn't understand her at all. And maybe it was mutual. She thought she knew him, but the Josh she loved wouldn't have said that.

As soon as his breathing slowed and she was sure he was asleep, she got up. Tiptoeing around the bedroom, she grabbed some clothes, basic cosmetics, and her overnight case, and went downstairs to pack. She wrote a note and left it under her engagement ring on the kitchen table. The note said:

Josh:

I couldn't sleep because of this rift between us. I think we need time apart so you can reconsider our engagement. I'm going to be an investigator, not a realtor. You have to accept that.

I don't see myself as jumping from crisis to crisis. But I do sometimes act on impulse—call it moral outrage, if you like. That's who I am, and I wonder if you can live with that. I guess you're wondering, too.

I can't imagine ever encountering another situation like Mary Ellen's murder. But if I did, I wouldn't behave any differently. So I want you to take time to consider whether you want to marry me.

Meanwhile, I've gone to stay with Steph. Believe me when I say I love you.

Always, Nicole

With little traffic, it took only twenty minutes to drive to Steph's apartment in West Hollywood. Nicole arrived a little after 3:00 a.m. and let herself in with the key her sister kept under a flowerpot by her front door—a practice Nicole had warned Steph against a number of times. She tiptoed in, carrying her overnight bag. She went into Steph's study, which doubled as a guest room, set her bag down and pulled out the futon. She must not have been as quiet as she thought because Steph appeared in the doorway, yawning, stretching and rubbing her eyes. She gave Nicole a puzzled look. "What's up?"

"Fight with Josh," Nicole said, tears spilling down her face.

Steph put an arm around Nicole and steered her into the living room where the two of them settled on the sagging couch that Steph had found in the alley behind her apartment house.

As Nicole was trying to pull herself together, Steph got up, went to a cupboard and pulled out a bottle of whiskey and two glasses.

Nicole looked at her sister incredulously. "For God's sake, Steph. At this hour?"

"You're a wreck," Steph said. "This will calm you down. Or I could roll us a joint. Your choice."

"No, no. Whiskey's okay, I guess. I just don't want to go to the office smelling like I've been up drinking all night."

"A little toothpaste, a little mouthwash," Steph said. "You'll be fine. Now tell me what happened."

Nicole did just that, recounting her scene with Josh.

Steph was quiet for a long moment before she said, "Your old pal Reinhardt and I talked about this before he went back to England. He couldn't understand why you'd chosen Josh. What was it he said? Oh, yeah"—at this point Steph affected a posh English accent—"'I'm surprised she's settling for suburbia. I thought she wanted a bigger life.'"

This made Nicole laugh. "Did Reinhardt imagine he was giving me a bigger life? He lived on another continent. Even if I'd gone over there to live with him—something he never did suggest—he was off the grid most of the time, engaged in some kind of covert ops. He wasn't about to give me any kind of life."

"True," said Steph. "But he did have a point. I mean, Josh is a lovely guy. He's gorgeous, he's nice, he's smart, and all that. But don't you sometimes wonder if his overprotectiveness is going to cramp your style?"

"I don't know," Nicole said. "I love him, and we have so much in common. And he gets me—" She broke off, realizing this was a claim she no longer could make. If Josh really did get her, they wouldn't be having this fight.

"Listen to me," Steph said. "The things I admire about you most are your chutzpah, your fearlessness, your sense of right. As a kid, I was so proud to be your little sister. And then last year you cracked that ring of crooks. You get off doing this stuff. Admit it."

"What are you talking about? It was terrifying, and I hated every minute of it." Nicole paused, reconsidering. "Okay, it was great at the end when they caught those guys and locked them up. The rest was a nightmare. But none of that matters. I'm in love with Josh. I want to be with him. I'm still hoping there's some way we can work this out." All at once something occurred to her. "If we're not back together soon, I'll have to look for another place to stay."

"I don't see why," Steph said. "You're welcome to stay in my guest room as long as you want."

"Thanks, Steph," Nicole said. "I know that. But after I testify, it will attract the paparazzi. Given my history with them, they'll follow me here. I'd never put you through that."

"Quit worrying. You and Josh will be back together in no time. He's crazy about you. You're not going to break up over this."

"I don't know. He said some things that made me wonder if we're right for each other." Nicole's voice trailed off. She put her untouched glass of whiskey on the coffee table and got up. "I'm whacked. Let's go to bed."

Nicole woke at 6:00 a.m., exhausted from too little sleep, and checked her phone. No messages. She'd hoped for word from Josh by now, saying, "Come home. It was all a misunderstanding." But it wasn't a misunderstanding. The idea of losing him made her feel ill.

When she got to work, she called Sperantza to tell him she'd learned something that might help Doshan's defense.

"I don't think it's wise to talk by phone," he said. "Let's discuss it over lunch. I'm downtown today. If you can make it, we could meet at the same place. 12:15."

"Okay," she said, "See you then." All morning, she kept checking her phone for messages. Each time she found nothing, she felt a little worse. She tried to reassure herself that she'd done the right thing leaving the way she did. She'd been honest in the note she'd left. She couldn't change who she was, and, even if she could, did she want to? But what if it cost her Josh? Once again, she found herself tearing up. On her way to the women's room to splash water on her face, she encountered Joanne in the hallway.

"Why Nicole," Joanne said. "What's wrong?"

"Allergies," Nicole said. "Drippy eyes."

"Santa Anas," Joanne said. "Isn't it awful? I had to take two allergy pills this morning."

Nicole hadn't even noticed the Santa Anas. Usually, the hot winds inflicted her with a runny nose, bad dreams, and a sense of foreboding. Much worse was the destruction they wrought. On a regular basis, Santa Anas turned a few sparks or a discarded cigarette into a wildfire that decimated thousands of acres of Southern California's forests and canyons. In her distraction, Nicole had no idea what the weather was like outside the ever-cool tower where she worked.

By the time she arrived at the restaurant, Sperantza was waiting in a booth in a second dining room at the back of the restaurant. Here it was relatively quiet.

As soon as Nicole was seated, a waitress arrived to take their orders: short ribs, the daily special, for Sperantza, and a niçoise salad for Nicole. Once they were alone, Nicole described her meetings with Alejandro and Kayla.

Sperantza's eyes grew wide, and he started to grin. "Nicole, this is exactly what we needed. We can subpoena Kayla as a hostile witness. Along with your testimony, this will create reasonable doubt."

Nicole put down her fork. "How? She'll deny telling me anything; she might deny ever meeting me. She's terrified of Drummond. He said he'd kill her if she told anyone."

"If we subpoena Kayla, she'll have to appear. We'll ask about Drummond and her rape charge against Alejandro. She can deny all she wants. But I'll call you as the next witness, and you'll explain she told you she'd do that because Drummond threatened to kill her. Then you'll relate what Mary Ellen told you. Your testimony will show he manipulated both girls into lying to the authorities and, in Mary Ellen's case, perjure herself in court. That pattern of behavior points to Drummond as a likely suspect in the murder."

Speranza stopped talking to take a swig of coffee and another bite of his meal. His eyes were darting about, and it was clear he was considering his strategy. He swallowed, put his fork down. "Obviously, Drummond is off our list of character witnesses. An amazing bit of detective work on your part, by the way," he said. "I'm surprised Slater missed this."

"Didn't Slater say that Drummond had an alibi for the night of the murder?" Nicole said.

"He did. I'm going to talk to him about that, make sure he checked it out thoroughly and didn't just rely on Drummond's word. I'm beginning to wonder if he cut corners on this investigation."

Nicole shrugged, remembering Slater's dismissive attitude when they'd spoken by phone. It was clear he hadn't put much time into this case. "Even if he'd found the Hemet High connection," she said, "it might not have done him much good. Kayla only talked to me because she recognized me from the tabloid stories last year. She thought I was some kind of celebrity." Nicole laughed. "But she sure wasn't happy when I suggested she testify in court."

§

She spent the weekend with her sister, hanging out, trying some new restaurants, and catching a couple of movies. All of that time, she kept checking her phone for a message from Josh, but there was no word.

On Monday, two days after she'd left Josh and two days before she was to testify, Nicole used her lunch hour to return to the house and pick up more of her things. As she'd expected, Josh was at work and the house was empty. Her heart ached as she walked through the place she'd come to regard as home. It was immaculate, tidier, in fact, than when she was in residence. She climbed the stairs to the bedroom. The bed was made, the bathroom spotless with freshly hung towels.

She gathered up some jeans and casual tops plus enough work outfits to last a week, tossing them on the bed. Then she went into the bathroom for the rest of her cosmetics and makeup. Since she was only taking two suitcases, she had to leave some items behind, but she'd made a significant dent in her wardrobe. She debated leaving her closet door open, to let Josh know she'd been there and moved out more of her things but decided against it. The idea she might have left for good could push him into making a decision before he was ready, and that could easily backfire.

Nicole headed straight for the short-term rental she'd arranged the day before. She'd looked at some online rental sites, not expecting to find much available for immediate occupancy. But she'd found something right away—a furnished, one-bedroom condo that was attractive and just a few blocks from her office. She'd taken it immediately, paying a week in advance. From the empty state of the closets and dressers, she concluded that no one lived here. Someone had invested in it for the rent it would pull in—$150 a night.

She still hadn't heard from Josh. It was hard for her to accept the idea that he was finished with her. Or was he was simply doing what she'd asked, thinking things over?

There were moments when she thought about what Steph had said. In a year or two, after the blush of romance had worn off, would she feel trapped in the quiet life Josh wanted? His love and companionship, motherhood, a career doing corporate investigations—would this fulfill her? She had no idea.

Before work, she'd been to the grocery store to stock up. The apartment came with linens, dishes, pots, and pans. Now, it was just past 1:00. All she had to do was unpack and put her clothes away. She could do that later. Instead, she decided, she'd head back to the office for the remainder of the afternoon. She didn't want to be here with time on her hands to think about her fight with Josh and what it meant for the future.

She arrived at the new rental, parked in front, and got her

suitcases out of the trunk. She bumped them up the short flight of steps to the front door, let herself into the lobby, and pressed the button for the elevator. She got off the elevator on the second floor, approached her apartment, and parked the suitcases next to the wall so they wouldn't topple over. Then she got out her key and unlocked the door. As soon as she stepped inside, she sensed something was off; someone was here. She took several steps back, getting ready to retreat when a man—a very big man—appeared in the kitchen doorway. It wasn't his size that frightened her as much as the grotesque mask he was wearing. It covered his entire head and looked like a cartoon rendition of Munch's painting *The Scream*. She turned and ran.

The man was fast, almost upon her before she'd taken more than half a dozen steps. She grabbed the handles of her suitcases, still standing at attention in the hallway, and thrust them in his path. He hadn't been expecting this, and he probably couldn't see much through the eyeholes of the mask. He tripped over the bags and went down with a crash. While he was getting up and shoving the suitcases out of his way, Nicole ran down the hall. Her heart was soon pounding in sync with the heavy footsteps behind her.

Just then a door opened at the other end of the hall. The masked man stopped and looked around. Nicole ran even faster, aiming for the stairwell. She was surprised to find her purse still on her shoulder. She reached in and dug around for her can of pepper spray.

The door down the hall slammed shut. By now Nicole had the spray in her hand. She risked a look behind. Beyond the man, the hallway was empty. Whoever had opened the door must have seen what was happening and decided to retreat.

She started running again, but he was too fast. Only moments passed before he grabbed her by the shoulder. She swung around and squirted the grotesque face with pepper spray. To her dismay, the spray liquefied when it hit the mask and ran down the slick plastic. But some must have made its way through the eye holes, for the man stopped and screamed, putting his hands to his face. Now free, Nicole hurled herself forward. Reaching the stairwell, she bolted down to the lobby and out of the building. She heard sirens as soon as she emerged from the front door. Two police cruisers pulled up. Nicole looked back into the lobby. Her pursuer was nowhere to be seen.

A policeman with a ruddy complexion and a shock of white hair introduced himself as Officer Greg Nielson. Nicole explained that she'd opened the door to her apartment, found a man waiting for her, and had been forced to flee.

"We'll take a look," Nielson said. Three of the officers started searching the building while Nielson accompanied Nicole up to her apartment. The suitcases were sprawled in the hallway. "Wait over there," he said, directing her to a spot about six feet from the door. He pulled out his gun and, holding it up as if to shoot, went inside.

A short time later, he was back. "The place is empty. Whoever it was is gone."

"When he started chasing me, I heard someone open a door down the hall." Nicole pointed toward where she'd heard the door open. "The guy in the mask stopped and looked around. I kept running, but I heard the door close again. Maybe whoever lives there saw us and called 911."

Nielson went down the hall, knocking on doors and shouting, "Open up! Police!" Before he got to the last door, it opened, and an elderly woman appeared.

"Oh, officer, I'm so glad you're here." She was breathless, as if she'd been the one running. "I'm Eleanor Poole. I saw this young woman being chased by a madman wearing one of those hideous *Scream* masks, as if the painting isn't frightening enough. I went right back inside and called 911." She turned to Nicole. "Are you all right, dear?"

"Thanks to you, I am. I think you just saved my life."

"Did you see anything else?" Nielson asked.

"I did," Eleanor said. "Just after I heard your sirens, I went to look out the window. I'm on the side of the building, you know, so that's the view I get. I preferred a place that isn't on the street. So much noise!" She paused, as if she'd forgotten where the conversation was headed.

"What did you see out the window?" Nielson prompted.

"Oh, yes. The man in the mask ran by, heading for the back alley. He turned left."

Nielson pulled a communications device with an antenna off his belt. He radioed his teammates to tell them which way the man had gone. He thanked Eleanor and accompanied Nicole back into her apartment.

Neilson closed the door and gestured toward the couch. They both sat down. "Do you have any idea who the intruder might be or why he might want to harm you?" he said.

Nicole explained about the trial, her role as a witness, and what she'd found out about Andrew Drummond. "You can see he wouldn't want me to testify. If he's the one who killed Mary Ellen Barnes, he'd want to shut me up. Obviously, I couldn't see his face. But he was really tall and muscular like a football player, which is what Drummond is."

"When are you going to testify?"

"In two days."

"We need to make sure you have protection," he said. "I'm going to call the station and alert them."

He made his call and gave a very brief description of Nicole, just her name, and the trial she was part of. After that, his side of the conversation became "Uh-hum" and "Yes, sir."

After Nielson hung up, he said, "You can't stay here. We'll put you up in a hotel or motel, depending, and you'll have to stay off the grid. You'll have an officer with you at all times until after your court appearance. You have a smart phone? Turn it off. Otherwise someone could use your GPS to track your movements."

Nicole pulled her phone out of her purse and looked at it. "First I have to tell the lawyer who's handling the case that I'm being intimidated as a witness."

Nielson nodded his head in agreement. "Go ahead. I have to make a call myself. Nicole went into the bedroom, closed the door, and dialed Sperantza. To her surprise, she got through right away. She told him about the man in the mask and the policeman's offer of protection.

"Tell him 'no.' We have our own security service. Nicer accommodations, better trained personnel for this sort of thing. But the police are right. You can't stay in that apartment, and you do have to turn off your phone and stay off the grid until after your testimony."

"What then?"

"Once you've testified, I can't see this guy as a threat to you. We'll wait and see what develops. If it is Drummond, he may very well be in custody by then. I'll call the security service right away. They should have someone there within the hour. Give me your address."

"I don't want to turn off my phone. What about my sister? What about work? What about my fiancé?"

"Call them now and explain. Leave a message if you must. Then turn your phone completely off and leave it that way. Oh," he added, "and make sure the police stay with you until our security arrives."

Nicole told Officer Nielson that she'd decided to use the security the attorney was willing to provide.

"Your choice," he shrugged. "When will he be here?"

"In about an hour. The lawyer wanted you or another officer to wait with me."

He glanced at his watch. She could see his hesitation. "It would be easier if you came with me. I'll drop you at the station. You'll be safe, and your bodyguard can pick you up there.

She made another call to Sperantza to rearrange the pickup.

On their way out, Neilson picked up the suitcases, still sprawled in the hallway. He took charge of them until they reached the patrol car, when he put them in the trunk. Neilson's fellow officers had disappeared in pursuit of Drummond, so it was just Nicole and Neilson on the ride to the station. She took advantage of the time to call her office, then her sister, to explain why she'd be out of touch for a few days. She couldn't bring herself to call Josh's cell. Part of her feared he wouldn't pick up when he saw her caller ID. Or maybe he'd answer, listen to her story, and say, "I told you so." There was also the possibility that he didn't care that she was unreachable because he had no intention of calling her.

After some thought, she called their home phone and left a message on the answering machine. She simply said she'd be out of touch for a few days without explaining why. She managed what she hoped was a cheerful tone, as if she were looking forward to the next few days and wasn't upset that he hadn't called her.

By now, the squad car had pulled up in front of the Wilshire Division station, an undistinguished building of red-and-beige bricks. Nielson pulled the suitcases out of the trunk. Nicole wheeled them up to the station while Nielson waited in his squad car. She opened the front door and turned to wave at him. He waved back and sped away, lights flashing.

Inside she found people waiting—some standing against the wall, some seated on crowded benches, and a few sitting on the floor. Most of them looked poor and unhappy, here for reasons every bit as fraught as her own. One of them, a Latino in a straw hat and sweat-stained T-shirt, got up from a bench and offered Nicole his seat. She thanked him but refused, pushing her suitcases against the wall so she could half-perch, half-lean against them. She kept her eye on the front door, watching for the man who would whisk her away from this corner of purgatory.

THIRTEEN

NICOLE WAITED THE BETTER PART OF AN HOUR. Occasionally someone would walk past to be admitted through a gate that led into the police station proper. This, she imagined, contained offices, interrogation rooms, and perhaps a lockup. Those gaining admission were generally cops, uniformed and plainclothes, sometimes accompanied by a "civilian" in handcuffs. None of them glanced at the waiting crowd. No one at the desk called a name, nor did any of those waiting approach the gate. Occasionally one of them would go up to the desk and ask a question, but they were soon back waiting.

At last a man who stood out from the law-enforcement types walked in. He was tall and nice-looking with bright blue eyes, close-cropped dark hair, and designer stubble. He was wearing a navy sportscoat, tan slacks, and a pale blue shirt. His brown, oxford shoes were shined to a high gloss, and the bulge under his jacket was unmistakably a gun.

He stopped in the middle of the room and scanned the assembled crowd until his eyes rested on Nicole. "Ms. Graves?"

he said.

Nicole got up, grabbed the handles of her suitcases, and headed toward him. He pulled out a card, which read, "Timothy Harris, Innovative Solutions Security," and handed it to her. While she was examining it, he reached for her bags and picked them up. "I'll be looking after you the next few days," he said in a low voice. "The car is in front." With that, he turned and headed for the front door, expecting Nicole to follow. The car was a generic gray sedan. It looked new. He opened the passenger door and waited for her to get in before putting the bags in the trunk and settling into the driver's seat. He was silent as he turned south on Fairfax and eventually joined the flow of traffic heading east on the Santa Monica freeway.

"Where are we going?" she said.

He looked around as if he'd forgotten she was there. "The Omni Hotel. It's near the criminal courts building." He fell silent again, concentrating on his driving. Nicole kept a firm grip on the armrests while he darted in and out of traffic lanes, cutting in on other drivers who honked in protest.

At last they exited the freeway and, barely slowing, screeched around a couple of corners until they came in view of a large L-shaped high-rise. Except for the rounded canopy over the entrance, the hotel's exterior was unadorned. Timothy drove into the crescent driveway, pulled Nicole's suitcases from the trunk, and left the car with the valet. The two of them walked into the hotel.

Inside, the Omni's decor was a far cry from the casual vibe of the Windward, where Nicole had stayed with Mary Ellen. The front door led to a giant reception hall with a cathedral ceiling. The room had no reception desk or seating for guests, just a gigantic arrangement of exotic flowers on a large glass table. On either side was a column flanked by a potted palm and a brass-railed staircase leading to an upper floor. Nicole paused to take it in, then rushed to catch up with Timothy, who was pulling her suitcases through a doorway to the next room. Here a wood-paneled reception room featured a check-in counter, concierge desk, and bellmen.

After Timothy checked in, he led Nicole to the elevators and up to the twelfth floor; he used his key card to open the door to a suite. Nicole looked around. The living room was furnished in expensive-looking, dark-wood furniture. Deciding to explore, she opened a door that led to a large bedroom. It featured a king-sized bed, a flat-screen TV, and a corner fireplace, not that she was likely to use it when the temperature outside was eighty degrees.

She was looking out the window when Timothy tapped on the open door and rolled in her suitcases. Without a word, he parked them by the closet and left, closing the door behind him. Nicole turned back to the window. It furnished an aerial view of downtown L.A.'s four-level freeway interchange, nicknamed "the stack." It was 5:00, and rush hour was well underway. Cars were crawling along, bumper-to-bumper in both directions.

She peeked into the room's white marble bathroom, then made her way down the hall to a second bedroom. Was this where Timothy would sleep? It was considerably smaller than her room, and there was no sign of occupancy. Thinking back, she remembered he hadn't brought in any luggage but her own.

She ended up in the living room where Timothy was perched on a chair next to the front door. She felt his eyes on her as she returned to her room, but neither of them spoke.

Nicole closed her bedroom door, turned the TV on to a mindless comedy, and lay down on the bed. She dozed off almost instantly. A knock at the door woke her. She got up and opened it, still a little groggy. Timothy handed her a menu. "It's almost 8:00," he said. "You might want to order dinner." He went back to his chair, and she closed the door.

After a quick look at the menu, she called room service and ordered a club sandwich, a green salad, and half a carafe of

Chardonnay. Then she turned on the TV. By the time her meal arrived, she'd watched the news and channel hopped until she came across a Seinfeld marathon, which she settled in to watch.

She was thinking of getting ready for bed when she heard the doorbell. She peeked out of her room. Timothy had opened the front door and was admitting a man with the same security-detail vibe. Spotting Nicole, Timothy said, "I'm leaving for the night. This is Henry Wynn. He's taking over. I'll be back in the morning." Henry nodded in Nicole's direction, and she nodded back before closing her door.

§

Her eyes popped open at 6:00 a.m., and she couldn't go back to sleep. She was depressed by the prospect of a full day stuck in the hotel room until her court appearance on Thursday. She couldn't use her cell phone; she had no Internet access and nothing to read. She couldn't imagine spending the entire day watching TV.. Around 10:00 a.m., she changed into sweatpants and a T-shirt. Passing through the living room, she told Timothy, "I'm going down to the hotel gym for a run."

"You're what?" he said with some annoyance. "You're supposed to stay in this suite where you're safe."

"I'm going crazy in here," she insisted. "I need a run."

"Alright," he said grudgingly. "Hang on a minute." He muttered to himself as he grabbed his coat from the closet and put it on to cover his gun holster. He waited outside the gym while she spent forty-five minutes running on one of the treadmills.

Back in her room, she lay on the bed and stared at the ceiling. She was still upset about Josh. Had he gotten her message? Was he trying to reach her? With her phone turned off, she had no way of knowing.

She forced herself to stop obsessing about Josh and let her mind wander. One of the questions that still bothered her was why Don Slater, Sperantza's investigator, had bailed on this case. She'd suggested things he should have looked into, but he hadn't. He'd been so disinterested that he hadn't even bothered to interview her. She didn't imagine he could possibly have a connection with Andrew Drummond. That would be too wild a coincidence. Yet something was definitely "off" about Slater and his attitude toward this case.

If she had access to a computer, she could log into her company's database and take a look at his background. That might shed some light on his behavior. It occurred to her that the hotel must have a business center with computers for the use of guests. She didn't want Timothy to go with her, not after he'd been so unpleasant about her visit to the gym.

She thought of the way Mary Ellen had snuck out of their hotel room. Nicole herself found herself tempted to do the same thing. She wasn't a prisoner here; she was perfectly free to leave. She arranged her pillows to look as if she were sleeping under the covers. Then she sat by the door, listening. It seemed like a long time before she heard Timothy get up and walk toward the hallway leading to the bathroom. When the door closed, she grabbed her purse and peeked out to be sure he'd left his post. Not only was the sitting room empty, but he'd left the key card on the coffee table. She picked it up on her way out of the suite.

The business center was located on the main floor, just past the registration desk. As soon as she walked in, she saw notices posted on both computers: "Out of order. We apologize for the inconvenience." She was disappointed. She was itching to find out about Slater. She considered her options. The main public library was a few minutes away by taxi, and this wouldn't take long.

The doorman called her a cab, and in a little over six minutes, she was entering the garden that fronted the blocky, cream-colored building which had served as L.A.'s main library since 1926. The structure's most eye-catching feature was the pyramid on top, decorated with an elaborate mosaic sun surrounded by bright-colored tiles. In the 1980s, the building had fallen into disrepair, then closed after two fires and damage from an earthquake. When it reopened, the original art-deco murals had been restored, the building redecorated, enlarged, and loaded with whimsical art. In all of L.A., it was Nicole's favorite building.

Heading through the garden, she noticed more derelicts than she'd seen here in the past. One of them, a skeletal young man with a massive growth of facial hair, got up from a bench and followed her up the stairs to the entrance. He dogged her steps so closely that she could smell him. From his physical appearance and aggressive behavior, she figured he must be a meth addict. To get away from him, she stopped at the central desk to ask where to find a computer to use, although she already knew she'd find several in just about any of the reading rooms.

As soon as the man had moved on, she walked down the corridor to Fiction. It was 11:00 a.m., and the room was empty. She sat at one of the tables and put her purse on the floor under her chair, just behind her feet. The computer was set to the library's catalogue. She quit out of this and started the browser.

As soon as she connected with Colbert and Smith Investigations, she logged in and looked up Don Slater, Los Angeles. Although it seemed a common name, there was only one in the entire city, age 36, which seemed about right. He was a native Angeleno, unmarried, with a decent credit record. He'd worked several years for a publication she'd never heard of called *To the Right Point*. After that, he'd been a barista while going to a community college. He'd eventually put in the hours and passed the test to become a P.I. After that, he'd worked at several law offices before joining Sperantza's firm. None of this was surprising.

Still curious, she decided to take a minute to Google him. His name popped up dozens of times on articles he'd written for a range of white supremacist and anti-feminist websites. He was especially active on *Aryan Nation* and *Boycott American Women*, where he railed against advocates of politically correct language who condemn racial epithets and derogatory terms for women. He argued that they were infringing on the First Amendment's guarantee of freedom of speech. He wrote on other, uglier topics as well, denigrating those who had the "misfortune"—his word—not to be born white.

Nicole was stunned. Slater's neglect of Doshan's defense had come from his own prejudices, as had his motive for ignoring her suggestions about the direction of the investigation. He wasn't going to take orders from a woman. She copied several of the URLs for his articles and emailed them to Sperantza. Slater might be a good investigator as long as it didn't run afoul of his bigotry. But if this was the way he thought, his boss should know about it.

She was getting ready to leave, when she felt something brush against her foot. Bending down to look, she saw someone crouched behind her chair, reaching through its legs in an attempt to grab her purse. He missed, and the purse toppled forward. He stretched further under the chair in another attempt. This time, she stamped on his hand with both feet, jumping up to bear her full weight on it. As she did this, her chair tipped, fell over backward, and hit the would-be purse-snatcher on the head with a loud smack. He let out a yelp of pain. Nicole scooped up her purse, holding it tight against her. When she turned around, she wasn't surprised to see it was the man with the bushy beard who'd followed her in.

A guard appeared at the door. "This guy bothering you, ma'am?"

"He was," Nicole said. "But I think I've bothered him back."

The guard pointed to a sign on the wall that Nicole hadn't noticed. In big letters, it said, "Watch your purse and other belongings." As she read it, the guard pulled the man to his feet and marched him into the hall. Nicole followed them outside, then turned left and passed through a breezeway onto Fifth Street. She felt a little shaky from the adrenalin rush brought on by the assault on her purse. Before long, a taxi stopped to pick her up and return her to the hotel.

Timothy was waiting in the hotel's big reception hall, and he looked angry. She gave him a nod, and he fell into step beside her as she headed for the elevator bank.

"May I ask where you've been?" he said.

"I went to the library."

"You're supposed to stay in the suite where no one will find you. If you really needed to go out, why didn't you tell me so I could go with you?"

"Because I didn't feel like arguing. You objected when I wanted to go to the gym this morning, and that's in the hotel."

"Next time, just tell me. You won't get an argument. But here's the thing: If anything happens to you, it's on me. You, of all people, should understand that."

"No worries," she said. "I'm staying put until tomorrow when I testify. Then you'll be rid of me."

They didn't speak again for the rest of the day. It was almost 1:00 p.m. by now, and Nicole was hungry for the first time in days. She ordered fish and chips and a beer from room service and spent the rest of the afternoon watching TV. The morning's outing had lifted her spirits. Maybe it was finding the backstory on Slater and being able to share it with his boss. On the other hand, it might have had something to do with her success in thwarting the purse-snatcher.

§

Nicole wasn't due at the courthouse until 9:00 a.m., but once again she woke at 6:00 and couldn't go back to sleep. She got up and set about getting ready. First was the matter of what to wear. She was limited to the clothes she'd brought along in the two suitcases she'd hastily packed at the house. She spent quite a while considering her options and trying things on. *If clothes and grooming mattered anywhere*, she thought, *it would be in court.* At last she settled on the plainest outfit she had: a navy two-piece dress. She added a nubby white scarf and navy heels. She pulled her hair back, attaching a faux chignon she usually saved for special occasions.

A little after 8:00 a.m., she checked herself in the mirror and gave a little laugh. She looked prim, like the principal of a private, all-girls school. Prim, she decided, wasn't a bad look for a witness. When she joined Timothy in the living room, he handed her a black, brimmed hat and a lanyard with a plastic press pass on it. She took a close look at the pass. It bore her photo and identified her as Mindy Schultz of KCVS. She did a double take. There was no such station, and CVS was a chain drugstore.

She gave Timothy a questioning look. "What's this?"

"When the media see the pass, they'll think you're one of them and ignore you. I've got one, too." He pulled a similar lanyard from under his jacket. This one had his name and photo. "You have sunglasses, don't you?" he said.

She nodded, pulled her sunglasses out of her purse, and put them on, along with the hat. She checked herself in the mirror over the couch. Now, wearing the small-brimmed hat, she bore a distinct resemblance to Mary Poppins wearing shades. The effect was silly enough to make her consider changing into another outfit, but it was too late. *Besides*, she thought, *she'd take off the hat before she went into the courtroom.*

Just outside the hotel, a car with a driver was waiting. Instead of a limo, which would have drawn attention, it was a maroon SUV. They were driven to a corner of the block occupied by the criminal courts building, where they got out, pushed their way through a crowd of media and curiosity seekers, and entered the building. No one seemed to notice them.

They managed to squeeze into an elevator. The button for the ninth floor was already lit. When they got off, she followed Timothy down a hallway to where Sperantza's red-headed associate, Kevin Volk, was waiting in front of a courtroom. Gold numbers on the wall by the entrance read 9-313. The doors were closed, and a sign said "No Admittance. Court in Session."

Timothy asked Nicole for her press pass. She took off the hat and the pass and handed them over, patting her hair to make sure the chignon was still in place. She and Kevin stood by the courtroom door. Timothy leaned against the wall, surveying the crowd.

Nicole wondered what they were waiting for. After a few minutes, the door opened and a young woman came out. She was all gussied up, and for a moment Nicole didn't recognize her. Today Kayla Jones' fair hair was worn loose around her shoulders. She was wearing a snug-fitting black dress, five-inch heels, and so much makeup she might have been headed out for a night at the clubs.

Startled, Nicole said, "Kayla!" The young woman gave her a withering look. Nicole shrugged, acknowledging the girl's anger. What, really, was there to say? That she was sorry Kayla had been dragged into court? She wasn't. It couldn't be helped.

A man—tall, athletic, with the bulge of a gun holster visible under his jacket—stood up and took Kayla's arm. With a wave of relief, Nicole understood this guy was Kayla's bodyguard. Sperantza had given Kayla the same kind of protection he'd provided her.

Kevin touched Nicole's shoulder, motioned for her to go in, and pointed to the witness chair to the left of the bench. As she entered, Nicole was surprised at how big the courtroom was and the large number of spectators—200, maybe more—seated in the visitors' section. Members of the press, who occupied the two front rows, seemed to recognize her and started murmuring. The judge banged his gavel to silence them. Doshan turned and nodded at her, his expression grim. Sperantza was standing, waiting for her to take her seat. At the prosecution's table were several attorneys, including one Nicole recognized from the news, Deputy District Attorney Frank Kendell.

Once she was seated, she looked at the jury. Most were Latino, three were black, and one was white. It was an older crowd, most with white or gray hair. There were seven women to five men. The single young person in the group was an attractive Latina in a business suit. She looked as if she might be a lawyer herself. The rest were casually dressed, ordinary-looking people who might have wandered in from the street.

Nicole was sworn in and asked for her name and occupation. Her mouth was dry, and her voice sounded hoarse when she answered. Once these formalities were out of the way, Sperantza began: "You were assigned by your employer, Colbert and Smith Investigations, to look after Mary Ellen Barnes during the civil trial that preceded this case. What did that involve?"

Nicole cleared her throat and said, "I was responsible for keeping her safe and away from the press. I also made sure she got her meals and that her other needs were met."

"Why couldn't Ms. Barnes do this herself?" Sperantza said.

"She was only nineteen and had never lived in L.A. except in a dorm on the campus of Oceanside University. She needed someone with knowledge of the city and the media to watch out for her."

"You had a conversation with Kayla Jones recently, didn't you?"

"Yes. This last Friday."

"Can you tell us why you contacted her?"

"I was upset by Mary Ellen's death, especially since it happened when I was supposed to be keeping her safe. I felt the police investigation wasn't thorough because they never looked at any suspects other than Doshan Williams. Since I have training in investigation, I decided to look into it myself. I spent a lot of time doing online research into the backgrounds of Mr. Williams's friends and teammates.

"It wasn't until last week that I found news stories about an alleged rape two years ago at Hemet High School. I've given Mr. Sperantza photocopies of those articles. The Hemet High incident bore a striking similarity to the original charge of rape against Mr. Williams. The accused quarterback at Hemet High was dropped from his team even though he was never charged with a crime. I contacted him, and he gave me the name of the girl who accused him, Kayla Jones."

"And did you meet with Ms. Jones?"

"Yes, I did."

"What did she say?"

"She told me she'd accused the athlete of rape at the instigation of Andrew Drummond, who threatened to publish X-rated photos of her online. According to Kayla, Drummond wanted to be quarterback at Hemet High. He thought up the rape accusation to get the existing quarterback kicked off the team. The plan worked, and Drummond took his place. What she told me was verified by a news article."

"Did Ms. Jones tell you she was willing to testify to this in court?" said Sperantza.

"No. She said she'd never testify. She told me Drummond had beaten her up and threatened to kill her if she ever told anyone that her rape accusation was false. Shortly after the assault, the X-rated photos of Ms. Jones were posted on the Internet."

After looking at his notes, Sperantza said, "Did you have a conversation with Mary Ellen Barnes the night she was murdered?"

"I did."

"Can you tell us what she said?"

"She said that Doshan Williams hadn't raped her. She'd lied to authorities because she was being blackmailed. The blackmailer had a video of her in a compromising situation, which he threatened to put online. She said it would ruin her life."

"Did she tell you the name of the blackmailer?"

"I asked, but she wouldn't say."

"When you looked into the background of Doshan's friends, did you find anything out about Andrew Drummond?"

"I did. He and two other football players on Oceanside's team went to Hemet High and were on the team there."

"What else did Ms. Barnes tell you?"

"She said Doshan Williams didn't deserve what was happening to him. She was going to recant her testimony the next day. She was afraid of the blackmailer's threat, but she said it didn't matter. She couldn't live with the lie she'd told."

"She said Doshan didn't deserve what was happening? Did she know him?"

"Yes. She said they'd met when he attended a few Bible study sessions."

"I understand you've been staying at a hotel under the protection of a bodyguard for the last few days," Sperantza said. "Can you explain to the court why this was necessary?"

"Three days ago, someone broke into my place and was waiting for me when I got there. He ran at me as if he intended to attack or even kill me. He chased me out of my apartment and down to the next floor. He was huge and wore a mask with the face from *The Scream* by Edvard Munch."

"Do you know who this was?"

"No. The mask covered his whole head. I could tell from his hands that he was fair skinned, and he was built like a football player. But that was all."

"Do you believe this incident was related to your appearance as a witness?"

"I can't think of any other reason someone would want to harm me," Nicole said. "Fortunately, he tripped over my suitcases. I got out my can of pepper spray and squirted him. Some got in his eyes, and the pain stopped him. That gave me time to get away."

"Have you received any other form of threat?"

"Yes," she said. "When I went to the Oceanside campus, a threatening note was left on the windshield of my car."

"What did that note say?"

"It said, 'If you know what's good for you, you'll mind your own business.'"

"What were you doing at Oceanside University that day?" Sperantza said.

"After Mary Ellen's murder, her roommate contacted me and said she had some information. I drove out to the campus to talk to her."

"Did you learn anything?"

"The roommate gave me Mary Ellen's journal," Nicole said. "There was also a Bible that Mary Ellen had notated in the margins. Neither book offered new information."

Sperantza turned toward the judge. "For the record, your honor, the defense has seen the journal and Bible, which have also been made available to the prosecution. There was nothing relevant in them." This said, Sperantza turned away from Nicole. "No more questions for this witness."

Kendell stood up to take his place. "About this intruder, Ms. Graves, did he say why he was in your home?"

"No. He didn't say anything at all."

"How do you know his behavior was related to this case? He could have been a burglar or a rapist. This could even have been a practical joke meant for someone else. Isn't that true?"

"Anything is possible. But from the way he came at me, it was clear he meant to do me harm."

"All right. But you have no evidence that his motive was related to this case, do you?"

"No."

"And the same is true of that note you found on your car windshield, isn't it? It could have been meant for anyone. In fact, how would the person who put it there know this was your car?"

"When I first arrived on campus and was getting out of the car, a bunch of students walked by, young men. They noticed me and made some sexist comments. One of them could have recognized me and would have known which car was mine."

"But you don't know with any certainty that the note was meant for you or even what it referred to, do you?" he said.

"No."

"Now, Ms. Graves, you do realize you're under oath."

"I do."

"Did you hear Mary Ellen Graves testify under oath in civil court that she'd been raped by Doshan Williams?"

"I did."

"Yet later that day, she told you the opposite was true. Is that correct?"

"That's correct."

"Can you repeat what Ms. Barnes told you after she'd testified to the rape?"

"She said it wasn't rape. She'd asked Doshan to walk her home. She knew him from Bible study, and she liked him. When he invited her to his room, she knew they were going to have sex. She also told me he'd asked her consent. She said she went to the school authorities and charged Doshan with rape because she was being blackmailed. She stalled for as long as she could, but time passed, and the blackmailer ran out of patience. He said if she didn't do it that very day, he'd post the video he had online."

"Miss Jones just told this court, under oath, that her testimony in a previous trial was true, that she had been raped by a member of the football team when she was in high school and that she hadn't told you anything to the contrary. Yet you expect us to believe that both Ms. Jones and Mary Ellen Barnes perjured themselves in court and you're the only person they told about it."

Nicole looked at Sperantza. Shouldn't he object to this question on the grounds that it was argumentative? He looked her in the eye and nodded. He wanted her to answer. "In Mary Ellen's case, that's correct. I don't know if Kayla confided in anyone else, but the basic facts she told me were verified by the news articles I found."

"Why would these women, who didn't know each other, both confess their darkest secrets to you? Especially in the case of Ms. Jones, who'd never met you before?"

Once again Nicole looked at Sperantza, and he gave a nod. "I can't explain it," she said, "except that I'm a good listener, and people do tell me things. It helps with my work."

Kendell looked down at a paper he was holding and adjusted his glasses. Then he said, "Tell me, Ms. Graves. Do you miss the attention you received from the media last year after the murder of your colleague?"

Even more argumentative, she thought. *This is downright insulting.* But she kept her voice even when she answered. "Of course not. That was horrible."

He turned away. "No more questions for this witness."

The judge nodded his head at her. "You are excused, Ms. Graves."

Nicole tried to catch Sperantza's eye as she left the witness stand, but he was busy jotting on his yellow pad. Doshan was staring straight ahead, looking even glummer than before.

Timothy was waiting just outside the door to accompany her to the elevator. Nicole followed him, overcome by a sense of defeat. She'd messed up her life, wrecked her relationship with Josh, and for what? Kendell had torn her testimony apart and maligned her character as well.

The media followed her out, shouting questions. She didn't listen, much less attempt to answer. When they reached the street, the car and driver were already waiting at the curb. Several motorcycles trailed behind them, causing the driver to circle around, take one-way streets, and detour into alleys until he lost them.

Nicole barely noticed the detours. She was thinking about her testimony. *What a mess.* She'd thought she was being selfless, perhaps a little heroic, in testifying for Doshan. But Josh was right, and she felt like a fool. She remembered the old adage, "No good deed goes unpunished," and realized that she'd just made herself the perfect example.

FOURTEEN

BACK IN THE HOTEL SUITE, Nicole lay on her bed with her eyes closed, going over the back and forth between the deputy D.A. and herself. She was startled by a knock on her door. It was Timothy, handing her his phone. "Your attorney—Sue Price." His words were clipped; he was clearly still annoyed.

Nicole took the phone, while Timothy retreated and closed the door.

"How're you doing?" Sue said.

"Not that great. The prosecutor ripped me to shreds. I'm going stir crazy in this damned hotel, and Sperantza insists I stay until the trial ends.

"I'm sure it went better than you think," Sue said. "Remember, it's not what the prosecutor says or doesn't say. It's who the jury believes. But here's why I'm calling. Josh is desperate to reach you. His father had a heart attack on Monday. He's been with his family at the hospital since then."

"I left a message on our answering machine at home," Nicole said. "I guess he didn't think to check. But he could have called

Steph. He has her number."

"He did," Sue said, "She explained why your phone was off, but she didn't know how to reach you either."

"What does he want?"

"He wants you to call him."

"A little problem with that," Nicole said. "They made me turn off my phone—in case it's being hacked."

"I'll be your go-between," Sue said. "Give me a message for him. I'll pass it on and get back to you."

Nicole was quiet for a long moment. Finally she said, "Let him know I was upset to hear about his father and what he must be going through right now. Tell him I love him, and I'm sorry, but I can't change who I am."

Sue gave a sharp intake of breath. "Oh, my dear. You two are so perfect for each other. Don't tell me you're breaking up."

"I don't know. He found out I was still looking into Doshan's case after I promised I'd quit. We had a fight, and I went to stay with my sister. He thinks I'm impulsive and reckless. What sent him over the edge was that I kept it from him. But if I'd told him, that would have made him angry, too. I don't want to have to defend myself for doing what I think is right. He also made it clear he doesn't respect my work as an investigator. I just can't see how it's going to work out."

"If you feel that way, it's better to find out now," Sue said. "I understand exactly what you're going through. Believe me, I do. This is one of the reasons I never married. I need to be my own person, not who someone else thinks I should be. I'll give Josh your message."

After they hung up, the hotel suite was silent. Timothy hadn't asked for his phone back. Maybe he assumed she was still talking to Sue. Almost without thinking, Nicole found herself calling Josh.

"Hello?" He sounded confused, no doubt by the unfamiliar caller ID.

"It's me," she said in a low voice. "I just wanted you to know how sorry I was to hear about your father. How's he doing?"

"It's touch and go. He's had a massive coronary. He's still in ICU. Even if he pulls through, there may be serious damage to his heart."

"That's awful. I'm so sorry. Sue says you've been at the hospital since Monday."

"Yeah, I'm pretty whacked out. But listen, we have to talk. We can't—" He stopped and she could hear voices in the background. "Wait," he said. The phone was silent long enough to make her wonder whether she'd been put on hold or disconnected.

At last he was back. "The doctor wants to talk to us. I've got to go." The phone clicked, and he was gone.

A few minutes later, Timothy knocked on the door and asked for his phone.

Reluctantly, she handed it back and followed Timothy into the living room. "I'm going down to the coffee shop for a snack," she said. "You can come, if you want."

"I thought we had an agreement that you'd stay here where it's safe. The coffee shop is open to the public. Anyone can just walk into that place."

"I'm not leaving the building. That was the deal. I agreed to stay in the hotel until I testified." She went to the front door, opened it, and turned to look at Timothy.

Not bothering to hide his irritation, Timothy grabbed his jacket and pulled it on to cover his gun holster. He trailed behind her to the elevator.

He insisted on the booth farthest from the entrance and took the seat facing the door. At 4:00 in the afternoon, the restaurant was quiet. While they waited for service, he took a careful look at those seated at the few occupied tables. Nicole ordered coffee and a piece of cherry pie. After a moment's hesitation, Timothy ordered the same thing.

While they waited, she decided to try to pull some personal

information out of him. In the two days they'd spent together, they hadn't had a single sustained conversation. He seemed disinclined to be sociable. Now that her testimony was out of the way, Nicole was suddenly curious. *Who is this guy? What's his story?*

"So, Tim—is it okay to call you Tim?—What do you do when you're not working?"

"Oh, I work out, read a bit, watch TV. You know, the usual." Timothy went silent, his eyes scanning the room.

He's avoiding my question, Nicole thought. *He doesn't want me to know anything about him.* "How did you get into private security?" she said. "Were you a cop?"

He looked at her. "I was with the military."

At this point, his phone rang. He pulled it out of his pocket and answered. "Harris, here." He was silent, listening. Then he said, "I'm sorry. You have the wrong number."

He put his phone on the table and gave Nicole a puzzled look. "Do you know a Josh Mulhern?"

"Yes."

"That was him, asking for you. How did he get this number?"

"I called him after I talked to my lawyer. She said he was trying to get in touch with me."

The phone rang again. After glancing at caller ID, Timothy gave Nicole an exasperated look and slid the phone across the table. "Keep it brief," he said. "And please tell him not to call this number again."

She picked up the phone. "Josh?"

"Who was that guy? Why did he say I had the wrong number?"

"That's my bodyguard, Timothy."

"Bodyguard?"

"Speranza thought I should have protection until the trial's over. Timothy takes his job very seriously." As Nicole said this, she glanced over at Timothy. He was looking in the other direction, pretending he wasn't listening. "I can't talk long," she said. "What's up?"

"I want you to come home. I'm sorry about what I said, you know, disrespecting your job. I didn't mean it. We can work this out."

"Oh, Josh, I don't know. Maybe you've made a mistake. Maybe I'm not the person you thought I was."

"I haven't made a mistake. I want you back. Please! When's a good time for me to call again?"

"My phone is off, and we can't use this line again." She noticed Timothy was running his finger across his throat, giving the cut-it-short signal.

"I have to go," she said. "I can't turn on my phone until the trial is over. I'll call you as soon as I can. Sorry to leave things up in the air. I do love you." She pressed the "end" button and handed the phone back to Timothy.

§

In the courthouse a few blocks away, Doshan was finding it increasingly hard to sit still. It was even harder to keep his cool and wear a neutral expression. Sperantza, in the chair next to him, was going over his notes. There were just two more defense witnesses. Once they were questioned and cross-examined, the defense would rest. Then came closing arguments, and the case would go to the jury. That could happen by the end of the day.

They'd originally thought Doshan might have to testify. But once the girl from Hemet and Nicole appeared, Sperantza said it was no longer necessary or even advisable. The two women had created reasonable doubt in the minds of jurors. That meant Doshan had nothing to gain by testifying. He might even damage the case if Kendell managed to rattle him into contradicting something he'd already said.

Sperantza called Larry Castelle, a teammate of Doshan's, as the next witness. After establishing Castelle's relationship to both Doshan and Drummond, Sperantza said, "Do you recall Andrew Drummond making any statements about becoming quarterback for Oceanside University's football team?"

"Yes. He told me a number of times what a great quarterback he'd been on his high school team. He said he'd be a hell of a lot better than Doshan. According to him, the only reason the school gave it to Doshan was because it looked good. You know, having an African American as its star."

"What was the nature of his relationship with Doshan?"

Kendell stood up. "Objection! Calls for speculation."

"Overruled," the judge said. "I'll allow it."

"When Doshan was around, Drummond acted like they were best buddies, but he was always bad-mouthing Doshan behind his back. One time he told me Doshan was heading for trouble because he forced girls to have sex with him, and that was going to get him kicked off the team."

"Did you ever observe Doshan behaving aggressively toward women?"

"Never. We used to go out as a group. You know, hang out at night on the beach, have a couple of beers, and sometimes girls would join us. They were always coming onto Doshan. We used to kid him about it."

Kendall, on cross-examination, tried his best to trip up Castelle, but the young man stuck to his story.

The defense's second witness was Josiah Williford, another member of the team. Once again, Sperantza asked the witness if Doshan was prone to violence.

"He never uses force except on the field. The only people I heard say that were Drummond and his sidekicks, Marshall and Sabatella. Drummond was always mouthing off, talking trash about people, especially Doshan. One time I heard him threaten to get Doshan."

"Can you tell us what he said?"

"It was when Drummond got benched after he fumbled a couple of plays. I was sitting right next to him. We were behind, and the game only had a few minutes to go. Suddenly, Doshan has the ball. Instead of passing it, he's headed for the goal line, running so fast it's unbelievable. The crowd is screaming. The other team can't get near him. He crosses the goal line, and we win. It was awesome!

"Then I hear a crash. It's Drummond hitting the bench with his fist. He's in a rage, muttering to himself. "You rotten son-of-a-bitch, Doshan," he says. "I'll fix you.""

"Were those his exact words?"

"Yeah. He was pissed because Doshan scored and everybody was cheering. I thought it was weird because it meant our team won. Besides, the two of them roomed together and always acted like bros."

Once more the deputy D.A. tried to discredit the testimony of the witness but without any luck. Williford insisted that he'd heard Drummond's threat against Doshan.

When Williford was dismissed, Sperantza announced that the defense had no more witnesses and was resting its case. Judge Lloyd banged his gavel. "We'll take a break now. I expect you to return promptly at 1:00 p.m."

Doshan checked his watch and stood up. It was 11:45. Sitting in court day after day was taking a toll on his body. He felt stiff and sluggish. He followed Sperantza into a small room adjacent to the courtroom that had been set aside for their use.

"How do you think we're doing?" Doshan's mouth was so dry he could hardly get the words out. He picked up a can of soda from the tub of iced drinks and downed it in a couple of gulps.

"Things are going well," Sperantza said. "Our witnesses did a great job. But there are no guarantees. Let's just hope the jury understands the concept of reasonable doubt."

Doshan did a couple of stretches before he sat down at the table with Sperantza. Each was absorbed in his own thoughts. Time was passing so slowly, Doshan wondered if the day would ever end. Then his mind leapt forward to what might happen once the jury made its decision, to the very real possibility that he might leave the courtroom in handcuffs, headed for prison.

When court reconvened, Deputy D.A. Frank Kendell presented the prosecution's closing arguments. He set up an easel for the posters he'd brought along. First was a timeline establishing Doshan's whereabouts the night of the murder. Next was a series of pull-out quotes from the audiotape of Doshan's initial interrogation, showing how he'd first denied, then admitted being at the Santa Monica Pier. Kendell seemed to think the fact that Doshan had changed his story was powerful evidence of his guilt.

More graphics followed, showing photos of the evidence he'd presented, explaining how each fit into the case against the defendant. Someone had spent a lot of time preparing the visual aids, which were colorful and easy to understand.

"This isn't rocket science," Kendell concluded. "Motive, opportunity, means. That's all you need to determine guilt in a murder trial. Doshan Williams had all three. Mary Ellen Barnes had accused him of rape, and he was furious. He wanted revenge. He was at Santa Monica beach that night. And look at him: There's no doubt he has the strength to kill Mary Ellen Barnes with his bare hands. There is no doubt he took the life of this innocent young woman. I have proved my case. Now it's up to you to see that justice is done by convicting Doshan Williams of murder in the first degree. Thank you."

When Kendell took his seat, Sperantza went over to face the jury and present his summation. He took a long moment to make eye contact with each juror. Then he said, "This case presents a multiple tragedy. First, we have the case of an innocent young woman who was brutally murdered after she was coerced into falsely accusing my client, Doshan Williams, of rape. And then, to make matters worse, the police and prosecution, relying on an incomplete, careless, and incompetent investigation, brought Doshan to trial for a murder he did not commit. Worse yet, they brought this charge against Doshan without looking into the possibility that someone else might be responsible for the crime."

Sperantza proceeded through each piece of evidence Kendell had presented, making the point over and over that the prosecution had looked no farther than Doshan Williams as a suspect.

"He talked about the DNA under Mary Ellen Barnes' fingernails, which the prosecution said was too deteriorated to use. But you heard our expert witness. He found the sample usable and said it showed the DNA did not match Doshan's." Sperantza pointed out the number of times the L.A.P.D.'s forensics lab had mishandled evidence. "And those are just the times they've been caught," he added.

"The prosecution was so desperate to prove their case that they used DNA on Doshan's cap, which proved nothing. Anyone could have taken that cap and planted it at the scene. We have the testimony from two teammates that Andrew Drummond, another team member, coveted Doshan's position. Drummond had told a lot of people that he would have made a better quarterback than Doshan. One witness heard Drummond threaten to 'fix' Doshan. Drummond's goal was to get Doshan off the team. Although Doshan didn't know Ms. Barnes intended to drop the rape charge, he did know he was innocent. Thus, he had reason to hope he would be exonerated in the civil trial. Why would he kill her when he knew he'd be the first suspect if anything should happen to her?

"As Nicole Graves testified, Ms. Barnes was about to recant her testimony. Ms. Graves also testified that someone threatened her, a defense witness, and broke into her house in an attempt to attack her. Whoever that was is likely to be the guilty party; that person wouldn't want Ms. Graves to reveal that Ms. Barnes was about to take back her accusation against Mr. Williams.

"Two people knew Ms. Barnes was about to recant. One was Nicole Graves, to whom the girl confessed. The other was whoever she went out to meet the night of her murder. It's my belief that she met with the blackmailer to beg him to take back his threat. We also have evidence that Mr. Drummond got to be quarterback in high school by blackmailing a girl into filing a fake rape charge against the existing quarterback. Who do you think would have a motive for killing Mary Ellen Barnes? If anyone wanted to 'fix' Doshan, what better way than having the police find Ms. Barnes murdered? Finally, the two prosecution witnesses, who swore Doshan violently attacked them, happen to be close friends of Mr. Drummond from their days at Hemet High.

"I hope you'll think long and hard about who detectives should be investigating for the murder of Mary Ellen Barnes.

"While you're deliberating, I want you to remember that you must find the defendant guilty beyond reasonable doubt. I believe you can see many holes in the prosecution's case—especially their failure to look at any other suspects. And once our evidence was introduced, they should have picked up Mr. Drummond for questioning. They have not.

"I view this as a failure on the part of Mr. Kendell and his assistant prosecutors to do the job they were hired to do. It's not only the duty of prosecutors to convict the guilty but to free the innocent. I trust you will look at the evidence in this case and find Doshan Williams innocent of a crime he did not commit."

Doshan was surprised to see Kendell get up and make another effort at tearing down Sperantza's closing argument. The deputy D.A. gave an abbreviated version of what he'd said before, this time without the graphics. He finished up with his mantra: "Motive, opportunity, means. Doshan Williams had them all. Now, ladies and gentlemen I know you will make the right decision."

The judge spent a few minutes giving the jury instructions and repeating the meaning of the phrase "beyond a reasonable doubt." When he was done, the jurors slowly filed out.

Once the spectators began to leave, Doshan stood up and followed Speranhtza and Kevin to their break room. It was half past three. Lunch had been cleared away, but soft drinks were waiting for them. The three of them sat at the table, while Sperantza explained what Doshan already knew: It could be days, weeks even, before the jury reached a verdict. "There's not much sense sitting around here all afternoon. We might as well go about our business and wait until we get word from the court."

Still, none of them was able to summon the energy to leave. They drank their sodas and went over the day's events.

They were still there an hour later, when there was a knock at the door. It was the bailiff. "The jury is back," he said. Speranza, incredulous, had him repeat himself.

"Is this good news?" Doshan said.

"I have no idea. I've never had a jury on a murder case come with a verdict this fast. It's either very good or very bad."

§

Back at the hotel, Nicole was engrossed in her book when she sensed a change in the sound coming from the TV. Even with the sound turned down, she noticed an audible hubbub and what sounded like shouting. She used the remote to turn up the volume. The camera was just panning into a close-up of the courthouse door when Doshan emerged with a huge grin on his face. He had an arm draped around Sperantza's shoulders. They were surrounded by reporters, all shouting questions: "How does it feel to be free?" and "What are you going to do now?" and "Are they going to arrest Drummond?"

Doshan held both arms up and made victory signs with his fingers. Then he talked to a few reporters who were close by. At last, he raised his voice so the TV microphones could pick it up. "It's great to be free. I'm grateful to my lawyer here, David Sperantza, and to Judge Lloyd for making sure I got a fair trial. That's all I have to say." He and his retinue pushed their way into a long black limousine that quickly started up and disappeared from view.

Nicole opened the door to the sitting room and called to

Timothy, "The jury found Doshan innocent!" As Timothy was turning on the sitting-room TV, Nicole started packing her clothes; her only thought was getting back to the privacy of her apartment.

When she told Timothy she was ready to leave, he seemed surprised. "Hang on a minute," he said, "I'm not driving you anywhere until Sperantza okays it."

"Fine," Nicole said. "Give me your phone and I'll call him."

She was able to reach Sperantza on her first try. "Congratulations!" she said. "You won."

"You played a major part in this, Nicole."

"Really? I felt like I let you and Doshan down. Kendell completely tore my testimony apart."

"Nonsense. You gave us an alternate theory. You inserted reasonable doubt into the trial. I don't know if Doshan would have been found innocent without your help."

"That makes me so happy," she said. "I'm free to go now, right? Timothy wanted to hear it from you."

"Hang on," he said. "I'd like you to stay put a while longer."

"But why?"

"The police are looking for Drummond. He wasn't on campus, so they're checking his parents' place in Hemet. You need security until he's picked up."

Nicole took a deep breath, trying to hold onto her temper. "I appreciate your concern, David. I really do. But I'm done. I'm not staying here another minute. I want my life back. If Drummond has fled, he's going to put as much distance between himself and L.A. as possible. He's not going to bother with me. Timothy can accompany me home and keep watch, if you insist."

"I think it would be wise," Sperantza said. "Let me talk to him."

Nicole handed the phone over and walked around the suite, checking for anything she might have forgotten. Timothy got her bags and waited by the front door. She was tired of his presence, and he was no doubt tired of hers. They proceeded to the elevator without a word.

FIFTEEN

As they waited for the valet to bring the car, Nicole pulled her cell out of her purse and turned it on. Josh answered after the first ring. "I'm just leaving the hotel," Nicole said.

"I'm out on a run," he said. "I'll be home by the time you get there. Can't wait."

"Wait a minute," she said. "I want you to understand. Nothing has changed. I'm staying at my apartment."

"But we have to sit down and discuss it," he said. "Things are going to be different from now on—I promise. Do you want me to come to your place?"

The sound of his voice, his conciliatory tone softened her resolve. "No. We're just getting into the car. We'll come to you."

"We?"

"Sperantza's insisting I still need a bodyguard. We'll see in you half an hour or so." After they hung up, she gave Timothy the address.

Josh was waiting in front of the house to greet them, still dressed in his running clothes. Timothy opened the trunk to get out her luggage. "Thanks," she said, "but just leave them in the car for now." Before he could close the trunk, Josh was there, pulling them out.

"No, Josh," she said. "I told you—"

"No worries." He smiled. "We can always put them back if you decide to leave."

She introduced Timothy to Josh and explained why Sperantza thought a bodyguard was still necessary.

"We'd better get inside," Timothy said. "You're an open target out here."

The three of them filed into the house, and Josh turned to Timothy and gestured toward the couch. "Make yourself comfortable. We're going upstairs for a bit. If you want anything to eat or drink, the kitchen is through the door behind you. Just help yourself."

Josh picked up the suitcases and started up the stairs. Nicole was about to tell him to leave the bags where they were. But already her resolve was weakening. She'd hear him out and then decide.

After setting the suitcases down and closing the door, Josh put his arms around her. His warmth felt unbelievably comforting. She melted against him and breathed in his scent, a little sweaty from his run, but still unmistakably Josh.

"We can have that talk now," he said, leaning in to kiss her.

The kiss left her a little dizzy, but she gently pushed him away, sat down on the bed and patted the space next to her, inviting him to sit.

"I'll go first," she said. "I promise to keep you informed about what I'm doing and what my plans are. But I have to be a free agent. I want to take on any assignment the agency gives me, no matter what it is. I enjoy doing these things. It's who I am."

Josh opened his mouth to speak, but she went on. "Odds are I'll never find myself in the middle of another murder case, or that my work will keep opening me up to danger. I'm not a cop or a soldier in Iraq, for God's sake. Most of the time I'm sitting in front of a computer. But I can't have you thinking you have veto power over what I do. And don't ever tell me to go into real estate again."

"I was wrong to criticize your career choice, and I'm sorry," Josh said. "It was in the heat of the moment, and I didn't even mean it. If I've been overbearing, I apologize for that, too. Some pretty terrible things have happened. But I agree. You have the right to make your own decisions. And if something you do worries me, I'll keep it to myself."

"But you'll still worry?'"

"Afraid so. Like you said, 'It's who I am.' Of course, I'm hoping you won't give me anything to worry about." He smiled, trying to make light of it. Getting up, he pulled her into his arms again. "So, you'll stay?"

"I will. But let's see how things go before we start thinking about a wedding."

"Really? You don't think I can keep my word?"

"I just want to take it slow." She snuggled her face against his neck. She still had concerns, but there was no point thinking about them now. Only time would tell if this was going to work. For now, she was happy to be home.

§

That night, the three of them ate dinner together. Josh easily drew Timothy out and got him to talk about himself. Timothy, it turned out, had been a Navy Seal for a dozen years before going into the private security business. Between work assignments, he was taking college classes online to complete credits for a teaching credential. Math was his chosen subject. "I'm two weeks on, two weeks off," he said. "It gives me a lot of time for school. The job isn't bad, and the pay is great. You get to meet some interesting people. Even if they're not that interesting, they're in—well— interesting situations. Something pretty extreme is going on if they need private security."

"Since you're a veteran," Nicole said, "doesn't the VA pay for school?"

"Right. The VA helps. But it's not enough to live on. They pay tuition, a stipend for books and supplies, and a modest amount for housing. But, unless I want to live in a dorm, I need a paycheck."

Later, when she was getting ready for bed, she found the blue velvet box with her engagement ring on her night table. She opened the box and stared at the diamond. She wasn't ready to put it on. Not yet. Not until she was convinced Josh really had changed and their relationship was on solid ground. She closed the box and put it in the night table drawer.

§

Several more days passed with no word from Sperantza or news of Andy Drummond's whereabouts. The three of them established a routine. Josh went to his office while Nicole worked upstairs in their shared office, telecommuting and catching up on work that had been neglected while she was gone. She wasn't sure how Timothy spent his time downstairs. At night, he slept on the couch. They'd decided it would be easier having a single bodyguard rather than two in rotating shifts. While she was working at her desk, she watched through the window when Timothy made an occasional foray out to the sidewalk to see what was happening on the street.

Mention of Doshan's trial and the search for Drummond all but disappeared from the news. One morning, a headline on XHN caught Nicole's eye. "Women's Group Drops Case Related to Doshan Williams's Trial." Next to the story was a video of a press conference Geneva Ford had called. She was standing in front of a microphone with her arm around a young woman. Nicole clicked the link to watch.

Geneva began with a brief statement that Women Against

Rape was abandoning its civil suit against Oceanside University. She didn't go into detail about why they'd dropped the case. But Nicole understood. Doshan had been found innocent of murder; he'd also been cleared of raping Mary Ellen. That meant Oceanside couldn't be accused of failing to protect her. WAR's entire case had fallen apart.

Geneva quickly moved on to introduce Evie Fisher, who was the plaintiff in the organization's latest case. It was against an accused rapist at Cal State University, Morro Bay, where the young man and Evie were students. Geneva was grim and determined, while the young woman wore a deer-in-the-headlights expression that reminded Nicole of the way Mary Ellen had looked when she first spotted the mob of reporters at LAX.

Of course, this young woman was not Mary Ellen. And it was unlikely that Geneva's new client was lying, as Mary Ellen had been. After talking about the particulars of the Fisher girl's case, Geneva said, "WAR is working hard to protect coeds from sexual predators, but college authorities fail too many victims by refusing to believe them. This makes them afraid to come forward. Just look at the case of Mary Ellen Barnes. Until the WAR took up her case, no one would take her seriously. If they had, she'd be alive today." Nicole replayed this part of the video several times, astonished by the way Geneva had twisted the facts.

That same day, there was an article about Doshan Williams that began on the front page of the *L.A. Times* and continued in the sports section. It said that Doshan was back playing quarterback for Oceanside and then recapped the story of what he'd been through since he was falsely accused of rape.

A week passed before Nicole finally got a call from Sperantza. "I wanted to give you a heads-up before I talk to Timothy. The police still have an APB out on Drummond. But his family said he took his passport and went to Mexico as soon as his name came up in Doshan's trial. The police checked the airlines, and an Andrew Stuart Drummond did board a United Flight to Guadalajara nine days ago. Authorities in Mexico are now searching for him. But Guadalajara is a hub for a number of airlines. He may have flown on to another country to avoid extradition. His mother took $5,000 out of the bank around the time he left, and the police think she gave it to Drummond to help him flee. They're looking at pressing charges against her for aiding and abetting. The point is, since we know Drummond has left the county, I think it's safe to discontinue your security. You okay with that?"

"Sure," she said. "It will be nice to have the house to ourselves again."

That night, Nicole set the table and lit candles, dimming the lights for a romantic evening with Josh. After they ate, they watched a little TV, then headed up to the bedroom to enjoy their newly restored privacy.

They were awakened by the phone a little after 2:30 a.m. Josh listened and said, "uh-huh" a couple of times and then, "I'll meet you at the hospital." He was immediately out of bed, pulling on his clothes. "My dad is having stomach pains, and my mom's afraid it's his heart. She's called 911. They'll probably take him to UCLA, so I'll head over there. She'll call me if they take him anywhere else."

Nicole started to get up. "I'll come with you."

"No," he said. "Go back to sleep. It could be nothing. I could hear my dad yelling in the background, 'It's just indigestion! Quit making a fuss!' But you know my mom. I'll call you if it's anything serious."

"You sure?"

"Absolutely. No sense in both of us getting up at this hour."

Nicole fell asleep as soon as Josh turned off the light and started downstairs. Awhile later she awoke and sat up, heart pounding. She'd thought she'd heard a noise, then she wondered if she'd dreamed it. Now the place was almost unnaturally silent. A chill went through her. She got out of bed and grabbed her robe. Without turning on the light, she tiptoed downstairs.

She headed for the security panel by the front door. The alarm wasn't set, and she figured that Josh, in his rush, must have forgotten. She hit the button to engage the alarm but nothing happened. She opened the closet door where the control box was located. The box, which was supposed to display a green light, was dark. She remembered noticing something a few weeks before. The light on the box had changed from green to flashing yellow. The system worked on electricity, but there was also a backup battery. She'd wondered if the flashing light was a signal that the battery was dying. She'd meant to call the security company and ask, but, in the crush of events, she'd forgotten.

She turned back to the alarm panel and hit the "panic" button. She'd never pushed it before, but she was certainly feeling panicky now. Nothing happened. She flicked the light switch for the entry hall. Nothing. The electricity was off.

Just then, she heard the crash of glass breaking somewhere in the back of the house. She grabbed her purse and ran out the front door in her bare feet. The neighbors' houses were dark but their porch lights were on. That meant the electricity was out only in her house. She thought of trying to rouse a neighbor to let her in, but she couldn't risk taking time to go around knocking on doors.

Her car was parked across the street. She ran to it and rummaged through her purse for the keys. She found them just as the front door of her house opened, and a dark silhouette appeared in the doorway. It had to be Drummond. He must have been waiting on the street, watching the house. When he saw Josh leave, he'd scaled the fence to their backyard and cut off the electricity. The noise that woke her must have been Drummond dropping to the ground when he went over the fence.

Nicole's hands were shaking, but she managed to get her key in the ignition and start the engine. Drummond had almost reached her when she slammed her foot down on the accelerator and made a tire-screeching U-turn, narrowly missing him. As she sped away, she could see him in her rearview mirror. He was heading for a car parked a few houses down. It looked like a junker, which she figured would probably be slower than her own relatively new car. She hit Ventura Boulevard going fifty-five miles an hour, heading for the freeway. Drummond's car was in better shape than it looked. He handily caught up with her and started tailgating her.

Nicole raced through every stop sign and red signal, hoping a police cruiser would spot them and pull them over. But no such luck. The buildings and businesses they passed were dark, and the streets were empty. She got onto the ramp of the freeway, pressing her pedal to the floor. Drummond was several car lengths back, falling farther behind after they shifted from the Ventura Freeway to the San Diego and began the climb up the steep hill. With this temporary reprieve, she took some deep breaths and began to formulate a plan.

She tore off the freeway at Santa Monica Boulevard, heading toward the beach. Before long, Drummond caught up. He began hitting her rear bumper successively, knocking her forward in her seat. She sped up. So did he, but she was able to stay far enough ahead to avoid any more attempts to bump into her.

To her left, she spotted an alley. She knew the West L.A. Police Station was one street south of Santa Monica Boulevard, adjacent to an alley. She prayed this was the one. She turned, tires screeching, into the alley. Drummond missed the turn and kept going. But almost immediately, she heard his tires squeal as he reversed course and followed. Halfway down the alley, where she remembered seeing the police parking lot, was a six-foot stone wall. Had she made a mistake and turned too soon?

When she reached the end of the alley, she made a quick left turn. And there it was. On her left, she could see part of the neon sign, just the letters ICE and, below them, ION. No police cars were in sight. Drummond, behind her, wouldn't be able to see the sign or have any idea where she was headed. She made another left, pulling into the driveway that ran past the station's entrance. Then she hit the brakes.

Drummond's car plowed into her. The crash was deafening. Since the collision came from the back, the airbags didn't deploy. Instead, she was jerked forward and banged her head on the steering wheel. The blow knocked her out for a moment. She opened her eyes with a start. Pain radiated from her forehead. Something was dripping into her eyes, and she could barely see. When she wiped it away, her hand came back covered with blood.

Meanwhile, police were pouring out of the building. In her rearview mirror, she saw Drummond get out of his car and start to run. She had to wipe her face again to watch while half a dozen cops pursued him. They quickly disappeared from view. Dimly, she thought he'd probably be able to outrun them. He was bigger, with longer strides, trained to run fast. Before long, however, Drummond reappeared, surrounded by cops. His hands were cuffed behind him.

Nicole wondered if they knew who he was. She tried to roll down her window so she could tell them, but it was stuck, as was her door. The impact must have bent the door, or the whole chassis. She knocked on the window and called out. But no one seemed to hear. Then the door on the passenger side opened, and a policeman said. "Your head's bleeding. We're calling the paramedics. Don't move until they get here."

"Wait," she said. "Do you realize who you just brought in?"

"Yeah. The guy who smashed into your car and tried to flee the scene." He hurried away before she could tell him it was Andy Drummond, who the police were looking for.

Minutes later, she heard a siren that grew louder and louder. A red paramedics van pulled up next to her. Two men jumped out to unload a stretcher board equipped with what looked like a red vice to hold her head. The paramedics used a piece of equipment to open her door. They lifted her onto the stretcher. That was when she blacked out.

She woke up in the hospital. Josh was by her side, holding her hand. She had a terrible headache, and she was confused. "What happened?"

"Drummond rammed his car into yours, and you hit your head. You've been unconscious for a couple of hours."

Nicole took hold of the bedrails and tried to sit up. The movement made her dizzy. Her vision broke into little pieces. She lay back again.

"You're not supposed to sit up yet," Josh said.

"Did they figure out who Drummond was?" she said. "I tried to tell them."

"They sure did. He's being charged with the murder of Mary Ellen Barnes, your attempted murder, and there's one more thing—" He lapsed into silence.

"What?"

"Drummond drove back from Mexico yesterday in some kind of psychotic rage. First he paid a visit to Kayla Jones's place. After she testified, Sperantza advised her to stay somewhere else until Drummond was picked up, so she was at a friend's. He trashed her place and spray painted death threats on the walls. Her building has CCTV, so the camera caught him going in and out."

"I'm glad she's safe. He might have killed her." Nicole closed her eyes, about to drift off, then opened them again. "I almost forgot. What about your dad? How is he?"

"He's fine. It was just indigestion, like he said. But they're keeping him on a heart monitor just in case." Josh was silent a moment, looking puzzled. "Can I ask you something? What were you doing driving around after I left you? When I got a call from the police that the paramedics were taking you to the hospital, it scared me to death. They said you were unconscious, but they wouldn't tell me any more than that."

Nicole explained. As she talked, she studied his face. He had that expression again, the one he got when he was exasperated with her. Was he blaming her for the encounter with Drummond?

Was he still angry that she'd broken her promise to stop working on Doshan's case? Were they about to loop back into that same old fight?

"Jesus," he said, holding his head in his hands. "I never should have left you by yourself like that. I should have had you come with me. We should have kept security around until Drummond was caught."

"It's not your fault, Josh," she said. "We couldn't keep Timothy around indefinitely. The police established that Drummond had left the country."

He gave her a wary smile, and his hands were trembling as they picked up hers. He leaned in to kiss her.

Awhile later, when the painkillers wore off, Nicole's head hurt. But her mind had cleared, and she was no longer in a fog. That was when she had an epiphany. She'd felt Josh was the perfect man for her, and she truly did love him. But she also understood she was completely wrong for him. She'd imagined she wanted what he did, but that wasn't true. She liked helping people in trouble, sticking her nose into messy situations and resolving them. She was good at it. At the same time, things happened to her and sometimes to the people around her—bad things. For the first time, she realized that this wasn't coincidence. It didn't happen to other people.

No matter how much Josh wanted a quiet family life with her—no matter how much she wanted to give it to him—she couldn't. They weren't right for each other at all. It surprised her that this realization, which meant the end of her and Josh, didn't cause more heartache. Instead it came almost as a relief. She didn't have to lie to herself anymore.

EPILOGUE

IT WAS A WARM, SUNNY SATURDAY AFTERNOON, and Nicole was in her new apartment. She'd started opening boxes filled with the household effects she'd put in storage when she moved in with Josh. The doorbell rang. It was Steph, who'd offered to come over and help.

"You don't look too broken up," Steph said.

"It's funny," Nicole said, "but I'm surprisingly okay. When we're done here, I'll take you out for dinner. I have reservations at that hot new restaurant, Chartreuse. It's right here in Westwood. We can walk.

"Later we can hit some clubs," Steph said. "You need to meet someone new. You know, get right back on the horse."

"No horses for me, please. I'm not ready." All at once, Nicole found herself on the verge of tears. Maybe she wasn't doing as well as she'd thought. She missed Josh, and the thought of Mary Ellen's death filled her with grief and regret. She turned back to the boxes, eager to think of something else.

They worked in companionable silence until 4:00 p.m., when they decided they needed expressos to boost their energy. A coffeehouse down the block was just minutes away. As they were leaving, Nicole's phone rang. She dug it out of her purse.

It was her boss, Jerry. "Sorry to bother you on a Saturday," he said. "We have an urgent case, and I think you'd be a perfect fit. It means going to London to persuade a runaway to come back to L.A. with you."

"What kind of runaway?"

"She's fifteen," Jerry said. "I gather she's a handful—spoiled and headstrong."

"And I'd be leaving when?"

"Tonight. The parents are springing for a first-class ticket. The father is CEO of the Merrimac Corporation, one of our clients. Are you up for it?

Nicole smiled. She was free to do anything she wanted, and this sounded interesting, although she knew how challenging teenagers could be. "Sure," she said. "It would be good to get out of town for a few days."

"I had a hunch you'd feel that way. Better start packing. Your flight leaves at 9:00, and you need to be at the airport earlier than usual. There's another terror alert, and security is especially tight."

After Nicole hung up, she told Steph about her new assignment, "We'll have to take a raincheck on our big night out," she said.

"London? First class? Fab!" Steph said. "I'll help you pack."

Nicole pulled a suitcase from the closet, chose a couple of outfits, and lay them on the bed. "Here," she said. "Could you put these in the hanging compartment of the suitcase while I pack my makeup and stuff?

Nicole disappeared into the bathroom with her cosmetics bag. When she returned, Steph was done packing the clothes and was busy tucking lingerie into the suitcase.

Nicole reached in and pulled out a filmy nightgown. "I'm bringing PJs. I won't be needing this."

"Who knows?" Steph said. "You might run into your old flame, Reinhardt."

"Reinhardt?" Nicole laughed. "I'd almost forgotten about him. Anyhow, he's sure to be out of town on one of his mysterious assignments. And I'll be saddled with a difficult teenager."

Steph took the nightgown out of Nicole's hands and put it back in the suitcase. "You never can tell," she said. "When it comes to you, anything can happen."

ACKNOWLEDGMENTS

ONCE AGAIN I WANT TO THANK my daughter Jennifer, son-in-law John, and granddaughters Anabelle and Lila for their unflagging interest and support. I want to thank my husband Bill for his feedback and advice and for rereading this book every time I made changes. A very special thank you to my brother-in-law Jeff, now retired from his criminal defense practice, who was an indispensable source of advice and information on the legal issues that came up in *Liar Liar*.

Thanks, too, to Cathy Watkins for her input about the business of private investigation and catching glitches in my plot. Also, thanks to Susan Scott, Joyce Brownfield, and Trish Beall for all their hard work in proofreading the book and keeping the story on track. And finally, thanks Sue Price, Jeannie Hahn, Claudia Luther, and my other friends who have been loyal boosters of my work.

ABOUT THE AUTHOR

LIAR LIAR: A NICOLE GRAVES MYSTERY is Nancy Boyarsky's third novel, following *The Swap* and *The Bequest*. Before turning to mysteries, Nancy coauthored *Backroom Politics*, a *New York Times* notable book, with her husband, Bill Boyarsky. She has written several textbooks on the justice system as well as articles for publications including the *Los Angeles Times*, *Forbes*, and *McCall's*. She also contributed to political anthologies, including *In the Running*, about women's political campaigns. In addition to her writing career, she was communications director for political affairs for ARCO.

Readers are invited to connect with Nancy through her website:

nancyboyarsky.com.

CPSIA information can be obtained
at www.ICGtesting.com
Printed in the USA
FFOW02n0859260518
46821797-48991FF